Murder
on a
Seagoing Tug

By

G. Sam Carr
CPO, USN (Ret.)

PublishAmerica
Baltimore

© 2006 by G. Sam Carr.
All rights reserved. No part of this book may be reproduced, stored in a retrieval system or transmitted in any form or by any means without the prior written permission of the publishers, except by a reviewer who may quote brief passages in a review to be printed in a newspaper, magazine or journal.

First printing

ISBN: 1-4137-9340-1
PUBLISHED BY PUBLISHAMERICA, LLLP
www.publishamerica.com
Baltimore

Printed in the United States of America

This novel is dedicated to the thousands of men and women I served with during my twenty-year career in the U.S. Navy and especially to those on the USS *Penobscot*, a fine seagoing tug and not at all like the one portrayed in this story. This is a book of fiction; any resemblance to persons living or dead is purely coincidental.

Chapter One

Day One—Morning—October 1962

"Chief McCain?" asked the pretty, slightly overweight, brunette receptionist as he stepped into the outer office of Commander Eastern Sea Frontier.

"That's right," he said smiling.

"Go right in—Commander Thomas is expecting you." He tucked his hat under his left arm and opened the door with his right.

Commander Frank "Tommy" Thomas, director of intelligence, rose to his feet, stuck out his hand and said, "I've been waiting for you Jack. How was the flight from DC?"

McCain stared up into the steel-gray eyes of his six-foot-two senior officer and said, "The trip was okay, but I haven't got a hint on why I'm here. Way I figure it is that you've got the Navy in some sort of trouble and you want me to bail you out."

"Not a bad guess. This time I'm really counting on you." The commander lifted an eight-by-ten glossy photograph off his polished, walnut desk and handed it to McCain.

McCain took a quick look at the bloated body of a light-haired young man dressed in navy whites, grimaced, and said, "What in the hell happened to him?" He handed the photo back to the commander. "That right side of his face is real ugly. You can see his cheek bones."

Commander Thomas dropped the photo onto the center of his desk. "That's Yeoman Second Class Lawrence Johnson. The experts say that the crabs and eels chewed his face away. You can't see it in the photos, but they took off a couple fingers too."

In spite of the formality, Commander Thomas and Chief Petty Officer McCain were lifetime friends and partners. They were born on the same day, in the same hospital, in Cheyenne, Wyoming, and although Thomas was senior in rank to McCain, when it came to age he was twenty minutes his junior.

Commander Thomas picked up the photo again and stuffed it beneath a stack of letters in a manila file folder. "Are you still curious what all this has to do with you?"

"Damn right. I know it has to be important or you wouldn't have booked me on a flight to Kennedy and had a marine corporal waiting to drive me down here. And I've got a good idea there's a lot more to it than that photo of a sailor turned into fish bait."

Thomas nodded. "As usual you're right. The photo is only part of it. The sailor was the yeoman on the USS *Lakota*. It's a seagoing tug home ported in Bayonne."

"Still don't see what that has to do with me."

Thomas stared at McCain for a second. "I want you to take Johnson's place on the *Lakota*. Here are your orders." He handed McCain an official manila envelope.

McCain took the envelope and said, "That's all you're going to tell me?"

Thomas sat down at his desk, leaned forward on his elbows and said, "You know better than that. Why don't you light up one of those stinking cigars and sit back while I tell you everything I know."

McCain extracted an Optimo panatela from the inside pocket of his khaki jacket and lit it with his Zippo. In seconds the room was engulfed in a cloud of smoke.

Thomas picked up a sheet of paper and waved it to clear the smoke.

McCain took another puff and said, "I'm not sure I like the sound of this. Seems to me that a chief relieving a second class might make someone suspicious?"

"Maybe," Thomas said. "But I think you can concoct a cover story. I want you to become friendly with the officers and it'll be easier as a chief." A worried look came over his face as he said, "This isn't a routine case. The city medical examiner says Johnson has been dead for at least three weeks. Yet, for some reason, his ship hasn't even reported him missing."

McCain put down his cigar, stood up and strolled slowly across the room. Suddenly he did an about face and said, "That is strange. Where did they find the body?"

Thomas also rose to his feet, walked around his desk, leaned against it, and said, "Johnson's head was bashed in. They don't know if he was hit and thrown in the water, or was thrown in and hit something. Whichever way it happened, they found bits of concrete embedded in his skull. But because he had some water in his lungs, they think he was still alive when he went in. Yesterday afternoon a harbor tug found him floating near the ferry slip on Staten Island."

McCain looked puzzled. "Why ain't the cops taking care of this? That ferry slip isn't government property, is it?"

Thomas took a pack of Pall Malls from his desk, pulled one out and lit it. He took another puff and said, "The cops are straining at their moorings waiting for us to identify the body."

"So, why don't you tell them?" He gave Commander Thomas a suspicious look and said, "You're hiding something aren't you?"

"Better not to press the issue yet, Jack. Take a strain. We haven't seen each other for six months; now you want to rush our visit. Too bad you won't be in town long enough to see Ruth and the kids. She's going to be real disappointed. By the way, I haven't had a chance to congratulate you on setting up that KGB mole in the Pentagon. I hear he didn't have a clue as to who did him in."

"Thanks," McCain said as he plopped down on the leather couch standing against the back wall of the mahogany-paneled office. "Are you going to tell me just what I'm getting myself into?"

"Well, let's put it this way. When I told the admiral the police might turn up something that could make the Navy look bad, he ordered me to stonewall it. Said he didn't want any surprises. We received Johnson's dental match yesterday but we haven't told Lieutenant Adams yet."

"Lieutenant Adams?"

"Yes, he's the commanding officer of the *Lakota*. The old man wants me to stall the police till you've had a chance to look around."

"So that's my job, just to look around?"

"You've got it, but of course if you can come up with all the answers, we'll appreciate it."

"Don't sound like such a big deal?" McCain reached into his jacket pocket and took out a note pad and pen. "Guess I'd better take some notes." He clicked down the point, looked Thomas in the eye and asked, "What makes you think the Navy will look bad? I doubt if this is the first swabby to drown in New York Harbor. And I doubt if it'll be the last."

After picking up the folder containing the letters, Commander Thomas took them out and laid all but one on the couch. "Eighteen of these letters are complaints from loan companies about *Lakota* crew members and their skipper for not paying their bills."

McCain shook his head and said, "Come on, Tommy, you don't really think this guy's death was because of some unpaid bills? You better come clean and let me have the rest of it."

With a wry smile, Commander Thomas held up the letter he'd held back. "I told you about eighteen letters. This is number nineteen and it's from the dead man—Johnson."

Chapter Two

Day One—Afternoon

Chief Petty Officer McCain stared out the window of the Bayonne Naval Supply Depot bus wondering what kind of a mess he was getting himself into. On the surface, the facts didn't appear too complicated. But Tommy left no doubt he felt there was a lot more to this case than met the eye. And McCain had never known him to be wrong.

At a distant pier McCain saw the mast of a small ship and figured it was the *Lakota*. But since he'd never been on a seagoing tug before he really didn't know what the ship looked like. He did know it was small for a navy ship and for sure the ship he was staring at met that criterion. He was a bit concerned on how he was going to fit in with the crew. But what the hell, a ship was a ship and probably wouldn't be much different than the destroyer he had served on right out of boot camp. Hard to believe it was fifteen years ago, he thought.

The driver stopped at the foot of Pier One and said, "Here ya are, Chief. That's the *Lakota* over there." He pointed to the ship McCain had been watching for some time. Only now he could see a portion of the faded gray superstructure showing above the edge of the pier. He stared at the ship for a second, then picked up his bag and headed for the steel structure that would be his home for the next few weeks.

McCain stood on the edge of the pier staring down at a ship that looked more like a tramp steamer than a commissioned ship of the line. The profile was almost identical to the hundreds of harbor tugs he'd seen in ports all over the world. Only the size was different. This one was almost three times larger than the other tugs, but was still a lot smaller than the 390-foot destroyer he once served on.

Taking his time crossing the narrow gangplank running from the pier to the forecastle deck, McCain spotted what he assumed, by the .45 strapped to his waist, to be the quarterdeck watch. The young sailor dressed in non-regulation dungarees, a frayed T-shirt and sneakers stared at McCain as he stepped aboard, saluted the colors and asked permission to come aboard. McCain held the salute waiting for the string-bean-shaped sailor with a toothpick in his mouth and a dirty white hat on his head to acknowledge the salute. Several ground-out cigarette buts cluttered the area around the man's feet.

Not wanting to get started on the wrong foot, McCain shrugged off his first impression and repeated his request for permission to come aboard.

From his perch on the jack staff, a ruffled seagull watched as McCain kept his hand in the salute position. The sailor seemed to have the same absent look as the seagull. When he apparently remembered what he was supposed to do, he returned McCain's salute and said in a Brooklyn accent, "What can I do for you, Chief?" Then without waiting for an answer, he resumed his slouched position against the rust-spotted superstructure.

McCain dropped the salute and said, "I'm Chief Yeoman McCain reporting for duty. Is the exec aboard?" His negative impressions of the ship and its crew were growing faster than his temper.

Brooklyn shook his head, and said, "Nope."

"Nope, what?" said McCain.

"The exec ain't aboard," he said nonchalantly.

"Well then, who's the duty officer?"

Brooklyn shrugged. "All the officers, 'cept Bos'n Greene, are ashore. The bos'n's in the wardroom. Guess he's got the duty."

McCain gave Brooklyn a stare that would freeze whiskey, waited a few seconds and said, "Would it be too much trouble to tell me your name and rate?" Because he hated looking up at anybody, the fact that the misfit sailor was a good eight inches taller than McCain didn't help cool his anger.

Then, evidently figuring he'd pushed the chief to his limit, the sailor jumped to attention and said, "I'm Rossi, radioman third class. I'll show you the way down." He picked up McCain's bag and started aft.

McCain, still boiling mad, tailed him down a steel stairway to the open catwalk running down the starboard side of the main deck. About twenty feet further aft, Rossi opened a door and led McCain into a good-sized room he recognized as the crew's mess. The bulkheads were painted pea-green and the deck was covered with alternating squares of gray and red asphalt tile. Scores of paperback books, soda cans, and other litter adorned the steel I-beams supporting the outboard bulkheads. At the furthest of the three round Formica-topped tables, a trio of sailors, dressed in dungarees and T-shirts, were playing cards. An overflowing ashtray sat alongside each sailor.

Rossi dropped McCain's bag and shouted, "This is Chief Yeoman McCain. He must be taking Johnson's place."

Well, somebody knows Johnson ain't coming back, thought McCain.

The card players stopped playing and introduced themselves as O'Neil, shipfitter second class; Wishbone, radioman first class; and Trumbull, engineman third class. At the center table, a skinny light-skinned black man leaned back in his chair watching the TV mounted high on the starboard bulkhead. Rossi jerked his head toward the man and said, "That's Dixon, the officer's steward." The third table was empty.

Leaning against a huge stainless steel refrigerator next to the door to the galley was a stocky, ebony-skinned man dressed in spotless white trousers and an equally white T-shirt. Around his ample middle was a white apron. On his head was a turned-inside-out white hat. From around its edges, McCain saw a thick crop of kinky salt-and-pepper speckled hair. He showed a full set of ivory-colored teeth and introduced himself as Rice, commissaryman first class.

McCain had a feeling he was going to like this man. And if his looks were any indication, his cooking ability should be pretty damned good. Rice was the first bright spot he'd seen since getting off the bus.

At the mess hall's forward bulkhead Rossi shoved a green drape aside and guided McCain into a dimly lit passageway. Pointing toward another green drape, he said, "That's the wardroom." Then he spun around and, like a rabbit escaping from a coyote, disappeared back into the crew's mess.

After knocking three times on the bulkhead next to the wardroom's green drape, McCain pulled the drape aside and peered into a small brown-wood-paneled room. In the center was a table surrounded by six chairs. On the far side of the table, stretched out on a leather couch, was an unshaven, middle-aged man. He was about five foot nine and wore khaki shorts; nothing else. By his side lay a half-empty bottle of Gordon's gin.

McCain eased himself around the table and reluctantly touched the shoulder of the sleeping man. "Bos'n Greene?" he whispered.

The man sat up so abruptly it startled McCain. His face was thin and weathered and his short hair jutted out in all directions. "Who the hell are you?" he said through a fog of spittle. The harried look in the bos'n's eyes made McCain believe he had just disturbed a bad dream.

"My name is Jack McCain, chief yeoman and I'm here to relieve Lawrence Jackson."

Greene, finally coming out of his trance, stuck out his hand and said, "About time they sent us a yeoman. That damn pussy Johnson went ashore about three weeks ago and we haven't seen him since. Paperwork's backing up and none of us know how to handle it."

After twisting off the Gordon's cap, he put the bottle to his lips and took a long swig. Then he must have realized what he was doing in front of a stranger and said, "I don't usually drink, but I've got this damn cough that don't seem to want to go away." He took another swig and offered McCain the bottle.

"No thanks. Too early for me," said McCain.

Greene screwed the cap back on. "How'd they find out Johnson was missing? The skipper wasn't going to say anything till he was gone thirty days."

Why would he want to do that? McCain wondered. Could it be because he knew Johnson was dead? Then realizing Greene was waiting for an answer, McCain said, "I don't know anything about him being gone. Is he over the hill or what? I pulled strings to get this assignment. Johnson's going to shore duty."

Greene's expression soured. "Oh. Oh. Looks like I let the cat out of the bag." He rose to his feet, reached inside his shorts and started scratching his balls. "Keep this under your hat; will ya, Chief?"

McCain nodded, wondering whether he was talking about scratching his balls or letting him in on an inside secret. Then McCain watched in horror as the bos'n withdrew his scratching hand and reached out to put it on McCain's shoulder. Trying not to disclose his feelings, McCain nonchalantly stepped back out of the bos'n's reach.

Seeming not to notice the rejection, the bos'n sat back down and started putting on his shoes. "What say we have a cup of mud? I'll give you the lowdown on this bucket of bolts." He got up, stuck his head through the green drapes and yelled, "Dixon! Bring two cups of coffee. Don't forget the fixings." He turned around, pulled out a chair for himself and pointed to the one opposite for McCain. "Have a seat. It'll probably be twenty minutes afore that lazy bastard gets here with our coffee."

McCain could have named a thousand other things he'd rather be doing, but knew he had to play the game if he was going uncover what Johnson's death had to do with the *Lakota's* officers and crew.

The bos'n leaned forward against the table. "You said you pulled strings to get these orders? I hope you got a kiss with them."

"Why do you say that?"

"Because you got fucked," he said grinning. "This has to be the worst ship in the Navy."

Trying not to sound stupid, McCain said, "I hope it's not as bad as you say. To tell the truth, I don't know a damned thing about seagoing tugs, but I wanted a homeport in New York and Bayonne is as close as I could get."

Bos'n Greene coughed, licked his lips, and took another swig of gin. "I've seen things on this ship that I've never seen before." He grimaced, clinched his teeth and with closed fists banged the table so hard the ashtray bounced a half-inch in the air. Then he yelled, "God damn it, Dixon. Where's that coffee?"

Shocked at the violent outburst, McCain waited a second then asked, "What kind of things?"

Greene lifted his right cheek and turned loose a loud fart before saying, "For one thing, we damn near had a mutiny."

"Really?" asked McCain.

Greene nodded. "Yep, Johnson filled our heads with a bunch of shit about navy regulations. Next thing you know, the exec called a meeting."

Suddenly the drape swung to one side and Dixon stepped in carrying two cups of coffee on a metal tray. He sat the tray down and mumbled just loud enough for McCain to hear, "Who shit their pants in here?"

Evidently the bos'n heard it too because he glared at Dixon for a minute then said, "Didn't I tell you to bring cream and sugar?"

Hate showed in Dixon's eyes. "Must not have heard you, thought you didn't use cream or sugar."

The bos'n glanced at McCain. "You want cream and sugar?"

"I can take it black," said McCain anxious to get back to the mutiny.

"Okay, Dixon. You can go, but you'd better damned sure pay more attention in the future."

Soon as Dixon backed out of the room, Greene said, "That's another example. On any other ship, that insolent little bastard would be cashiered out of the Navy."

McCain didn't respond. He was far more interested in things bigger than cream and sugar and he also wondered if the bos'n had in fact shit his pants.

Greene glanced up at the twenty-four-hour clock on the bulkhead, then turned to his right and turned on the TV. "Time for the ball game," he said. "We'll talk later."

McCain was in no mood to watch a ball game. Plus having had all he could take of the bos'n's gin-reeking breath and lingering body gas, he downed his coffee and said, "Bos'n, before you get comfortable, would you show me the ship's office and then where I'll be bunking tonight."

Greene looked at McCain with an expression saying he couldn't believe he was passing up the chance to stay and watch the Mets. But then he shrugged his shoulder and said, "Sure, Chief."

McCain trailed Greene down the short passageway till he stopped and knocked on one of the doors. "This is Chief Quartermaster Tom

Hall's stateroom." He then pointed to another door across the narrow passageway and said, "That's Chief Jackson's room. He's ashore and his room's probably a mess. You're better off bunking with Hall for tonight. Tomorrow the three of you can figure out who's senior and gets a room by himself."

Next door to Hall's room was a small screen-fronted compartment containing two desks and two file cabinets. McCain tried the door and said, "Is this the ship's office?" He already figured out that it was and couldn't wait to get in there and start going through the files and personnel records. There had to be something on the indebtedness letters in the personnel files. Maybe he'd even find something to shed a light on Johnson's death.

"That's it. You'll be sharing it with the storekeeper."

"Looks kind of small for two people," McCain said as a faint voice came through the door to Hall's room saying, "Come on in."

Greene opened the door and McCain saw a slender, clean-shaven man with light brown hair wearing khaki trousers and a white T-shirt sitting on the bottom half of a double bunk. His hazel eyes staring through black horn-rimmed glasses left no doubt the man did not enjoy being interrupted. "Something wrong, Bos'n?" he asked.

McCain and Greene stepped into the box of a room with bulkheads painted the same color as the crew's mess. It seemed as if everything below deck, except the wardroom, was painted in a sick-looking pea green.

"Tom. Meet Chief Yeoman Jack McCain. He's Johnson's relief. How about letting him share your room tonight? The XO can decide who bunks with who in the morning. Most ships it would be based on date of rank, but on this ship, who in the hell knows." With that, Greene turned and went out the door.

Hall pulled out a straight-backed chair and offered it to McCain. Before sitting down, McCain looked around. Everything but bare essentials had been stripped from the small room. Besides the bunk bed, there was a metal clothes closet, a small stainless steel sink, a mirrored medicine cabinet, and a combination chest of drawers and desk. Two identical chairs completed the furnishings.

McCain sat down and said, "Nice room, Chief. Lot cleaner than the rest of the ship."

Hall took a handkerchief from his back pocket and polished his glasses. "I know what you mean. I've been trying to get off this ship for a year. The old man keeps disapproving my request. He says I'm too important." Hall put on his glasses and said, "The trouble is that he and the XO can't get along. They use me as a go-between."

McCain wondered if he was still in the U.S. Navy or if aliens had scooped him up and plopped him down on a ship from another planet. Finally he said, "I can't believe this ship is as bad as you and the bos'n say it is."

Hall bit his lower lip for a second. "Believe me, it is. But it's nothing that a good CO couldn't fix. Of course we'd also need some time in port to get the work done."

"Why don't they get along?"

"Don't know for sure. About a month ago, the XO came to me and said he and the bos'n and chief engineer were thinking about taking over the ship and wanted me to join them." He slipped his feet into a pair of shoes, stood up and said, "I've got to go up to the chart house and make sure the charts are ready for tomorrow."

"Did you join them?" McCain asked.

As he was putting on a neatly pressed khaki shirt, Hall said, "Not on your life. I talked them out of it." He moved in front of the mirror and combed his hair. "None of it would have happened if Johnson had minded his own business."

McCain rubbed his chin, stared at Hall for a second and said, "The quarterdeck watch, Rossi, said that Johnson was over the hill. Do you think it's because of his part in this?"

Hall started to say something, thought better of it and stopped. He was going out the door when he turned and said, "Maybe you'd better talk to Captain Adams." Then as if to change the subject, he said, "You can hang your uniforms in the closet and there's an empty drawer under the bunk you can use."

Hall seemed all right to McCain. Not only was he squared away, but obviously loyal to his CO and knew when to keep his mouth shut. He thought he was lucky to get as much out of Hall as he did. There was no doubt that if anyone knew both sides of the story, it was Hall. He'd have to find a way to get the quartermaster to open up. If he didn't know all the answers, it was at least a place to start.

Chapter Three

Day One—Evening

After a delicious supper of grilled ham, candied sweet potatoes, and fresh-baked cornbread, McCain retreated to the ship's office and started rummaging through Johnson's desk. Finding nothing of interest, he was checking out the old IBM electric typewriter when he heard the rattle of the metal door. He looked up to see, standing in the doorway, a handsome man of average height with salt-sprinkled black hair and matching moustache. Spotting the lieutenant bars on the man's collar, McCain jumped to his feet.

"At ease, Chief," the lieutenant said as he stuck out his hand. "The bos'n said you were in here. Glad to have you aboard."

McCain stared into a pair of tired and troubled eyes. "Captain Adams?" he asked.

The lieutenant nodded slightly and said, "That's me." He pulled out the storekeeper's chair from beneath the desk and straddled it. "On the *Lakota* we don't pay much mind to formalities. You can call me Skipper or Cap'n." A grin spread across his weather-toughened face. "You can even call me Lieutenant, but if you do, I'll figure you're mad at me. By the way, what do you think of our little ship?"

McCain was tempted to tell what he really thought about his little ship, but instead, returned his smile and said, "Well, it's different than anything I've ever served on." He reached down and took a folder from the desk. "Cap'n, I've been going through these papers and it looks as if we've got our work cut out for us. In fact, I'm having a hell of a time figuring out what needs to be done first."

"Like what?" Adams asked.

"Well, for one thing, I can't find copies of any reports notifying the Navy and local police that Johnson is over the hill."

Adams folded his arms, shrugged and said, "That's because we're seamen on this ship. What the hell do we know about paperwork? We just figured Johnson took off with some of his off-the-wall friends. I expect he'll be back any day now."

McCain was itching to ask what Adams meant by "off-the-wall" but brushed it off, smiled, and said, "He'll be pissed when he does. He's got a damn good set of shore duty orders waiting for him. I doubt if he'll get them now."

Adams shrugged and said, "That's his problem."

The CO appeared to be one cool cat. Was it possible that he already knew Johnson was dead? Hoping to get some helpful reaction, McCain said, "Of course if he comes back tonight, we can cover for him."

Adams shrugged again. "You mean to tell me you're just here to take his place?"

Why would he be thinking otherwise? Seeing an opening, McCain frowned and being as serious as he could, said, "Why yes, sir. For months I'd been trying to get a ship out of New York. The detailer owed me a favor, so when he discovered Johnson was eligible for shore duty, he cut us both a set of orders. Why would you think otherwise?"

Adams grinned and turned a light pink as he said, "I don't know. Guess I'd forgotten that you yeomen have the Navy by the balls."

McCain grinned and nodded his head. "We do have it pretty good. But let's get back to Johnson. I've been going through his service record. Near as I can tell, he's never been in any type of trouble before. Why would he go over the hill now?"

Adams took out a Chesterfield, lit it and puffed till he'd filled the tiny office with a plume of smoke. "How would I know what got into Johnson?"

The fish did for sure, thought McCain. He looked Adams in the eye and asked, "Captain, do you know who Johnson hung around with?"

"Probably. Not much goes on on this ship without me knowing about it. I can't see that it makes much difference, but he mostly hung out with Scott Trumbull, engineman third class. Some think they're a little too close."

Well, there's another vague reference to Johnson's friends. Might as well lay my cards on the table. "Captain, what did you mean when you said Johnson probably took off with some of his off-the-wall friends? Why do you call them off the wall?"

Adams took a quick puff, snuffed out his cigarette, and said with a grin on his face, "Way I hear it, Johnson's queer as a three-dollar bill. Of course I have no way of knowing if it's true or not."

Taking a couple seconds to let the unanticipated words sink in, McCain shook his head and said, "Damn. That's heavy stuff. Hell, he's got a top-secret clearance. If what you say is true, seems that they should have picked something up in his background investigation. But on the other hand I did read a report once that claimed only a handful of homosexuals is discovered by their clearance check."

"Just telling you what most of us think," Adams said nonchalantly.

"Strange," McCain said as he opened a file drawer and removed Trumbull's personnel record. He sat down, leafed through the manila folder, and then said, "According to this, Trumbull's got a clean record. I suppose that could mean he's just never been caught."

Adams stood up. "I wouldn't know. Anyway, like I said, welcome aboard. Would like to stay and talk some more, but I've got to make sure the ship's ready for getting underway tomorrow. We're pulling out around noon."

"Going to sea so soon?" McCain said trying to act surprised. "I was hoping I'd have time to get to know the ship a little better and have a chance to clean up some of this backlog." The fact was that Tommy had already told him that the ship was going to Guantanamo Bay and they'd be gone for at least a month. He said it'd give him time to get some facts together before Johnson's death went public.

McCain jerked the cover off the typewriter, looked up at Captain Adams, and said, "That means I'll have to make a sailing diary to send to PAMI. We'll have to show that Johnson's not on board."

Adams, looking agitated, asked, "What do you mean, have to?"

Recognizing he was hitting a nerve, McCain said, "I've made out AWOL reports for the exec's signature. I'll get them in the mail before we get underway."

"Maybe you will and maybe you won't," Adams said. "What the hell is PAMI? And why did you make them out for Posey's signature?"

McCain expected some reaction to Posey's name, but his not knowing what PAMI stood for was hard to believe. "PAMI stands for Personnel Accounting Machine Installation. As to Mr. Posey's signature, I just assumed he would be the one to sign. On every ship I've ever served on, the XO signed all the enlisted personnel papers."

"Not on my ship," Adams said. "And what's more," Adams leaned down and stuck his nose in McCain's face, "Chief, we'll get along just fine if you remember that I give the orders and do all the signing." He waited for his words to sink in, and then said, "If Posey tells you to do something you come to me. One more thing, you tell him about this conversation and I'll have your ass."

Suddenly McCain realized what Hall was talking about. "Yes, sir," he said. "I'll retype these papers and bring them to your cabin." He picked up the competed forms and ripped them in half. Hoping to calm Adams down, McCain asked, "By the way, Cap'n, any idea how long we'll be gone?"

"I'd say three or four weeks. We'll stop overnight in Norfolk to pick up a barge and then nonstop to Gitmo. The Seabees need some sand for concrete." The sharp edge seemed to have been taken off his words.

"Last time I was in Gitmo," said McCain, "it looked to me like it was all sand."

Adams moved to the door, turned and said, "You're probably right. It's full of sand, but not the type needed for concrete. We'll be hauling river-bottom sand from Kingston." With that, he closed the door and headed up the companionway to the bridge.

McCain lit up a cigar, rolled a new form into the old typewriter and started typing. Between strokes, he wondered if Tommy had any idea of the screwed-up mess he'd handed him. How could the Navy let this ship get into this condition? And how could such a concentration of misfits wind up on one ship? With the exception of that TV show *McHale's Navy*, he'd never heard of a ship being run like the *Lakota*, let alone seen or served on one. And he hadn't even commenced to dig. Maybe he'd better call Tommy and ask for help. At least try to talk him into stopping them from getting underway. There were too many foul-ups to be accidental and he was beginning to doubt that he'd be able to sort them out by himself.

McCain was working on the last form when Adams popped his head in the door and said, "When you need me, I'll be in the wardroom."

Twenty minutes later McCain went into the wardroom and found, sitting around the table, Bos'n Green, Captain Adams, and a chief warrant machinist. The machinist had a husky build, a plain face except for a once-broken nose, and a crew cut. The bos'n introduced him as Jim Haggen, the chief engineer.

McCain already knew who his was. He'd read Haggen's file and saw that he had been in the Navy for twenty-four years and now lived in Brooklyn with his wife and two sons. McCain stuck out his hand. "Glad to meet you, Mr. Haggen."

Haggen accepted the hand, gave it a quick pump, and said, "Welcome aboard, Chief."

With the formalities over, McCain pushed the papers and a ballpoint pen to Adams, who said, "Thanks, Chief, want a cup of coffee?"

"No thanks, Captain." The fact was that McCain really did want a cup of coffee but not in the wardroom. Soon as he could get out of there, he was heading for the crew's mess, where he could have his coffee and at the same time see if he could pump some of the men about Johnson.

In the crew's mess, Rossi and Wishbore were playing acey-duecy, Dixon was reading a Captain Marvel comic book and Trumbull was watching *Lucy* on TV. McCain went straight to the huge stainless steel coffee urn, grabbed a mug and filled it. He blew across the steaming surface and sat down next to Trumbull where he pretended to watch TV as he searched for a way to break the ice.

At the first commercial, McCain turned to the blonde boyish-looking sailor and said, "The CO tells me you're a good friend of Johnson." A harrowed look leaped into Trumbull's eyes. "So what?" he asked.

"I have to send out AWOL notices. Any idea where he could be?"

Trumbull looked around for a second and then leaned closer. "Wait till the show's over. We'll take a walk."

McCain nodded, got up and thumbed through a stack of pocket westerns. He chose a dog-eared copy of Louis L'Amour's *Law of the Desert Born* and started leafing through it. Then seeing that *The Lucy Show* was about to end, he stuffed the book into his back pocket and stepped out onto the main deck, where the moon was full and a damp, musty odor of fish and salt hung in the air.

When Trumbull stepped through the hatch, McCain was leaning against the rail puffing on a fresh Optimo. "Sorry for the intrigue, Chief. The people on this ship have big ears. You've got to be careful what you say. Let's walk aft."

It took a whole cigar and a half-hour of cautious questioning to drag any information out of the reluctant Trumbull. In the cool damp night air, with drops of moisture forming on the gray metal deck of the fantail, McCain was able to glean that Johnson was indeed a homosexual and that he had a crush on a bouncer in a queer joint named The Pink Poodle. Furthermore, Trumbull had accompanied Johnson to the gay bar on the night he disappeared. While there, Johnson and this bouncer named Jerry Marsh had a lover's quarrel. Then Trumbull said he was so embarrassed by the way Johnson was carrying on he got up and left.

Trumbull's knowledge about Jerry Marsh was as sparse as the cash in a sailor's pocket before payday. He did say that he didn't believe Marsh was a homosexual and that the only interest he had in Johnson was as an easy source of money and gifts. Money that Johnson may have borrowed from the CO or exec.

It was at the very end of the conversation that Trumbull dropped the bombshell. He'd started walking forward when all of a sudden he turned, came back, looked McCain square in the eye and said, "Find Johnson's diary, it'll probably tell you everything you want to know."

The words hit McCain like a double shot of 151-proof rum. "Johnson kept a diary?" he asked.

Trumbull said, "He called it a journal." With that said he spun around and headed back to the crew's mess.

McCain stayed to mull over what Trumbull had just said. As he looked out at the busy harbor traffic with their glowing lights and blowing horns, he had a gut feeling Trumbull hadn't told him everything he knew. It was enough to start forming the puzzle but he'd need a lot more to put the pieces together. McCain hoped Trumbull was right about the contents of the journal, but first he had to find it.

Chapter Four

Day Two—Early Morning

Breakfast offered McCain his first opportunity to meet Chief Engineman Pete Jackson. Jackson had rust-colored hair, untrimmed beard and was wearing greasy dungarees. The bill of his khaki chief's hat was badly scuffed; the vinyl cover was in even worse shape.

While Jackson introduced himself, McCain noticed the foul odor of stale beer, cheap wine, and unwashed armpits. He did have one thing in his favor. That was that he was only an inch or two taller than McCain. At least he wouldn't have to look up at Jackson.

They were seated at the table closest to the galley which was reserved for the three chief petty officers and three first-class petty officers. McCain looked across the table at Jackson and Hall. They were as different as the *Lakota* was to the other ships he'd served on. Hall sat erect and ate with perfect table manners. Jackson slouched in his chair and stabbed a folded piece of bread into his sunny-side-up eggs. When he lifted the bread to his mouth, a glob of slimy yolk dripped onto his shirt. Jackson stuffed the bread into his mouth, washed it down with a gulp of coffee and let out a belch. Hall looked as if he was going to be sick.

So far, both chiefs seemed to be friendly and willing to accept McCain as one of them. By the end of the day though, there was a good chance they'd both hate his guts. When he checked the personnel files, he discovered he was senior to both of them. That meant the "odd couple" would be sharing a stateroom.

The reputation of yeomen being wheelers and dealers seemed to satisfy the crew's curiosity as to why McCain was chosen to relieve Johnson. That coupled with the old adage that it wasn't a good idea to make an enemy of the ship's yeoman caused most of the men to go out of their way to be friendly. Evidently they didn't feel the same way about Johnson. With the exception of Trumbull, the rest of them seemed happy to see him gone.

Just before breakfast, McCain had discussed Johnson with Rossi and Seaman Steed. His interest perked up when Steed said, "Now we can build up the recreation fund again."

"What do you mean by that?" asked McCain.

Steed looked straight at McCain and said, "A couple days before he went over the hill, I asked him for some money to buy three new softballs for the team. He said he couldn't because the fund was out of money."

"Johnson had control of the money?" McCain asked.

"He was treasurer and custodian," Steed answered.

"Did he say why there was no money?" McCain asked.

Steed said, "I asked him, but he wouldn't tell me. He just said that if we needed new softballs we should take up a collection from the team."

"Did you do that?"

Steed shook his head. "No. I went to Mr. Posey and complained."

"How'd you make out with the XO?"

"He just said that Captain Adams had the money and there wasn't anything he could do about it."

Rossi broke in, "Wasn't only the rec fund."

"What else?" asked McCain.

Rossi threw up his arms and said, "Johnson was a real bastard. He wouldn't do a thing for the crew without getting paid for it."

"Like what?"

Rossi gestured with his hands again and said, "Like last month when I lost my fucking ID card. Naturally I went to Johnson. He laughed and said it would take about a month to get a new one. Then he came right out and said that if I greased his palm with a ten spot he'd be able to get one of the yeomen on the base to make me up one right away."

"Did you give him the money?"

Rossi shrugged, "What else was I going to do? I couldn't go ashore without one."

"Did he say who he had to give the money to?"

"He mentioned some name, but there was no doubt in my mind it was going into his own pocket." A call from the mess deck saying that chow was ready broke up the conversation.

After eating his fill of bacon and eggs, McCain refilled his mug with coffee and took it to the ship's office. Before going in, he stopped long enough to study the miserable working space shared by the yeoman and storekeeper.

The room was just long enough for two small single-pedestal metal desks and two 4-drawer file cabinets. An old straight-backed chair with a ripped seat cushion stood between the two cabinets. Between the desks and rear bulkhead there was barely enough room to pull out the desk chairs. Every inch of bulkhead was covered with hanging clipboards.

On the side of the storekeeper's file cabinet was pasted a color poster of a naked blonde with tits the size of muskmelons. On Johnson's side was a calendar decorated with the picture of the Fire Island Lighthouse.

McCain stared glumly at the pile of work to be done and decided he had to find a better place to work. There was no way he could dig into the files without explaining to the storekeeper, Tobey, what he was doing.

McCain had met Tobey that morning. The storekeeper had a dark complexion and a French-looking pencil-line mustache that would have let him fit well in New Orleans. McCain didn't find much to like or dislike about the man, but he sure as hell didn't want to be cooped up in the tiny office with him.

He was leafing through a pile of papers when McCain heard, "Chief McCain? Okay to come in?" The speaker was a smiling young lieutenant (junior grade) wearing neatly pressed work khakis.

McCain grinned and said, "Mr. Posey, I presume. Come right in."

Posey stepped into the office and sat down in the storekeeper's chair. McCain set aside the papers and twisted his chair around to face the XO.

Handsome as Posey was, he had troubled eyes. McCain broke the ice by saying, "You want to start, or should I?"

"I'll start by saying how glad I am to see you," said Posey. "Johnson's been gone for over three weeks and his work has really piled up. I wanted to ask headquarters for a replacement, but Captain Adams wouldn't hear of it."

McCain wondered if he could trust this young officer. Better not, he thought. But it wouldn't hurt to test him a bit. "Mr. Posey, why won't Captain Adams let you sign any papers? And why doesn't he want me to take any orders from you?"

Posey's face turned a bright pink. "Who says...?"

Before Posey could finish, McCain said, "Captain Adams told me last night and it surprised the hell out of me. I've never been on a ship where the XO didn't do most of the paperwork. I figure there must be some reason for it."

His face quickly changed from pink to red as Posey shrugged and said, "Adams is the CO. He has every right to run his ship the way he feels it should be run."

Seeing he had put Posey on the defensive and feeling a bit sorry for him, McCain changed the subject my asking, "What do you think of Johnson? Why would he go over the hill?"

Posey shrugged, thought for a second and said, "He was a good yeoman. I think he knew his job."

McCain took a deep breath and asked, "Whose idea was it not to report him missing?"

"Wasn't mine," Posey said defiantly.

Hoping he had loosened him up, McCain said, "So it was the captain's. Why do you suppose that was?"

"You'll have to ask him." Posey got to his feet. "That's a moot point now. Jim Haggen told me you had Adams sign the papers last night."

McCain liked Posey. His record said he'd graduated in the top ten percent of his academy class, his first ship was a tanker and he'd received several commendation letters for the way he handled his duties. McCain wondered how much of a risk it would be if he took Posey into his confidence. This was going to be a lonely job and it would be nice to have someone to share his plans with. But if it turned out that Posey was the wrong person, he'd blow his cover and probably the whole case. He'd better wait awhile.

Before Posey could get out the door, McCain stepped up to him and said, "Mr. Posey, as the senior chief, I'd appreciate it if you would tell Hall he has to move in with Chief Jackson. Then I'd like to move the ship's office into my stateroom. It won't take much work; the shipfitter can weld a bracket to hold the file cabinet. I can use the drop-down desk for my typewriter."

Posey looked as if I'd just thrown him a curve ball. "I suppose I'd better check with Captain Adams."

Pleadingly, McCain said, "Mr. Posey, there's way too much work to do, and I can't do it in this fishbowl. If you don't think you can give the necessary orders, just say so and I'll give them myself. I'd like to be moved in before the captain even knows about it. It'll only take about an hour and I can have it done while he's on the bridge." He paused and studied Posey's expression for a couple seconds. "It's my guess you'll probably benefit most from this switch."

Now looking curious as well as perplexed, Posey said, "I don't understand what you mean by that and I'm not sure I want to. But you're right. I'm the XO and I'll give the orders. If Captain Adams don't like it, it's too fucking bad." He looked as if the word "fucking" left a bad taste in his mouth.

McCain knew the pressure he was putting on the young officer and almost felt sorry for him. It was obvious his outburst of independence was staged for McCain's benefit and it was something he shouldn't have had to do. Adams must have already broken him to the point where he'd chosen flight over fight. He hoped he hadn't baited Posey into a bigger bind than he was in already. When he finally finished his investigation, he'd talk Tommy into helping Posey get assigned to another ship. There was still time for him to revert back to the efficient young officer he was on the tanker.

In less than two hours, McCain's new combination living quarters and office was ready for occupancy. Because it was only a temporary arrangement, he had the shipfitters just tack-weld the file cabinet to the bulkhead. Even though the typewriter looked out of place on the leaf of the desk and papers were spread from one end of his bunk to the other, McCain was happy with the results. Most important of all was that he was now secluded from Tobey and the rest of the crew. He was so busy getting his office moved he hadn't even stowed his personal gear. But that could wait till they got underway. He checked his Timex. Two and a half hours to go. Just long enough to inventory and pack Johnson's gear. He shook his head and wondered if Captain Adams even knew it had to be done. Just to make sure, he'd fill him in before he got started.

McCain knocked on Adams's door and waited several seconds. Assuming Adams wasn't there, McCain did an about face and started up the ladder to the bridge. But before he'd climbed three steps the cabin door opened and Captain Adams stuck out his head. When he saw it was McCain he pulled his robe around him and opened the door halfway.

From his position on the ladder, McCain was able to look past Adams and into the cabin, where he spotted a big-bellied blonde standing at the foot of Adam's bunk. This was really unbelievable and so unexpected he just stood there unable to move. Finally he said, "Captain, I'd like to talk to you for a minute."

Adams stepped into the passageway and closed the door behind him. "Couldn't this wait, Chief?"

McCain removed the unlit cigar from his mouth and said, "No, sir. Normally I'd have gone to Posey but you said…"

"I know what I said. What do you need? I'm busy."

McCain felt like saying that he'd already figured that out, but he held his feelings in check and explained that regulations called for them to inventory and pack Johnson's gear.

Adams looked aggravated; as if he didn't want to make a decision. "Are you sure we have to do this?"

"Yes, sir. In a few more days, Johnson will be a deserter. Even if he turns himself in, he'll never come back to the *Lakota*."

Adams shrugged. "So what?"

McCain stuck the cigar back into the corner of his mouth and rolled it from one side to the other. What kind of a person was this captain? Did he already know Johnson would never be coming back? "For sure Johnson will be court-martialed. We have to turn in his records and gear so they'll be available when he's picked up."

"So what do you want from me?"

"I'll need a witness to help me with the inventory. If you have no objections I was thinking of having Mr. Posey help me."

Adams's face turned scarlet. "Damn right I have objections. You can use anybody but him." He took a deep breath and then said, "I'll take that back. Get the bos'n to help you."

"Aye aye, sir." McCain started to leave, then turned back and said, "There is one more thing, Captain."

"What now? Damn it, I've got a lot to do before we get underway. Get it off your chest and get back to work."

"Sorry, Skipper. I just wanted you to know that Chief Hall is now in with Jackson. I'm by myself and I've moved the ship's office in with me."

"You what?" He looked as if he was going to explode.

In the few hours McCain had known Adams, he'd lost all respect for the man. McCain knew he was bordering on insubordination but the thought of that woman inside the cabin made him not give a damn. If he had to put up with this misfit officer, he was going to get some pleasure out of it. Ignoring his obvious disapproval, McCain said nonchalantly, "It's much better this way. I can get more work done and so can Tobey." He then took out his Zippo and relit his cigar. "Soon as you see how nice it looks, you'll agree with me. Want me to explain how I laid it out?"

Adams's hands shook. His bottom lip twitched. "Damn it, McCain, I said I had things to do. Don't bother me anymore today." He backed into his cabin and slammed the door.

McCain looked around. Seeing that there was no one in sight, he pressed his ear to the door. He could hear voices, but couldn't make out any words. Disappointed, he gave up and went down the passageway to the wardroom. Bos'n Greene, looking more like a human being than he did the day before, and Haggen were having coffee.

Haggen looked up and said, "Morning, Chief. What can we do for you?"

When McCain explained what he wanted, the bos'n turned to Haggen. "Jim, I've got too much to do. Would you take care of it for me?"

Before Haggen could answer, McCain said, "The captain was pretty explicit about who he wanted."

Greene laughed. "Don't worry about it. He's got so many problems he won't even remember what he said. By the way, did you meet Kitty?"

Assuming he was talking about the woman in the cabin, McCain said, "You mean Mrs. Adams?"

"No. Kitty is his pregnant girlfriend. His wife's in Norfolk. She's also pregnant."

McCain felt his contempt for Adams rising even higher. "Okay, I'm just following orders. Would one of you meet me in the crew's quarters in ten minutes? We'll need bolt cutters to open Johnson's lock."

When McCain reached the bottom of the ladder located outside his cabin and leading down into crew's quarters, Haggen and Shipfitter O'Neil were waiting for him in front of Johnson's locker. O'Neil held a bolt cutter in his right hand.

The two-by-three upright aluminum locker was the sum total of personal storage space granted to each of the *Lakota's* enlisted men. A combination lock hung in the hasp on the door.

Stacked between rows of three-tier bunks, other aluminum lockers were scattered around the compartment. Each bunk was identical: a pillow on one end, a folded blanket on the other. The mattresses were covered with white sack-like covers instead of sheets. Every bit of available space was used for storage or sleeping.

O'Neil guided the bolt cutter's jaws over the u-shaped bar of the lock. One squeeze of the handles ended the lock's days of protecting Johnson's possessions. McCain removed the now-useless lock and opened the door. "Good job, O'Neil." He turned to Haggen, "I don't think we'll need O'Neil any longer."

As O'Neil started up the ladder, Haggen said, "Do me a favor, chips. Chief Jackson and the electricians are working on the main electrical board. If it looks like they can't get it repaired in time to get underway let me know." Haggen's gaze shifted to McCain, "That's where I should be right now instead of down here going through Johnson's gear. You sure you need me?"

This was going to be easy. Since McCain had come down the ladder, he'd been thinking of some way to get Haggen out of the picture. The last thing he really wanted was a witness, but the inventory form called for it. Now it looked as if he'd get what he wanted without breaking a sweat. With any luck, he'd find the journal or something else that might shed some light on Johnson's murder. That is if he was in fact murdered. There was still a slight chance it was an accident. But he sure wouldn't put any money on it.

McCain staged a worried expression, shrugged his shoulders and said, "Regulations call for the inventory to be done by two people. But if you believe I'm not going to steal anything and are willing to sign after the fact, I'll take the chance."

Haggen glanced in the locker. "Don't look like there's anything in there worth stealing." He turned back to McCain, grinned and said, "For damn sure you can't wear his clothes."

Not appreciating the dig about his height, McCain said, "On second thought, maybe you should stick around. We should be done in an hour or so."

Haggen's smile was quickly replaced as he said, "Give it another thought, Chief. Adams will be mad as hell if we can't get underway on time. I'll sign later. It'll just be between you and me."

McCain nodded, turned to the locker, pulled out a narrow drawer and looked inside. "Don't look like there's any jewelry. Where will you be when I'm done? I've got to give a signed copy to the base master-at-arms."

"I'll be in the engine room."

Haggen was still rushing up the ladder when McCain bit down on his unlit cigar and went to work. After removing neatly stacked piles of shorts, socks, shoes, and uniforms, McCain ran his hand under his supply of T-shirts and felt a bunch of letters held together with a rubber band.

Without bothering to remove the rubber band, McCain flipped through the stack checking return addresses. There were none he recognized, but the letters might prove to be very interesting. He laid them aside. He'd read them later in his room. In the back of his mind, McCain still hoped he'd find the journal. But there was no sign of it. On the top shelf, he found a key ring with three keys on it. One looked like the key to the ship's office. He wondered what locks the other two would open.

It took McCain almost thirty minutes to list everything other than the letters and keys. When he finished packing the sea bag, McCain matched up the grommets and secured them with a new bronze, navy-issue padlock. He then shoved the letters inside his shirt and pocketed the keys.

He checked his watch. Time was flying. Only two hours to type up the inventory, get it signed, and delivered to the base master-at-arms

Chapter Five

Day Two—Mid-Morning

Back in his room, McCain pulled one of the letters from the stack and scanned through it. It was from a torpedo man third class on the USS *Barracuda*. The "My Dearest Larry" salutation was enough to let McCain know the writer and Johnson were more than mere shipmates. The rest of the letter was even mushier but gave no clue as to who might want to see Johnson dead.

The second letter was from a female accusing Johnson of trying to break up her marriage. McCain checked the address and saw that she was living in base housing. The fact that she had access to Johnson might be a lead. Better have Tommy look into it.

Resisting the urge to go through more of the letters, McCain pulled his chair up to the drop-leaf desk, slid the IBM Selectric from its storage space and typed an original and three copies of the inventory list.

Then with the inventory lists rolled up in his right hand, McCain rushed through the mess deck, through the crew's head and down the ladder into the diesel-smelling engine room. Two giant General Motors diesel-electric engines stood in the center of the large compartment. Forward of the engines, Haggen, Jackson, and a couple white hats were busy at work. McCain handed the list to Haggen, who, taking no interest whatever its contents, quickly scribbled his name and handed it back.

With that out of the way, McCain went back to the ship's office, where Tobey was making some entries in a ledger book. When McCain asked if Tobey recognized any of the keys from Johnson's locker, Tobey took the keys. He studied them for a second and said, "Sure, I know what they're to. This one is to the ship's office, and this one is to our storeroom on the pier." He held up the third key. "This one is to the stationery supply cabinet inside the storeroom."

"Supply cabinet?" McCain thought of the journal. "Who else has a key to the cabinet?"

"I suppose there's one in the master key file. But Johnson was the only person that needed one."

All the essential elements of a good hiding place, McCain thought. "How do I get to this cabinet? I need some envelopes. I think I'll deliver Johnson's sea bag and stop there on my way back."

Toby got up from his chair, and said, "Hell, Chief, I've got some time. Tell me what you need and I'll get it for you."

Definitely not the words McCain wanted to hear. To give him time to dream up a legitimate sounding turndown, he lit up a fresh cigar and by the time a ring of smoke reached the overhead, McCain had his plan. He rolled the cigar into the corner of his mouth and said, "Damned nice of you, but I don't have time to make a list. Besides I want to see what's on hand in case I have to order more."

Tobey shrugged and sat back down.

McCain then said, "There is something you can do. Would you get the duty driver to put Johnson's sea bag in the pickup?"

"Sure thing," said Tobey as he headed for the crew's mess.

McCain went back to his room and got his hat. The clock above the mirror showed that in ninety minutes they'd be on their way to Norfolk.

When McCain stepped onto the pier, he was met by a young, red-headed seaman standing beside a battered gray Chevrolet pickup truck with USN stenciled on the doors. Johnson's sea bag stood all alone in the truck bed. The seaman, grinning through a field of freckles, said, "Chief, I'm Seaman Curtin, the duty driver. Where we headed?"

McCain gave Curtin his hand and said, "Glad to meet you, Curtin. First stop will be the base master-at-arms office, where we'll get rid of Johnson's gear." He scampered around to the passenger side, stretched to reach the running board, and pulled himself into the cab. "They ought to put a ladder on these old trucks," he said with a grin.

Seaman Curtin looked at the chief like he didn't know whether to laugh or simply ignore him, choosing the later he pumped the gas pedal three times and turned the key. The engine fired. He let out on the clutch. After a dozen or so jerking bumps, they were on their way.

Before the engine had a chance to get warm they pulled up to a one-story brick building. "Here we are, Chief. Want me to carry the sea bag?"

"Sure would appreciate it. It's almost as big as I am." McCain slid out of the cab and headed for the door marked "Base Master-at-Arms." Curtin followed with the bag atop his right shoulder.

Inside, behind the counter stood a squared-away second-class boatswain's mate wearing undress blues. Around his right bicep was a black band embellished with MAA in gold letters. "Can I help you, Chief?"

McCain explained what he wanted and gave the man the sea bag. He then asked if there was a phone he could use. Not wanting to risk Curtin overhearing his conversation, McCain said, "You can wait in the truck. I'll only be a minute." As Curtin turned to leave, McCain said, "On second thought, I've got some letters that have to go in the mail. You can run them up to the mail drop and pick me up on your way back." He took three letters from his inside pocket and handed them to Curtin.

Soon as Curtin was out the door McCain turned to the sailor behind the counter and said, "Boats, I have to make a call to 90 Church Street. You got someplace that's private?"

"Sure, you can use the duty officer's phone. There's no one in his office."

"That'll do fine," said McCain. He pushed open a swinging counter gate and rushed into the vacant office. While waiting for Tommy's secretary to pick up the phone, he thought about Tommy and him growing up in Cheyenne. Tommy's dad was president of the country club. McCain's mother kept the clubhouse clean and did the cooking. Even though Tommy got to play golf while McCain was limited to caddying, they became the best of friends. Upon graduation from high school, McCain joined the Navy. Tommy went to Harvard.

Shortly after McCain got out of boot camp his mom died. She'd had cancer for years and McCain never knew it. But with her gone, there was no reason to go back to Cheyenne. When Tommy graduated law school, he too joined the Navy. Then, unknown to one another, they both were given orders to the Naval School of Justice in Newport.

Tommy was a lieutenant (junior grade). McCain was a yeoman second class. It turned out that they were both attending school as part of the commissioning crew of the USS *Boston*, the nation's first guided-missile cruiser. Tommy was to be the legal officer. McCain was to be his legal yeoman.

McCain had never forgotten how surprised they both were when they discovered they would be serving together. After they graduated and reported aboard the *Boston*, they never lost contact again. And even though McCain worked for Tommy they felt more like brothers than colleagues.

When Tommy's secretary finally put him on the phone, McCain gave him a rundown of what he'd learned. Then before Tommy had a chance to reply, McCain said, "Tommy, you know I've never backed away from anything in my life, but this might be too big for one man. Maybe you should stop the ship from getting underway."

"Too late, Jack. Just do the best you can. We haven't got time for another plan and the cops are getting anxious to find out the name of the deceased. We're in this together; I'm going to check out the bouncer this afternoon. So stop worrying, I'm sure you can handle anything that comes your way. Give me a call from Norfolk and let me know what you've uncovered. Most of all, find that journal. And when you do, make damn sure no one else sees it. It has to be the key to a lot of unanswered questions."

McCain took a deep breath and hoped Tommy's confidence in him was well-founded. "Is that all, Tommy?"

"One more thing; about the time you're passing Ambrose Lightship, your radioman will be receiving a dispatch saying Johnson is dead. That should untie your hands a little." McCain heard a chuckle on the other end when Tommy said, "Have a nice trip. Don't get seasick."

After hanging up the phone, McCain used the duty officer's sparkling-clean ashtray to grind out his cigar. Why he was smiling he didn't know. There sure wasn't anything funny; especially since Tommy was sitting up there in that plush office while he was going to sea on a rust bucket manned by a bunch of incompetent weirdos. McCain wondered if Tommy's cruel sense of humor was related to his six-foot-two height. Maybe it was from a lack of oxygen up there. Oh well, time to get back to work.

McCain departed through the outer office and headed for the door. Before going out, he turned and said, "When my driver gets here, tell him I've walked back." He lit up a fresh cigar, checked his watch and headed for the storeroom. He still had forty-five minutes.

The storeroom was located on the first floor of a two-story building that ran down the center of the pier. Thinking logically, McCain entered a door directly across from the *Lakota*. Inside he discovered that the storeroom was made of two-by-fours covered with heavy wire mesh. He tried one of the keys from Johnson's locker. It didn't work. He tried another. This time the lock snapped open.

Standing against the rear wall was a two-door plywood cabinet also secured with a bronze padlock. This time McCain hit pay dirt on the first try. The inside consisted of five plywood shelves crammed full with office supplies.

With only a little more than a half-hour to go, McCain started searching for Johnson's journal. The lower shelves were easy to reach but brought no results. As he was maneuvering a five-gallon can of paint into position to stand on, the door opened and Tobey stepped inside. "See you found the office supplies. The envelopes are on the top shelf. I'll get you a box."

McCain started to refuse, but couldn't think of a reason for rejecting the offer. "Thanks," he said. "This is one of those times when being short is a real pain." Disappointed, knowing his search was finished, McCain said, "Looks like we've got a good supply of everything we need. Just get me a handful of 'franked' envelopes. That should hold me till we get back."

As Tobey locked up, McCain checked his watch. Twenty minutes before sailing time. If only he could get back in there; maybe the journal was on that top shelf. They were halfway across the pier when Captain

Adams appeared on the port wing of the bridge. He saw the two men below and started screaming, "McCain! Where the hell you been? I want to see you up here immediately." With his lower lip quivering, he turned and walked into the pilothouse.

"That was some friendly greeting," McCain said. "Any idea what's eating him?"

Tobey grinned. "He's probably worried about coming back from sea and finding Kitty like he left her."

"You mean pregnant?"

"Hell, no; well fucked." Tobey shook with laughter. Obviously he was a man who appreciated his own jokes.

McCain left Tobey laughing on the pier and took his time going up to the bridge. He stepped into the pilothouse and found Adams standing with feet spread and arms crossed. His voice shook as he said, "Chief! Don't you know it's the yeoman's job to pick up the pay records before we get underway?" With a closed fist he pounded on the chart table. "Without those records the crew can't get paid," he growled.

McCain wondered if he was more concerned about his own pay than the pay of the crew. "Sorry, sir. I should have thought of that. I'll run over to the disbursing office right now."

McCain was about to turn to leave when Adams shouted, "McCain! You stand fast." He put his hands behind his back and started pacing. "Posey is picking them up." He stopped and glared at McCain for several seconds. Then he gritted his teeth and said, "We might as well get something straight right now."

Talk about overreaction, McCain thought. Wondering whatever it was they had to get straight he was forced to wait while Adams rushed out on the starboard wing and spat over the side.

When he came back in, he said, "Don't forget, I came up through the ranks. I know exactly how you fuckin' yeoman operate." Beads of spittle formed in the corners of his mouth. "If you used your pull to get on my ship thinking it'd be a plush job, forget it." He wiped his mouth with his handkerchief. "Far as I'm concerned, you're not a damned bit better than Johnson. You're going to do everything he did, including serving as my bridge talker. And I've told Posey to put you on the underway quartermaster watch list. Got that straight, mister?"

McCain found himself in dire need of a cigar, but figured it was be a bad time to light up. He'd run up against other officers like Adams and he knew that they were usually looking for an argument. The only way to handle them was to "yes" them to death. Deny them the backtalk and you've won the battle. McCain snapped to attention and blurted out, "Yes, sir. Anything else, sir?" He wondered if Adams could read his true feelings.

Adams glowered for a bit, then said, "That'll be all for now. When I set the sea detail, you report to the bridge. And from now on I want to know when you leave the ship."

Was Adams afraid of something or just being chickenshit? McCain grinned and said, "Aye, aye, sir." With a bigger grin he then said, "And if you're not aboard I'll let the XO know I'm leaving."

Looking as if he'd just won a victory, Adams said, "That's the way I want it."

Chapter Six

Day Two—Early Afternoon

Five minutes after special sea detail was set, as Adams had directed, McCain was once again in the pilot house. This time he was wearing a set of sound-powered phones; the communication system of choice used on navy ships because they need no outside source of power. The set consisted of large padded earphones and a mouthpiece mounted on a breastplate hanging from a strap around his neck. The breastplate also supported the junction box that connected the mouthpiece and earphones to the telephone sound system. This was not a new experience for McCain. He'd been captain's talker on other ships so he was fully aware of what was expected of him.

In addition to McCain, also on the bridge was Captain Adams, his second in command, Posey, Tobey as the quartermaster, and Seaman Curtin as helmsman. Adams looked down at the pier, and shouted, "Slack one, three and four. Hold number two." McCain pushed the button on the mouthpiece and repeated Adam's words exactly as they were uttered.

With the starboard side to the pier and the stern facing the channel, the ship would either have to turn completely around or go out stern first. McCain didn't consider himself a ship handler but backing out seemed to be the best option.

Once again Adams called down to the line handlers on the pier, "Cast off one, three and four lines." The sailors lifted the lines off the corresponding bollards while the *Lakota* crew pulled them aboard.

Soon as the lines were clear, Adams said, "Right fifteen degree rudder, back slow." The turning screw sent a vibration through the ship's hull as the *Lakota's* stern swung to port. Adams then said, "All stop. Ease number two." When slack appeared in the line, he yelled, "Cast off number two." While the crew was heaving in the line, Adams said, "Back slow."

Within minutes they'd backed into the channel and had swung the bow to where it was pointed out to sea. "Ahead one-third," said Adams. McCain was impressed. Adams had handled the ship like a rowboat.

While waiting to be dismissed from special sea detail, McCain eased over to the chart table to see if he could get an idea of the course laid out for the first leg of the trip. Near as he could tell they'd be passing Ambrose Lightship in a couple of hours. He was hoping it would be sooner; he was anxious to see the crew's reactions when they heard about Johnson's death. Off to starboard McCain spotted the Staten Island Ferry slips where Johnson's body had been discovered.

McCain took another look at the ferry slips and then back to the pier in Bayonne. Only a few thousand yards separated the two. Was it possible that Johnson was killed on the *Lakota* and thrown overboard? If the tide was on its way out, the current could have easily carried the body to where it was found.

After Adams secured the sea detail, McCain was on his way down from the bridge when he stopped on the first landing and stepped into the chart house to see Chief Hall. It would be their first conversation since McCain had commandeered his stateroom. He wasn't sorry about what he'd done, but he took no pleasure in forcing Hall to share space with a slob like Jackson. The ball was now in Hall's court; he was senior to Jackson and if he put his foot down Jackson would have to clean up his act.

McCain found Hall bending over the chart table laying out the next leg of the journey. He looked up, saw McCain and said, "Well, what do you think of our little ship now?"

"Looks like Captain Adams is a damned good seaman," said McCain. "I can't say much for his ass-chewing though. Hell, I've had better by ensigns." He took a half-smoked cigar from his pocket, struck life to his Zippo, and lit up.

Hall shrugged. "He is a good ship handler, but that's about all I can say about him. And that's a shame. I've heard that he was an outstanding CPO." Hall paused and shook his head. "I guess the freedom of having his own command led to temptations that he'd never had to deal with before."

For Hall's benefit, McCain turned his head and blew out a large puff of smoke. "Sounds like that could be the case. Anyway, I just stopped by to let you know that there's nothing personal about me wanting my own stateroom. It was no reflection on you." McCain thought for a second, "Nor Chief Jackson, for that matter."

Hall stuck out his hand. "No problem. If I was the senior chief, I'd have done the same thing. I don't think Jackson likes it too much though." McCain shook his hand as Hall kept talking. "He'll get over it. It's not that Jackson is a bad guy, he just drinks too often and showers too seldom." He picked up a sheet of paper and said, "I see by the watch list you're going to be Posey's quartermaster."

"That's the old man's idea," said McCain.

Hall grinned. "Ever stand a quartermaster watch before?"

"Nope," said McCain.

Hall reached behind him, pulled a tall stool from beneath the chart table and sat down. "Don't worry about it. It's easy. You'll be keeping the ship's log and help Posey stay on course by taking sightings. He'll show you everything you need to know." He rolled up the chart he was working on. "Hell, pay attention and you'll be standing OOD watches before we get back."

As McCain was about to leave, the door separating the chartroom from the radio shack opened and Rossi came out carrying two empty coffee mugs. He saw McCain, grinned, and said, "You standing in a hole, Chief?"

McCain gritted his teeth and kept silent. As Rossi passed on his way to the mess deck, McCain stuck out his foot and sent Rossi pitching forward over the hatch combing. His feet remained inside the chartroom; the rest of his body sprawled on the landing.

Then McCain stepped alongside Rossi's prone body and said, "Don't you know you've got to watch your step. These little ships are dangerous for you tall guys." He reached down, grabbed Rossi's belt and pulled him to his feet. Pieces of shattered coffee mugs were scattered about the deck. "Make sure you clean up that mess," McCain said gently.

Rossi's face turned scarlet. "You tripped me!" he slurred.

McCain blew a puff of smoke in his direction, and said, "Damn it, Rossi, don't blame me if you can't walk and chew gum at the same time." He gave Rossi a wry grin and turned to Hall. "You didn't trip him, did you, Chief?"

Hall shook his head, chuckled, and said, "I didn't see anyone trip him."

Making no bones about being pissed off, Rossi bent down and started picking up the broken china. As he was doing so, McCain heard him mutter something about fucking chiefs. Then he thought he heard Johnson's name, but was unable to get the frame of reference. McCain wondered if there was bad blood between Rossi and Johnson. He made a mental note to see what he could find out about their relationship.

Before leaving, McCain glanced around the chart house. The major piece of furniture was the chart table and high stool Hall was sitting on. On each side of the knee well were wide cabinets for storing charts.

Two bulkhead shelves held various navigation books and bound volumes of "Notice to Mariners." To the right of the radio shack door was a polished hardwood case. "What's in the fancy box?" McCain asked.

Hall slid off his stool and moved over to the case where he lifted the lid exposing what looked like a clock. "This is the ship's chronometer. See how it's mounted on a pair of gimbals."

McCain nodded and knew why, but evidently Hall thought he should educate him.

"No matter how the ship pitches or rocks," said Hall. "It'll always stay level. Every day at noon, it has to be wound. When you're on the twelve-to-four watch, it'll be one of your jobs." He closed the cover.

"Tomorrow, I'll show you how to wind it."

Wanting to change the subject, McCain pointed to an electronic instrument mounted on the inboard bulkhead, and said, "What's that?"

Hall reached up and turned a knob. Wavy lines formed on the screen. "It's our Loran receiver. You'll learn how it works on this afternoon's watch."

This was all interesting but it wasn't giving McCain any dope on the murder. Besides he urgently had the need for a cup of coffee. "I've learned enough for now. What say we go down and have a cup of mud?"

"Sounds good to me," Hall said.

As they were on their way out of the chart house, Radioman First Class Ben Wishbore stuck his head out of the radio shack and said, "How about telling Rossi to get his ass up here with my coffee." Wishbore had thick black hair and wore a handle-bar mustache. Earphones covered his ears.

McCain glanced at Wishbore, then at Hall and said, "I'd sure hate to have to work in that little room with an SOB like Rossi."

Hall nodded.

"How long before we reach Ambrose Lightship," McCain asked.

"Won't be long," said Hall.

They were on their second cup of coffee when Rossi came bounding down the ladder and burst into the mess hall. "We just got a message. Johnson's dead. Must have had an accident. They say he fell in the harbor and drowned."

Acting as surprised as the others, McCain asked, "Did they say when it happened?"

Rossi gave McCain a dirty look before saying sarcastically, "I didn't read the message. You'll have to ask Wishbore, he copied it."

McCain left his coffee and went up to the radio shack, where a thorough reading of the dispatch confirmed that Tommy had included just enough info to let Captain Adams know one of his crew was dead. Only McCain and the killer (if he was on board) knew how Johnson died.

McCain checked his Timex. In less than an hour he'd be relieving Tobey as quartermaster of the watch.

Chapter Seven

Day Two—Afternoon

At 1530, McCain threw some water on his face, brushed his crew cut, and climbed the two flights to the bridge. He had to admit that he was a bit ambivalent about standing a quartermaster watch for the first time, but was determined not to screw up. In no way did he want to give Captain Adams the satisfaction of chewing him out again.

Arriving early, McCain took his time looking over the log and then watching how Tobey handled his duties. Chief Hall's words that standing watch would be easy kept running through his mind, but for some reason he kept doubting them. There had to be more to it than keeping the log and getting coffee for the OOD.

Bos'n Greene stood in the pilothouse, his binoculars to his eyes staring through the windshield. McCain rose up on his toes and stretched to peer over his shoulder. He didn't see anything but rolling water crowned with gentle whitecaps. He left the bos'n and joined Tobey on the starboard wing of the bridge. McCain was impressed with Tobey and how he was completely at ease as he pressed his eye to the pelorus scope. Then he mumbled something to himself, swung the scope a few degrees to take another sighting, then swung it again to take a third. Then he rushed to the chart table and where the three sightings intersected he wrote the time—1535—on the course line Posey, as navigator, had laid out for them to follow.

McCain decided to give it try himself, but immediately found himself in trouble; the pelorus stand was too tall. He tried standing on his toes but he still couldn't see through the scope. It really pissed him off that he wasn't going to be able to do everything Tobey had done. There had to be another way. He stepped back, studied the pelorus stand, and noticed its flared base. He had an idea. He put his right foot at the top of the flare, wrapped his left leg around the pedestal for balance and tried again. It didn't work. He still couldn't line up anything on the beach. Besides he felt his foot slipping off the painted surface.

McCain turned around to look for something else to stand on. Bos'n Greene and Tobey stood laughing. Even the helmsman was grinning. He felt the blood rush to his face. Tobey must have noticed and said, "Don't worry, Chief, when I get off watch I'll get you something to stand on."

Using the radar was a bit easier. He'd stood watches in combat information centers and knew how to chart other ships in the area. However, this process was a bit more complicated because to fix the ship's position, he'd have to compare the shoreline's radar image with the navigational charts. He'd never done that before. But according to Tobey, they seldom relied on the radar for piloting; most of the time it was land-based navigational aids. When out of sight of land, they used Loran or the stars.

At exactly 1545, Posey relieved Bos'n Greene. Tobey signed out and McCain logged in that Posey had assumed the duties of OOD and YNC McCain the duties of quartermaster of the watch. Then McCain logged their course, the condition of the sea, a description of the clouds and the direction and speed of the wind. He wouldn't have to make another entry till they changed course or something noteworthy happened.

Posey glanced at the log and said, "Well, Chief, looks like you've done this before. Now how about taking some sightings?"

McCain stared at Posey wondering if he'd heard about his problem and was setting him up. Then deciding it wasn't worth worrying about he said, "Sorry, Mr. Posey, I can't just yet. Tobey is bringing me something to stand on. After he gets here, I'll get you all the sightings you need. Fact is, I'm looking forward to it."

Suddenly the sound of footsteps running up the ladder caught their attention. It was Tobey carrying a red plastic milk case. "Try this, Chief."

McCain placed the case at the foot of the pelorus stand, stepped up, leaned over, and looked through the scope. It was perfect. "Thanks, Tobey," McCain said as he turned to face Posey. "What bearing you want? By the way, you mind if I smoke?"

Posey went to the chart table and said, "Not at all; how about taking a bearing on that smoke stack, that oil storage tank and that radio tower."

At 1700, an hour into the watch, a casually dressed Captain Adams came on the bridge. In his hand he held a radio message form. Ignoring Posey, Adams handed McCain the form and said, "We received another dispatch from headquarters. The admiral says we have to conduct a line-of-duty investigation on Johnson. Can you do that?"

McCain studied the form for a minute. It was no surprise; Tommy was just doing what McCain had suggested on the phone. He looked up at Adams and said, "I've done one or two of them before. They need it before they can pay Johnson's death benefits." He couldn't help but notice how the message seemed to irritate Adams. Was it the word investigation? "I'll get started first thing in the morning," he said.

Adams nodded. "Okay, but remember, nothing leaves the ship without me seeing it first."

As Adams turned to go below, McCain snapped to attention, and said, "Yes, sir, Captain. I got your message this morning. Still can't sit down without a cushion." He was disappointed, Adams, seeming preoccupied, didn't bother to respond.

Soon as the captain was out of sight, Posey beckoned McCain to join him on the starboard wing. When safely out of the hearing of the helmsman, Posey put his hand on McCain's shoulder and said, "I get the impression you're not too fond of our captain?"

McCain removed the cigar stub from his mouth and spit over the side. "You've got that right. Take a look at this ship and its crew. How can anyone respect a CO that lets his command get in this condition? I'd say that's enough reason."

Posey didn't say anything. He didn't have to, the look in his eyes, and the nodding of his head, said he agreed with McCain. He was again tempted to tell Posey his real reason for being on board, but decided to think about it a bit longer. They would be together on the four-to-eight watch in the morning. If he decided to tell him, he'd do it then.

Posey lifted his binoculars, peered out over the bow and said, "I'm trying to spot our next sea buoy." He lowered the glasses. "If I were you, I wouldn't keep giving the old man a hard time. He can get damn mean. A few weeks ago Johnson talked me and the rest of the officers into taking Adams on. I've been paying for it ever since."

McCain blew out a puff of smoke and watched the wind carry it aft. Then he nonchalantly said, "You talking about the mutiny?"

Posey's head snapped in McCain's direction, a quizzical expression covering his face. McCain smiled, "The bos'n mentioned it. But he didn't give me any details."

He looked relieved as he said, "I wouldn't call it a mutiny, but some things are better not being talked about." Then without another word, Posey stepped inside the pilothouse, bent over and pressed his face against the rubber face mask shielding the radar screen.

McCain went to the chart table and checked the location of the elusive buoy on the map. He then looked over his shoulder and said, "Can you pick it up on radar?"

"I've got a blip that could be it. Should be dead ahead." Posey raised his binoculars again.

McCain opened the drawer to the chart table, grabbed a pair of binoculars and went outside. While searching the horizon, he thought about Posey's warning and his reference to Johnson. Could Posey have had something to do with Johnson's murder? It didn't seem likely. But who could it be? And what about the debt letters? He'd looked them over before coming on watch. Six of the ship's enlisted men each owed both Household and Beneficial Finance Companies three hundred dollars plus interest. But how could that have anything to do with Johnson's death? Was it possible that Johnson played a role in their obtaining the loans?

He wished he could take a look at their loan applications. All six men were single third-class petty officers or above. Not the type to need money from finance companies. And except for Rossi, not the type to walk away from their obligations. He decided that after he got the line-of-duty paperwork out of the way, he'd make it a point to talk to each of them.

The rest of the letters were addressed to Captain Adams. All from the same companies complaining that he hadn't answered their pleas for assistance in collecting the money his crew owed them.

Suddenly, in the distance, he spotted a small dark object. Was it the buoy? He watched it for another minute and, pointing at the object, said, "I think I've got it."

"You're right, Chief, that's it. See if you can get a bearing on it?"

McCain mounted his milk crate and peered through the scope. "Looks like 186 degrees." Good, he thought, he was getting the hang of this real fast.

Posey moved alongside and said, "We're right on course."

As the buoy drew closer, they didn't have a chance to continue their conversation. Posey stayed in the pilothouse. McCain stayed on the starboard wing till it was almost time to be relieved. To enable the watch-standers to have time for supper, the four-to-eight watch was split into two dog watches. The first dog watch was only an hour and a half long.

At exactly 1720 McCain logged that he had been relieved by Boatswain's Mate Third Class Billy Joe Tucker; that Chief Hall had assumed the duties of OOD; and that Seaman Haley had taken the helm. New Jersey was off to starboard and he was hungry as an Atlantic City slot machine.

Chapter Eight

Day Two—Evening

By the time McCain made it down from the bridge, most of the crew and all of the chiefs had finished eating. He had the table to himself as he tore into a heaping plate of baked Virginia ham, sweet potatoes, string beans, and corn bread. It was the third good meal he had since reporting on board. The *Lakota* had many things wrong with it, but chow wasn't one of them.

McCain finished his first plate and went into the galley for more ham and another hunk of corn bread. As First Class Commissaryman George Rice cut McCain a slice of what was left of the ham, McCain said, "I'll tell you, Stew. That's the best corn pone I've had since I left Wyoming. A dab or so of honey would make it perfect."

The generous smile on Rice's jet-black face indicated that he was proud of his work and appreciated the recognition. Once again, McCain was impressed with how neat and clean Rice was. He'd been cooking all day, but there wasn't a spot on his whites. Along with Chief Hall and Posey, Rice stood out from the rest of the crew. "Glad you liked it, Chief," Rice said as he grabbed a clean plate off the dish rack and gently placed two generous chunks of his golden masterpiece it its center. He handed the plate to McCain and said with a twinkle in his oversized eyes, "I do believe I can rustle up some honey. Give me a minute and I'll bring it out."

After placing the plates containing corn bread and ham on the table, McCain grabbed his empty mug and refilled it at the coffee urn. This would be his first chance for a one-on-one talk with Rice. He was hoping to find out why anyone with twenty-four years of perfect conduct could suddenly start being a deadbeat. Something had to be wrong. And, as in most cases, the only way to get this type of answer was to ask the one involved. He'd watch for an appropriate time and place to question Rice about it.

Rice came out of the galley carrying a pot of honey with the handle of a small dipper extending above the rim. He set the pot in front of McCain, drew himself a cup of coffee and sat down opposite the chief. "That there honey is my private stock. Most of this crew wouldn't appreciate it, so I don't share it with them." He took a sip of coffee, and said, "You're different. I don't mind sharing with you."

McCain liked the sound of that. He had a smile the size of Rossi's arrogance on his face when he ladled a thick stream of honey over his square of corn bread. He returned the dipper to the pot and slid his plate closer to his chest. Then, leading forward, McCain gingerly lifted the honey-dripping cake and took a bite. It was every bit as good as it looked. "Stew," he said, "this must be Wyoming honey; haven't tasted anything this good in years."

Rice's thick lips parted in a wide grin. "I believe it comes from the Dakotas, but you've got it right. It's good eatin'." Rice got up and said, "Watching you makes me want a piece myself."

While waiting for Rice to return, McCain glanced around the mess deck and saw that, except for him and Rice, it was empty. A good time to try to get the information he was looking for.

When Rice moseyed out with his chunk of corn bread and sat down again, McCain said, "Glad we've got this chance to talk. I saw in your record where you've put in your papers to transfer to the fleet reserve. Any idea what you're going to do when you get out?"

"Sure enough; I'm going to open a little restaurant in Newport." Rice sipped his coffee. "That is if the mortgage is approved. My wife, Odelia, is taking care of that."

"Is Odelia your first wife?"

"Yes, sir. It took me a long time to find the right woman. Only been married a year, but she sure was worth waiting for." He took another sip. "I called her before we left. She thinks she's pregnant." He grinned. "Imagine an old man my age having a new baby."

"You're not old, but how do you feel about it?"

"Just grand. A bit scared, but just grand. I'm starting a new life; I've had enough of going to sea. I can't wait to sleep every night with Odelia. She's a fine wife and is going to be a fine mother. She's smart too; got two years of college."

McCain took a deep breath and said, "Stew, I don't exactly know how to tell you this."

Rice gave him a questioning look.

"It's about the money you owe. I'll help you write to the finance company and tell them how you're going to start repaying."

Rice's eyes got as big as the cake plates. Looking as if he was about to choke, he said, "What money? I don't owe nobody any money."

McCain wondered what in the hell was going on. He'd questioned enough people to be pretty sure Rice wasn't lying. "You didn't borrow money from Household and Beneficial Finance?"

"Not for me, I didn't. No, sir. Captain Adams needed some money and wanted to borrow it from me. I told him I don't loan money to nobody." Sparkling drops of sweat formed on Rice's black brow. "He had some papers he wanted me to sign and take them into town and deliver them to those two companies. When I handed them the papers, they looked them over and then handed me three hundred dollars. I brought the money back and gave it to the captain. Nobody said nothing about me making payments. Far as I'm concerned, everything's fine."

McCain tightly gripped his cup. This was not what he expected. "You borrowed money for Captain Adams?"

Rice's lower lip twitched. "No, man. I didn't borrow no money. I just went into town and got it for the captain. He said I wouldn't have a thing to worry about."

McCain shook his head and said, "Didn't you think that was a little strange?"

Looking as if he was going to be sick, Rice said, "Only thing strange about it was when he told me not to mention it to any of the officers or men." He stood up and stacked the empty plates. "Tell you the truth, I'd forgotten about the whole thing. Johnson asked me about it once, but didn't say why he was askin'."

Johnson must have suspected something, McCain thought. "When did Johnson ask you about it?"

Rice shrugged. "A few days before he went over the hill." He picked up the plates and carried them into the galley.

As McCain finished his coffee, he kept hoping Rice would come back out. When he saw that he wasn't, McCain took his mug into the galley and dropped it in the sink. He then placed his hand on Rice's shoulder, and said, "Thanks for the honey, Stew. About that other thing; don't worry about it. It's probably some mistake."

McCain wondered if he'd get similar stories from the others. How did Johnson fit in? Could it have anything to do with his death? Were the two investigations turning into one?"

Rice, who had been carving more ham, put down his knife and wiped his hands on his apron. Concern still showed in his eyes as he said, "Chief, I sure hope you're right. Mostly everyone knows I just do my job and don't get too friendly with anyone. But when your skipper needs a favor; well, you do what you gotta do. Never hurts to have the old man on your side." He picked up his knife and another thin slice of ham dropped onto the carving board.

"Thanks again, Stew," McCain said. "I really did enjoy the corn bread and honey. Now I've got some work to do."

Back in his room, McCain pulled out his desk chair, sat down, and lit a fresh Optimo. When fully engulfed in smoke, he reached in the desk drawer and pulled out the stack of debt letters. He quickly learned that, in addition to Rice, the letters implicated Smith, quartermaster third class; O'Neil, shipfitter second class; Wishbore, radioman first class; Billy Joe Tucker, boatswain's mate third class; and last but not least, pain-in-the-ass Rossi.

He found it very curious that no two of them fit into a pattern. None of them were close friends, and except for Rossi and Wishbore, they didn't even work together. And he'd already seen enough to know that there was no love lost between Rossi and Wishbore. He doubted that either of them would confide in each other. If Captain Adams wanted to pick people who would keep secrets from one another, he picked the right bunch.

In the line-of-duty investigation, he'd have to ascertain that Johnson's death was not due to his own misconduct. He knew the Navy usually didn't want to create additional problems for the deceased's family, so he'd give Johnson the benefit of the doubt about being AWOL and assume he died while in a pay status. If possible, he'd like to list it as a suicide, which the Navy normally considered a sign of insanity. But in his gut, he knew Johnson didn't kill himself. He just hoped he'd be able to find the person who did it.

He got up and paced around the little room. Was it possible that he was killed accidentally? To know that, he'd have to find someone who was with him when he went into the water. And unless he missed his guess, that someone would be a murderer and not a witness to an accident.

McCain was sure Tommy realized that with the *Lakota* at sea, he couldn't furnish all the answers. Tommy also had to know that Johnson couldn't be responsible for his own murder and that this line-of-duty investigation was just a façade to give McCain an excuse to question the officers and crew and maybe come up with a motive for murder.

In his message, Tommy was smart to call it an accident. But it was 180 degrees from what he had said on the phone. Tommy must have the same hunch McCain had: foul play. McCain's opinion grew stronger by the hour. Every time he turned over a rock, he found another reason to give credence to the murder theory.

He checked his Timex: 2000. Maybe he should try to get some sleep. At 0330 he had to get up and go on watch. In fact, he was looking forward to it because on the bridge he'd be alone with Posey and the helmsman. It would be his first good chance to pump Posey without Adams being around.

After twenty minutes of tossing in his bunk, McCain decided he wasn't sleeping and was wasting his time. Thinking that some fresh air might help, McCain took a fresh pair of khaki pants out of his locker and ran his hand down into the legs to break up the starch. He slipped them on and stepped into the passageway outside his door.

When he pulled aside the drape to the crew's mess, he found the room packed with movie watchers. A projector mounted on the starboard bulkhead purred as it projected John Wayne followed by a group of hard-riding cowboys across the room and onto a screen mounted on the port bulkhead.

Ducking low to avoid the projector's beam of light, McCain rushed through the crowded room and into the head. He then took his time passing the engine room ladder and entering the towing-engine room, where he stopped to take note of the three-inch wire rope coiled around the huge towing drum attached to the towing engine. He'd never seen a cable that large before.

On the fantail, there wasn't a soul in sight. The night air and sky was beautiful. Funny how the stars always looked closer when you were at sea. He walked to the rail and peered down at the flickering phosphorescent specks adding life to the black water below. He'd seen them hundreds of times before, but the sparkling specks still mesmerized him. He could watch them for hours.

Suddenly a metal object banged off the deck and hit McCain in the leg. He reached down and grabbed a foot-long dog wrench just as it was about to go over the side. He looked around. It had to come from the bridge or maybe from outside the radio shack or chart house. McCain was someone's target; but who? He went back to his cabin to think about it.

Chapter Nine

Day Three—Early Morning

What was that? Knock, knock, knock. Someone was at the door. McCain yawned and stretched his arms. It seemed as if he'd just dropped off and his sleep was hard to shake. When his mind finally focused, he realized it was Tobey telling him it was time to relieve the watch. Another knock. He rubbed his eyes and called out, "Come on in."

Tobey opened the door, stuck in his head, and said, "Hate to wake you up, Chief, but it's that time. Don't rush. Grab yourself a cup of coffee and bring it up with you." He backed out and closed the door.

McCain reached up and switched on his reading lamp sending a blast of blinding light into his sleep-laden eyes. Soon as his eyes adjusted, he forced himself out of his bunk and threw some water on his face. When sufficiently awake, he donned his work khakis and headed for the crew's mess. His watchmate, helmsman Seaman Steed, stood before the urn filling his mug with steaming mud-colored coffee. McCain reached into the dish rack, grabbed himself a mug, and waited for Steed to finish. When Steed turned and saw McCain, he said, "Hell of a way to make a living, right, Chief?"

Although conversation was the last thing on his mind, McCain forced a grin and said, "Sure as hell is. But I suppose after about fifty years, one could get used to it."

Steed laughed, sending coffee sloshing over the mug's brim. He quickly put it down on the table and said, "Fifty years, ha—ha—ha;

won't take me fifty years. One more to go on a four-year hitch and I'm out of here."

Not seeing the humor in what he said, McCain shrugged his shoulders, stepped up to the urn and claimed his share of its contents. Steam and a strong aroma rose to fill his sinuses. "Boy does that smell good," he said before glancing at Steed and saying, "Guess the Navy ain't for everyone. Wait up. I'll make the climb to the bridge with you. By the way, how'd you like the movie last night?"

"Ain't no such thing as a bad John Wayne movie. But the way you scooted through the mess hall without even glancing at the screen, I guess you don't think so."

McCain blew on his coffee and tried to take a sip. It was too hot. "I like John Wayne, but I needed some fresh air." He pictured the flying dog wrench and said, "Did you notice if Rossi was at the movie?"

"Funny you ask," said Steed. "You'd no sooner left the mess deck when the film ran out. While Curtin was changing reels, Rossi got up and said he was going up to the radio shack. A few minutes later, he came back."

On their way up to the bridge, they met Bos'n Greene, who had just been relieved by Posey, coming down. Greene looked tired and old enough to have been a messcook at the last supper. But now his face didn't have that bloated look he had when they first met. Greene stopped and squeezed to one side to let Steed and McCain pass. Before continuing his journey down, he said, "Have a good watch. It's a beautiful morning, the sea is like glass."

In the pilot house, McCain joined Tobey at the chart table, where he filled McCain in on the ship's course and speed. In addition, he warned McCain that there was a blip on the radar that he should keep his eye on, and what the next navigational sighting would be. He then signed the log and left the bridge.

McCain checked the radar screen and saw the blip of a ship five degrees to port of their present course. It was still several miles away and of no immediate concern. He then went out on the starboard wing, where Posey stood scanning the horizon through his binoculars. "Good morning, Mr. Posey. See anything out there?"

Posey lowered his glasses. "According to the radar, we've got a ship up ahead. Looks as if our courses might cross."

"That a problem?" McCain said.

Posey laughed. "Only if we do it at the same point at the same time. Don't think there's any danger, but we'll keep close watch on it. If necessary, we'll slow down till he gets out of our way." He lifted a blue-rimmed wardroom saucer and cup off the bulwark. "Let's go inside and see if you remember what you learned on our last watch."

At the chart table, Posey turned to McCain and said, "See if you can tell us where we're at."

McCain felt like a schoolboy and Posey the teacher. He started to say something sarcastic, like asking if Posey was a high grader, but he didn't. Fact was, compared to the rest of the officers; McCain thought Posey was the only one deserving to wear gold braid. Haggen, the chief engineer, wasn't too bad. But the bos'n and skipper were disgraces to their uniforms.

Bending over the chart, McCain located the 0400 mark on the dead-reckoning course. He noted the nearest landmarks on the chart before stepping out onto the open wing, raised his binoculars and studied the lights on the coastline. After a minute or so, he said, "I'd say that's Ocean City, Maryland. But to make sure, I'll take a couple cuts." He looked for his milk crate. It was missing. "Anyone know who took my box?"

Posey stepped into the pilothouse and came back with the milk crate. "The bos'n told me where he'd stuck it. Said it was in his way."

After positioning the crate at the foot of the pelorus stand, McCain climbed up and took three bearings. Then he rushed to the chart table and, using the protractor, made a light pencil mark where the three bearings came together on their course line. This was easy. He turned to Posey and grinned. "Just like I told you; that's Ocean City, Maryland. We're right where we should be."

McCain was surprised how good he felt when Posey said, "Chief, that was great. You sure you've never done this stuff before?"

He found himself close to beaming when he answered, "Sure haven't. But I'll let you in on a secret. I always wanted to be a boatswain's mate. Almost made it, too. Out of boot camp, I was sent to a tin can and put on the deck force. When the yeoman discovered I could type, he talked the XO into taking me off chipping paint and assigning me to the ship's office. They sent me to yeoman school and made me a pencil pusher." He caught himself just as he was about to disclose how he got his job as an investigator.

A couple minutes later he took a swig of coffee, swirled it around in his mouth, started to swallow, changed his mind and spit it over the side. "That got cold fast," McCain said as he sent the rest of the mug's contents into the black water below. "Come to think of it, this yeoman job would be pretty good if it wasn't for all the paperwork." It was his favorite line and he always ended it with a laugh. This was no exception but evidently Posey didn't think it was so funny. McCain shrugged his shoulders and let the subject drop.

At 0500, the oncoming ship changed course. No longer in any danger of colliding, McCain went out on the port wing to watch the sun come up. Many times he'd watched the sun rise at sea and it never failed to impress him. It started as a glow on the eastern horizon. A few minutes later, with the upper edge of a bright orange ball showing above the surface of calm water, he heard footsteps behind him. He turned and saw it was Posey.

"Isn't that beautiful, Chief? This is my favorite watch. The ship and the world come to life on this watch." He paused for a second. "Maybe someday, it will be a morning like this when mankind finally realizes that there's room for all types. And the strong will stop trying to force their will on the weak."

McCain stared at Posey and saw a faraway look in his eyes. "That's pretty deep stuff," he said. "What are you really trying to say?"

That strange look in his eyes grew more intense. Suddenly Posey seemed to realize where he was and with an expression that made McCain think that Posey would like to take his words back, said, "I didn't mean anything. Sometimes I get carried away. Especially when I see how beautiful nature can be."

McCain eyed Posey for a moment. "Mr. Posey, do you suppose we can talk for a bit?"

"Sure, Chief. What's on your mind?"

He took a deep breath and said, "When I first came aboard, the bos'n told me that you and the officers tried to take over the ship." He felt sweat running down his back. Mutiny was not a pleasant subject to talk about. "When I mentioned it to Chief Hall, he said he talked you out of it. I've heard these things happen, but never been on a ship where it did."

Posey blushed and looked as if he wanted to run and hide. "It was the biggest mistake I ever made. I've been paying for it ever since." He sighed. "At the time, I felt it had to be done. I'm much smarter now."

McCain shook his head. "What on earth was the captain doing that made you think it was necessary? I went through your record and it shows you to be a good officer. But good officers don't take part in mutinies."

Posey pulled out his handkerchief and wiped his forehead. "I'm sure you know the captain's got a wife and girlfriend? Both women were after him for money. To keep them off his back, as soon as we'd come in from a tow, he'd go to headquarters and volunteer for another trip. Sometimes it would be the same day. The married men were complaining. Even the single men had had enough." He stepped inside and checked the radar.

When he came back out, he seemed to be more relaxed. "One day when Johnson and I were discussing the problem, he broke out the Navy Regulations and showed me how, for the good of the command and the Navy, the XO could relieve the CO. At the time, I thought it was the thing to do."

"Holy shit," McCain said. "What happened next?"

"I called a meeting of the chiefs and officers to show them the regulations. All but Chief Hall wanted to go through with it. Hall wouldn't budge. Then the bos'n changed his mind. After that, I was all alone."

McCain pictured the scene in his mind. It was like watching a bad movie. "Does the CO know about the meeting?"

"He does."

"How'd he find out?"

"That was what we finally agreed on. On our way back to port, we called another meeting. This time we invited Captain Adams. I explained how we felt and warned him that if he didn't arrange for some time in port, we'd take the matter into our own hands."

"How'd the captain take that?"

"He went into orbit. Called us a bunch of stupid bastards and dared us to try it again. Then he said he held me responsible. Now he runs hot and cold. Sometimes he treats me like a human being, but mostly he makes me feel lower than whale dung."

McCain was tempted to tell Posey he should feel that way, but figured the young officer was already paying for what he'd done and there was no use piling on. "Was Johnson at the meeting?"

"No," said Posey. "When I told him about it later, he was almost as mad as the old man. He said we'd screwed up and he'd take care of Adams himself."

Almost swallowing his cigar, McCain asked, "What did Johnson mean by that?"

"Don't know," Posey answered.

"You weren't curious?"

"I was. But he'd already gotten me into enough trouble. Maybe I didn't really want to know."

McCain shook his head again. "Sounds to me that you officers got yourselves into real trouble; Johnson may have planted the idea, but you're the ones who took the action."

Posey nodded. "I know you're right, Chief. I really don't want to talk about it any more." He turned and walked slowly to the other wing of the bridge.

McCain spent the rest of the watch wondering if that's why Johnson wrote to the admiral. The letter had said that he wanted a meeting; that he had something the admiral should know. But what on earth was it? He supposed it could have been about the mutiny but that didn't seem right to him. If only he could get his hands on Johnson's journal.

Chapter Ten

Day Three—Afternoon

At 1200 hours, the *Lakota* made its approach to Pier Three, Naval Operating Base, Norfolk. An hour later, with the ship securely moored, the crew was filing through the galley heaping their plates with huge portions of golden-brown fried chicken, mashed potatoes smothered with gravy, and corn-on-the-cob.

Jackson, Hall, and McCain were seated at the chief's table and were being served by the duty mess cook. Dixon shuffled through the crew's mess heading for the wardroom. In one hand he had a platter of chicken; a bowl of potatoes in the other. A moment later his was back for the gravy and corn.

McCain picked up a luscious-looking drumstick, bit down and tore off a chunk. Soon as he swallowed, he turned to Chief Hall and said, "I heard the XO say we're staying here overnight. How come?"

Hall used his napkin to wipe his mouth, and then said, "The yard tugs will be bringing a barge down from Little Creek. Won't be here till about 1600; we'll miss the tide. It's better to wait till morning."

Chief Jackson shoved a whole thigh in his mouth and brought out a stripped bone. Still chewing with bits of chicken dropping from his lips, he said, "Bos'n Green and Haggen asked if they could go to the Chief's Club with me. You guys want to come along?"

Hall gave Jackson a "God forbid" look and said, "Think I'll take in a movie."

McCain thought for a second before saying, "I haven't been to the club since I was on the *Albany*. Do they still call it the finger bowl?"

Jackson grinned, "Hell, it's worse than ever. Their main rule is that any woman, doesn't make a damn who she's married to, can come in the club. But unless she's with a chief, she has to come in alone. If you can't pick up something in there now, you'd better turn queer."

The odds sounded so good McCain said, "Guess I'll tag along. You wearing civvies?"

"Naw, Green and Haggen will be in civvies. I'm wearing khakis."

"Good, I'll do the same. What time we leaving?"

"The bos'n can't leave till the barge is alongside. Probably be about 1800 by the time he squirts some Old Spice in his armpits and finds a clean pair of socks."

McCain looked at Jackson wondering if he would at least do as much. "I've got some office work to do and I have to go to the post office. I'll meet you at the club." That should give him plenty of time to find a phone and give Tommy a call.

It was 1600 on the nose when McCain entered a Chief's Club phone booth and called Tommy's office. A second later, Tommy's voice came booming through the ear piece. "How does it feel to be at sea again?"

McCain smiled and said, "I'd sure as hell rather be back in DC with some cute chick. But other than getting my ass chewed out by the CO, causing friction among my fellow chiefs, and having someone try to knock my head off with a dog wrench, things are going pretty smooth."

Tommy said, "Glad to hear you're having a good time."

Expecting what came next, McCain held the phone away from his ear till Tommy's laughter died down. "Go ahead, laugh your ass off. I'm up to my balls in alligators, and you're getting a kick out of it."

Tommy laughed again before saying, "Now that I think of it, it won't take many gators to reach your balls."

"Cut the fuckin' comedy. Did you check out that bouncer?"

"Went to the bar myself and spoke to him about Johnson. He told me that Johnson was in there that night and came on to him pretty strong. He also claimed that when he saw how serious Johnson was, he told him that he was straight and had a wife and two kids."

"How did Johnson take that?"

"He went into orbit and started screaming about all the money he'd spent on gifts for the bouncer."

"How'd they wind up?"

"The bouncer said he was about to throw Johnson out, but the sailor Johnson was with grabbed his arm and dragged him out of the place. Said it was the last time he saw Johnson."

"Did he know the sailor's name?"

"Nope, said he'd never seen him before."

"It may have been a third-class engineman named Trumbull. But I've got more checking to do before we can be sure."

McCain caught a movement over his shoulder and stopped talking to take a better look. Strolling toward the lounge was a petite brunette with a Natalie Wood face. She was dressed in a tight, black lace dress with the hem riding well above her knees. "You got anything else, Tommy? This phone call must be costing the taxpayers a bundle."

"What's the rush, Jack? Got some broad waiting for you?"

Funny how Tommy always figured him out. "Not yet," he said. "But I just saw one that looks very interesting. By the way, I mailed a letter to your home address. I put in everything I've learned so far. I'm going to hang up; I'll give you a call from Gitmo."

"When are you leaving Norfolk?"

"Tomorrow morning, high tide. We should be in Cuba on Thursday."

"Okay, Jack. Go chase the little mermaid. But don't fall in love and miss your ship or I'll have to send someone down there to investigate you."

With Tommy still laughing, McCain hung the receiver on its hook and headed for the lounge. He pushed open the door and found himself in a dimly lit room. Across the back wall was a black-leather bar lined with matching bar stools. Scattered throughout the premises were clusters of posh easy chairs surrounding glass-topped cocktail tables. In the far corner, two couples with drinks in hand huddled around one of the tables.

A Latino bartender stood behind the bar polishing cocktail glasses.

A bored waitress wearing a v-necked white blouse and short black skirt leaned against the bar sipping soda. On the right corner stool sat the girl, her left leg crossed over her right. The hem of her skirt now lingered halfway up her thigh.

McCain edged closer. She was even more beautiful than he first imagined. He fought back the urge to reach out and caress the silky tanned skin of her thigh. Instead, he took a deep breath and slid onto the stool to her left. "Mind if I anchor here?" he asked.

She looked at him with soft blue eyes and said with lips made to be kissed, "It's your club, Chief. I'm just a guest."

He glanced at her provocative body. Sex, as clear as if it were in Day-Glo paint, was written all over her tiny frame. If Bo Derrick was a ten, this chick was a fifty. "My name's Jack McCain," he said.

She wrapped her manicured right hand around the first joints of McCain's fingers and squeezed gently. "My name is Joan. Did you say Jack McCain? I don't think I've ever seen you in here before." Her smile was as sweet as Rice's honey.

For a second, McCain thought about his promise to meet the guys. But for now he only wanted the goddess holding his hand in her satin smooth fingers. "Haven't been here in years," he said.

"What'll you have, Chief?" asked the Latino.

To be alone would be just fine, he thought, but he looked at the bartender and said, "Give me a CC and ginger." He turned to Joan. "You ready for another?" he asked.

She glanced down at her glass. It was half-full of crushed ice and what looked like a daiquiri concoction. "I'm good for now, thanks. You were saying?"

He pulled out a twenty and laid it on the bar. "I started to say I haven't been here in years. It's a lot fancier than I remember."

"Are you going to be in Norfolk for long?" She had a curious glint in her eyes.

McCain shook his head. "Now that I've met you, I'm sorry to say we're pulling out tomorrow."

Her body seemed to quiver before she said, "That makes things a lot easier." She smiled and slid closer. The hem of her skirt moved higher. "What ship are you on?"

McCain pulled his gaze from the new patch of skin and said, "The seagoing tug *Lakota*."

Her eyes lit up. She started to say something, evidently changed her mind, picked up her glass and took a sip.

"You've heard of the *Lakota*?" he asked.

She smiled. "Is your CO a lieutenant named Adams?"

"You know the skipper?" he asked.

She nodded. "I live across the street from his wife." A slight wrinkle crossed her brow. "I don't think she knows he's in Norfolk."

McCain waited till the bartender put down his drink then touched her arm and said, "Small world."

She gave him another one of those groin-stirring smiles and said, "Why don't we move to a table? It'll be cozier and a lot more private."

She was making him as nervous as he was on his first visit to a whorehouse. He was willing to do anything she asked. "Good idea," he said. "Let me take your glass."

He picked up a glass in each hand and followed as she led him to a table far away from the other two couples. "This table okay?" she asked. Without waiting for his answer, she sat down on one of the low chairs and crossed her legs. McCain caught a flashing glimpse of white panties.

McCain dropped into the chair next to her and asked, "What makes you think Mrs. Adams doesn't know we're in town?"

"Because she's expecting her boyfriend. At least she was when I left the house." She glanced at her watch. "That was only an hour ago."

How many twists was this case going to take? No time to worry about it now. He leaned toward her. "Sounds like you're married?" The last thing he wanted was trouble from a jealous husband.

She must have read the concern in his eyes and said, "My husband is a lieutenant commander. But don't worry. His ship is in the Med. He won't be back for another month."

McCain let out a deep sigh of relief and asked, "What ship?"

She took his two hands in hers, making his skin tingle, leaned toward him and said, "Look, Jack. You've been around for a long time. You know what goes on when couples are separated for months on end. I'm sure he's taking care of his needs over there. Now if things go right with us and you're willing, I'm going to take care of mine. But it's better if we don't know all there is to know about one another." She moved closer and kissed him on the lips.

He hoped she didn't notice his knees shaking as he said, "Any way you want it. But why aren't you in the Officer's Cub?"

"You know the answer to that. If I left the 'O' club with anyone, you can bet my old man would find out. In here, nobody gives a damn who you're married to. You wait till tonight; I won't be the only officer's wife in the main ballroom."

McCain downed his drink and motioned to the waitress to bring another round. His eyes went back to Joan. "You want to stick around till the ballroom opens?"

"That's up to you." She smiled, wrinkling up her nose like one of those rabbits in a Disney movie.

God, what this woman was doing to him. He glanced down to see if the bulge in his pants was noticeable. To make sure it wasn't, he crossed his legs and checked the time. Still an hour before Jackson, Haggen and Green showed up. "I promised a couple guys off the ship that I'd meet them here at six. How about us getting a bite to eat? Afterwards I'll introduce you to them, and then we can go on our way."

The words no sooner left his lips when he got the horrible thought that maybe she wouldn't like the idea, so he said, "Of course we really don't have to meet...."

The waitress placed their drinks in front of them. McCain laid a ten spot on her tray and said, "Keep the change." She shrugged and went back to the bar.

Joan picked up her purse. "A bite to eat sounds good. Should we eat here or go off base?"

McCain said, "I don't have a car. But we can still go into town. I'll call a cab."

Joan ran her tongue across her lips and said, "No problem. My car is outside." She reached in her bag, brought out a set of keys and handed them to McCain. "You drive," she said.

Chapter Eleven

Day Three—Evening

After a delicious meal of Maryland crab, another drink, and several hot juicy kisses, McCain was feeling on top of the world when he pulled Joan's Olds into the Chief's Club parking lot. Before getting out, Joan stared into the rearview mirror and applied fresh lipstick. She blotted her lips with a tissue then said, "Let's go meet those friends of yours and get it over with." As McCain opened the door for her, she gave him that wrinkled nose again and said, "Those kisses have got me hot as jalapeno pepper."

With Joan holding tight to his arm, they entered the Chief's Club and went directly to the main ballroom. The place was gigantic. Running across the far end was an oversized bandstand. A twenty-five-foot-wide dance floor started at the bandstand and stretched forward fifty or sixty feet. It was made of inlaid hardwood and looked better than most high school gymnasiums. Six bars, three on each side, were spaced equally along the length of the room. Every other bit of space was used for tables and chairs; hundreds of them. Because it was early, not many of them were occupied.

When McCain spotted Green, Haggen and Jackson at a table halfway between the main entrance and the bandstand, he put his arm around Joan's waist and headed in their direction.

Haggen's look of disbelief told McCain he was the first to spot them moving in their direction. Haggen's mouth started wagging and immediately the others twisted in their chairs.

Jackson jumped to his feet, came toward them, and said, "McCain, glad you made it." His gaze ran up and down Joan's body stripping her of all her clothes. "And who's this lovely little chickadee?" He was grinning like a raccoon in a cornfield.

Without answering, McCain gave him a dirty look and led Joan to the table and introduced her to Haggen and Green as a longtime friend. When finished, he turned and did the same to Jackson. He was glad he'd warned her of what to expect before she met the three men. Jackson had already dripped beer on his shirt and tie. Green, dressed in an old threadbare sports jacket, was obviously loaded. Haggen was the only one that looked presentable. The grimace on Joan's face told McCain that she wasn't pleased to be in the presence of his shipmates.

"Sorry we won't be able to stick around for long. We promised Joan's family we'd be home for dinner." Sometimes it amazed McCain how convincingly he could lie. His lie must have also amazed Joan, because her grimace changed to a wide smile.

Haggen spoke up, "At least stick around long enough to have a…"

Without waiting for Haggen to finish, Jackson reached for Joan's arm and said, "I got a better idea. How 'bout taking us home with you?"

Joan jerked her arm away and squeezed closer to McCain. He was ready to deck Jackson but decided it would really screw matters up, so he said, "Sorry, guys, but that isn't in our plans. Besides the bos'n looks like he's happy right where he's at."

Greene squinted through red eyes and said, "If you assholes want to go with McCain, go ahead. Bos'n Greene don't need no fucking baby-sitters."

That was the final straw. McCain took Joan's hand and, without saying another word, guided her toward the door. As they walked away, McCain heard Jackson say, "She looked like a stuck-up bitch anyway. McCain'll never get into her pants."

Joan raised McCain's expectations by giving him a grin followed by a wink. Out in the parking lot, he said, "I'm sorry I put you through that. Where do we go from here?"

She stopped walking, gently took his chin in her hand and kissed him. "Don't worry about it, Jack. I can see you're not like them." As they resumed their walk to the car, she said, "You've got the keys. I'll give you directions."

The drive to Virginia Beach seemed to go on forever. Finally she told McCain to turn into a development of medium-sized houses. After several more turns, she pointed to a white ranch and said, "That's it. Pull into the driveway." Then reaching above the visor she pushed the button on the remote control and said, "Drive right into the garage. We'll get out inside so no one will know you're here."

McCain glanced in the rearview mirror and wondered if the unlighted house across the street belonged to Captain Adams's wife.

Soon as the garage door hit bottom, Joan took over. "You stay here while I make sure all the shades are down." While waiting in the dark, McCain wondered if Ruth ever cheated on Tommy. Ruth was the only girl he ever loved. All the others were stand-ins. But because Tommy could give Ruth more than he ever could, he was happy for the two of them.

After Joan beckoned him inside, she took him on a quick tour of the kitchen, dining room, den, living room and two bedrooms. The entire house was exactly the way he had expected it to be. McCain's mother always said you could tell how a woman keeps her house by the way she keeps herself. No doubt about it, Joan took good care of herself and her house. After the tour, she led him into the den, where she pointed to a rolling bar and said, "While I change into something more comfortable, why don't you fix us a drink."

At the bar, McCain hesitated and called to her in the bedroom. "I'm not sure I know how to make a daiquiri."

"No problem," she called back. "I'll have a glass of white Zinfandel. There's a bottle in the fridge."

As McCain filled two crystal goblets with the pinkish-colored wine, his mind pictured Joan coming out wearing a sexy see-through negligee. Underneath she'd be wearing bikini panties and no bra.

He was debating whether the negligee would be black or red when she came out wearing jeans and a loose-fitting sweatshirt. Gliding up to him, she took the glass from his hand and set it down. Then she wrapped her arms around his neck and kissed him with such passion that what she was wearing no longer mattered. After sending his brain spinning out of control she leaned back and said, "Should I put on some music, or the TV?" She had the sexiest voice he'd ever heard.

He wasn't considering music or TV, but this was one of those times when you had to haul in and wait for high tide. Hopefully it wouldn't be long. "Whatever you want to do is fine with me," he said.

"Okay, let's see if we can find a movie that will put us in the mood for later."

He almost blurted out that he was already in the mood. Instead, he pulled her close to him and gave her another long kiss. When they broke apart, they went into the den and Joan turned on the TV. Soon as a picture came on the screen, she changed channels till she hit an old movie. Then she took his hand and led him to the blue satin couch opposite the TV.

Once together on the couch, the kisses and groping started. Halfway through the movie, whose name, cast and plot remained unknown, McCain said, "If we don't do something soon, it's going to be too late."

Joan got up and flipped off the set. "Can't let that happen. We'll go in the guest room. The master bedroom is only for me and Bill."

McCain didn't care if they went down to the basement. He was ready.

Inside the guest room, Joan picked up an electric clock. "I'm setting the alarm for 5 a.m., I can't risk having any of my neighbors seeing you. You'll have to be out of here before daylight." When she finished setting the alarm, she turned to McCain and asked, "Have you got a rubber?"

A knot formed in his gut as he shook his head. Was this going to be the end of their tryst?

"No problem," she said. "I'll get one of Bill's." On the way out of the room, she looked over her shoulder and said, "Get undressed. I'll be back in a minute."

By the time she came back, he'd removed everything except his shorts and was covered up in bed. She was wearing a white terry-cloth robe. She untied he belt. The robe dropped to the floor. Her naked body sent his brain spinning out of control. He took a deep breath. She was beautiful.

After throwing back the covers and removing his shorts, she turned off the lamp and lay down beside him. Within seconds they were locked in each other's arms. Five minutes later, when he could take it no longer, he said, "Better give me that rubber."

It took less than a half-hour before they were both exhausted. When he came back from the bathroom, after getting rid of the rubber, Joan was turned on her side with her back toward him. He eased back into the bed wishing he had a cigar. Then he realized that since he'd met Joan he hadn't smoked a single Optimo. He wondered if he should compliment her on changing his smoking habit, but decided to wait awhile and let her speak first. He hoped her silence didn't mean she was sorry for what they'd done. He was still thinking about it when he dropped off to sleep.

Chapter Twelve

Day Four—Early Morning

McCain had no idea how long he'd been sleeping when he heard a man shouting. At first he thought he was dreaming, but soon realized it was coming from somewhere outside the house. He checked the clock: 3:05 a.m.

Now there was a woman screaming. He reached over and gently shook Joan. "Joan, Joan, something's going on. I think we'd better check it out."

She stirred a bit and rolled onto her back. Rising up on her elbow, she said, "Sounds like your skipper has met his wife's lover." She quickly grabbed her robe and stood up.

McCain followed her into the living room and watched as she pulled aside a shade and peeked out. He moved to the other side of the window and did the same. The Adams house was ablaze with lights. Framed in the lights, he saw a woman he assumed to be Mrs. Adams standing between Captain Adams and a sailor wearing dress whites. He turned to Joan. "Can we open this window? I want to hear what they're saying."

"No, don't try. They might hear you." She let her side of the shade drop back into place. "Put your clothes on. We'll go out back and sneak around the house. There's a hedge there. We can hear, but they won't see us."

She was right. From behind the hedge they were able to hear every word coming from across the street. All the shouting was between Adams and his wife. The enlisted man stood there accepting his role as the subject of the conversation.

"What kind of a whore are you?" Adams yelled.

Mrs. Adams screamed back, "Don't call me a whore, you cheating son of a bitch. Ever since we've been married, you've been fucking everything that walked."

He yelled again, "You're right, you're not a whore. Even that stupid gunner's mate wouldn't pay to get into your rotten crotch."

The sailor gritted his teeth and with clinched fists headed for Adams. She grabbed his arm and said, "Tony, don't pay him any mind. Go in the house. He won't stick around long." The confused-looking sailor headed for the door.

Once he was inside she moved closer to her husband, jabbed her finger into his chest and said, "I have to screw around. You don't send me enough money to eat and pay the rent. If it wasn't for Tony I'd have been evicted by now."

"Is that his kid you're carrying?" Adams growled.

"No it's not, idiot. It's yours. But Tony'll be a better father than you'll ever be." Her voice sounded meaner than ever. "At least he's a man."

"Man. You call that piece of shit a man?"

"Damn right I do. At least he sticks to women."

"What do you mean by that?"

"You know damn well what I mean. Your yeoman, Johnson, wrote me a letter and told me all about what goes on between you two. Said he gives you more sex than me and that slut, Kitty, combined. So you just turn your ass around and go back to your lover."

McCain held his breath waiting for Adams's reply. There was none. She'd won the argument. Without denying a single allegation, Captain Adams turned and retreated down the street.

McCain was dumbfounded. Was Johnson telling the truth? Was that the only letter he wrote? Did Adams already get even? Why in the hell didn't Tommy get someone else for this case? He looked at Joan. "Did you hear what I heard?"

"Shush." She raised a finger to her lips. "Let's go back inside."

After shutting the kitchen door, she said, "I knew about the letter, but wasn't going to mention it. Is it true your captain and ship's yeoman are having an affair?"

He grinned and shook his head. "I'm the ship's yeoman now and after tonight you should know I'm not gay." He paused for a second. "But this guy Johnson was the yeoman before me." He wondered if he should go on and decided he would. "Johnson won't be having any more affairs. Five days ago they found him floating in New York Harbor. His head was bashed in."

Joan's mouth dropped open. "You're kidding?"

"Afraid not. They're looking for the killer now."

She looked up at the clock. "This has been some night. I think it's time I took you back to your ship."

A half-hour later when Joan dropped McCain off at the brow of the *Lakota* he found Tobey in the process of relieving Billy Joe Tucker as the quarterdeck watch. As if nothing was out of the ordinary McCain picked up a *Reader's Digest* that Tobey must have brought with him and started leafing through the pages. When Tucker went below, McCain asked Toby, "Is Captain Adams aboard?"

"Not according to Tucker, he isn't. The other officers and chiefs have been sacked out for hours. Looks like you and the old man are the only ones that scored."

Without answering, McCain walked across the deck and looked over the rail. "I see they got the barge alongside. Any idea what time we're pulling out?"

"The XO said 0900."

McCain glanced at the clock above the quarterdeck log. "Think I'll try to get a couple hours' sleep."

He went into his room and changed into work khakis. Then he stretched out on his bunk and attempted to drop off. But the words of Mrs. Adams kept running through his mind. Was it possible that Johnson and Adams were getting it on in the captain's cabin? If they were, someone must have seen Johnson coming or going. The *Lakota* was too small to keep something like that a secret. Maybe he only did it once or twice. If it did happen, was it before or after the mutiny attempt? Had Johnson set the old man up?

After thirty minutes of his mind racing in circles, McCain gave up on trying to fall asleep. He slipped on his shoes, lit a cigar, and went into the crew's mess. He'd downed about a third of his mug of coffee when Captain Adams opened the door. When he tried to step over the hatch combing, he tripped. Grabbing the edge of the ice machine to keep from falling, he said, "Fucking piece of shit."

McCain wondered if Adams was talking about him, Mrs. Adams, the ice machine or the *Lakota*. Adams then forced himself to stand up straight and took a bearing on the door leading to officer's country. Then either not seeing McCain or ignoring him, he went forward on unsteady legs.

Adams was no sooner out of sight when Tobey came in and asked, "Did you see the old man come through?"

"I saw him. Sets a nice example, doesn't he?"

Tobey got himself a mug of coffee. "That's the drunkest I've ever seen him. He pulled up in a taxi and started arguing with the driver. He said he didn't have any money and wanted the driver to take his watch in payment. When the driver refused, I paid his fare and helped him out of the cab and across the gangway."

McCain stared at Tobey in disbelief. He never would have believed a CO could stoop so low. He wondered if the crew was aware of their captain's poverty. Then acting as if it was a completely new subject, McCain asked, "Does he have money troubles?"

Tobey nodded. "Big ones." He took a sip of coffee. "So damned big he cleaned out the recreation fund. He's stiffed so many guys that no one will loan him money anymore."

"Does he owe you money?"

"No. A few weeks ago he got hold of some loot and paid back two or three of the crew. But then something screwy started happening. I think it had something to do with some finance companies."

"What makes you think so?" McCain asked.

"I figured it out," said Tobey. "I haven't told anyone else about it though."

"How'd you figure it out?"

Tobey paused and took a deep breath. "I noticed that every day when the mail came in, Johnson went through it." He took another sip. "You know how small that office is?"

McCain nodded.

"Well, one day I saw Johnson pulling out letters addressed to some of the crew. When I asked him why, he said it was the captain's orders."

"Did you happen to notice what crew members and who the letters were from?"

"I didn't see them all, but one was for Rice, and I think Rossi and Wishbore had a couple. The ones I saw were from Household and Beneficial Finance."

"After Johnson went over the hill, did you take care of the mail?"

"Nope. I figured it'd be my job, but the old man said he wanted to see all the mail first. As soon as it came on board, it was delivered to his cabin." Tobey finished his coffee and took the mug into the galley. "I'd better get back on watch. See you later, Chief."

McCain had wondered why, that shortly after they left Bayonne, Dixon delivered a stack of incoming mail to his office and said that the captain said it was okay to pass it out. Now that he found out what was going on, he knew he had to put a stop to it. The next mail delivery would be in Gitmo. He didn't know exactly how he was going to do it, but Adams wasn't going to censor that batch. He checked his Timex; still time to take a stroll before breakfast.

Dawn was breaking as McCain moseyed back to the fantail, where he used his handkerchief to wipe the dew off the port bit before sitting down and lighting up a fresh Optimo. He'd barely had an ash formed when he noticed Trumbull coming toward him. This could be the chance he'd been waiting for to bring up that night Trumbull and Johnson were in the gay bar. "Hey, Trumbull, you're up early."

Trumbull took a seat on the other bit. "Couldn't sleep. Too many things on my mind."

"Like what?" McCain asked.

"I really don't want to talk about it," Trumbull said.

"Why?"

Trumbull took a deep breath, and said, "Captain Adams says that you're bad news. He warned me to stay away from you 'cause you're too friendly with the XO."

So, McCain thought, he'd touched a nerve in the old man. "What's wrong with that?" McCain asked.

"The captain thinks Mr. Posey is out to ruin him by turning the crew against him."

Sounded like Adams might have a speck of paranoia. "Do you think the captain is right?" McCain asked.

"Don't know for sure," Trumbull said. "But everyone knows they hate one another."

"Do you know whose side Johnson was on?"

Trumbull nodded. "Up till a few weeks ago, he tried to play both sides. But I know he liked the XO better than Captain Adams."

"How do you know that?"

"By what Johnson let slip out one day. He said he'd had all he could take of Captain Adams. And then that afternoon something else happened. The officers and chiefs had a meeting with the captain. After the meeting, Johnson was really pissed off about something. Didn't say what it was. But he was fit to be tied."

"He didn't tell you anything?"

Trumbull thought for a second. "Only that he said to get a job done, you had to do it yourself."

"Do you know what the job was?"

"Nope. He clammed up after that."

McCain tossed his cigar into the water and watched it float away. "Remember when you told me about the night you and Johnson went ashore together?"

"Yeah, I do. Probably should have kept my mouth shut."

"Why?"

"Captain Adams told me I should have…"

McCain heard what sounded like fear in Trumbull's voice. Why would Adams object to McCain knowing that Trumbull and Johnson went ashore together? It didn't make sense, but as he watched Trumbull, he had a strong feeling that the man had something else he wanted to say about that night. McCain decided to force the issue. "Remember when you told me that you left Johnson at the Pink Poodle?"

Looking as if he was trying to figure out what was coming next; Trumbull stared at McCain without answering. Finally he said, "I remember what I told you."

"Was that the truth?"

Trumbull hung his head. "Not really."

"You left with him, didn't you?"

Trumbull's head snapped up. His eyes were as big as poker chips. "How did you know that?"

Protecting his cover, McCain said, "It was just a guess. But that's no big deal. Maybe you should tell me what you did after the two of you left the Pink Poodle."

Trumbull's voice quivered as he said, "You won't tell the captain I told you?" There was no doubt that he was frightened.

Trying to calm him, McCain said, "I won't tell anyone. This is just between you and me."

Trumbull looked as helpless as a beached whale. He sighed deeply then said, "Johnson and that bouncer, Marsh, got into an argument about money. Marsh wanted Johnson to give him twenty dollars. Johnson said he didn't have it. Said he'd give it to him the next day."

So far the info Tommy had given him was checking out. "What happened then?"

"Marsh got mad. Said if he couldn't count on Johnson, he didn't want anything to do with him. Johnson tried pleading with Marsh, but Marsh wouldn't change his mind. Johnson started screaming and demanding that Marsh give him back the gifts. Especially the Rolex watch."

"Any idea where Johnson got the money for a Rolex watch?"

"No, I don't. But Johnson was making such a commotion that Marsh and another bouncer grabbed him and started dragging him toward the door. I then volunteered to get him out of there."

"Where'd you go?"

"We were on our way back to the ship. But when we got to Bayonne, Johnson wanted another drink. So we stopped at Ziggy's bar, a joint right outside the main gate."

"I've never been there," McCain said. "But go ahead."

"We'd just sat down at the bar and ordered a drink when Captain Adams came in and took a seat alongside Johnson. The captain didn't look too bad, but it was obvious he'd been drinking."

"So what happened?"

"From the minute Captain Adams sat down, I felt as welcome as a dose of clap. Completely ignoring me, they started whispering about something. Whatever it was, they sure didn't want me to hear. So I finished my drink and went back to the ship."

McCain spit over the side to wet his lips. What a break, he thought. This meant Captain Adams could have been the last man to see Johnson alive.

Trumbull stood up and said, "Chief, I've got to go get washed up for breakfast. Please don't say anything…"

"I didn't hear a thing," McCain said as he pretended to zip his mouth closed.

He watched Trumbull walk away as he mulled over what he'd just learned. No wonder Adams didn't want Trumbull to say anything. It was getting to look more and more like Captain Adams was the man responsible for Johnson's death. Was it possible that Johnson told him about the letters to his wife and the admiral? McCain doubted the journal would answer that question, but it might give him the reasons Johnson wrote the letters. Maybe even say if the stuff he'd written to Mrs. Adams was true.

He rubbed his gut and realized he was hungry. On his way to the mess deck, he, for the first time that morning, noticed the sun rising over the horizon.

Chapter Thirteen

Day Four—Morning

All through breakfast, McCain kept thinking about his talk with Trumbull. Things didn't look good for Captain Adams. Not only was Adams the last known contact with Johnson, but from what McCain had learned in the past two days, Johnson had supplied Adams with a couple good motives: sex and money. Probably two of the most popular motives for murder.

Now the thought of going back to sea with this madman made him damned uncomfortable. Worst of all, if someone else was murdered he'd have it on his conscience unless he got ashore long enough to give Tommy a call. He checked his watch: 0745, a little more than an hour before their scheduled departure. But for sure he couldn't make a call unless he first got permission from Captain Adams to leave the ship. It was going to be hard to come up with an excuse that Adams would buy. Most of all, he had to be extra careful not to give his suspicions away.

When he stopped by the wardroom, all the officers, except Adams, were having coffee. When Haggen spotted McCain, he grinned and said, "How'd you make out with that little fox? She was some looker."

"Told you she was just a friend." He looked at Posey and said, "I have to go ashore for a few minutes. Will you give me the okay?"

Troubled doubt showed in the executive officer's eyes as he said, "I'd like to, but you know what the captain's orders are."

"Yeah, I know, but he's probably sleeping. Think this is important enough to wake him up?"

Posey, looking like he'd found a way out, said, "He's awake. I had Dixon go in there a few minutes ago."

"This is a damned pain in the ass," McCain mumbled as he knocked on the CO's door.

"Who the hell is it?" came faintly through the closed door.

"Chief McCain."

"What do you want?" His voice louder this time.

McCain felt stupid talking to a door as he said, "I have to go ashore for a few minutes. You said I have to check out with you. Remember?"

"I remember. Request denied."

"But this is ship's business. I have to go ashore."

The door swung open. Adams stood there, shaving cream covering the left half of his face. The white foam made his red eyes look like cherries on an ice cream sundae. "What kind of business?"

McCain stared at Adams. How he'd grown to hate the son of a bitch. "I've got to drop off a copy of the sailing diary. You know, like I did when we left Bayonne."

"Give it to Posey. Let him deliver it. Maybe he'll get lost and miss the ship." He used his right leg to slam the door.

McCain was tempted to knock again, just to piss him off some more, but decided not to. He then pondered ignoring the order and going ashore anyhow. But if he did, Adams had every right to restrict McCain to his room. An eight-by-ten box was no place to gather the evidence he needed to put Adams away. He'd just have to make the best of it.

An hour later, jumping the gun on the setting of the special sea detail, McCain, wearing his sound-powered phones, stood on the starboard wing of the bridge looking down at the large open barge tied alongside. He was wondering why the barge's stern was tied to the *Lakota's* bow when Posey came through the door. McCain looked at him and asked, "How come it's backwards?"

Posy grinned and said, "When we get out into the open channel, we'll cast it off. It'll do a 180 on the tow line and wind up in the right position."

McCain nodded. "Makes sense. Too bad I can't say the same for a lot of the other stuff that goes on here."

Suddenly, Adams's voice came booming out of the pilothouse. "McCain, get in here. If Posey ever makes CO you can be his talker. Right now you stick to me like stink on shit."

Nice guy, McCain thought. He wished he could have called back that it was too bad Posey wasn't the CO. He had a hunch the *Lakota* would be a much better ship. He stepped into the pilothouse and stood behind Adams, who was leaning against his elevated bridge chair. "Sorry, Captain. I thought we had a couple more minutes."

An idea McCain couldn't resist flashed through his brain. He looked Adams in the eye and said, "I must be losing my hearing. I didn't hear you sound special sea detail. Guess that's what happens when we come rolling in during the wee hours of the morning."

Obviously infuriated, Adams glared at McCain for a second before he dashed across the pilot house and grabbed the PA system mouthpiece. He blew twice to make sure it was working, then said, "Set the special sea detail."

The atmosphere on the bridge was as cold as a whore's heart. Adams stood on the port wing; taking turns shouting orders to the line handlers on the pier and to Posey at the engine order telegraph. McCain repeated every word into the sound-powered mouthpiece hanging on his chest. Before he realized it, they were away from the pier and heading for Chesapeake Bay.

Thirty minutes later, when well clear of the Hampton Roads Bridge Tunnel, Adams gave the order to cast off the barge. Once freed, the rust-colored monster swung completely around and would up with its bow tethered by twenty-five feet of tow wire to the *Lakota's* stern. Adams then gave the order to let out two hundred feet of wire. Evidently satisfied with the way the barge was riding; Adams secured the special sea detail and went below.

As McCain coiled the long phone wire, Posey moved alongside and whispered, "Chief, please stop baiting Captain Adams. Each time you do, he takes it out on me."

McCain saw real fear in the XO's eyes and felt sorry for the young officer. "I had no idea that was happening," McCain said in a low voice. "I'll knock it off." He took the neck strap and wrapped it around the cord. "Why don't you stand up to him? Put in for a transfer? Do something; what in the hell can he do to you?"

Posey looked down at the deck. "Chief, all my life I knew I'd be making the Navy my career. I almost screwed it up when I listened to Johnson. I'm not going to chance it again."

Trying to make Posey feel better, McCain said, "If something does happen and you need a witness, you can count on me. It's a damned shame the way he treats you. I feel like writing a letter myself."

Posey's head snapped up. The corners of his mouth twitched. His eyes showed even greater fear. "Chief, I beg you; don't do me any favors. This will all blow over; you know as well as I do that a bad fitness report will be the end of my career."

So that was it. McCain put his hand on Posey's arm and asked, "Is there anything I can do to help?"

Posey thought for a second, then said, "Well, maybe if you went to the captain and tried to patch things up…"

McCain cut in. "Rumor has it that he thinks you and I are out to get him. You know anything about that?"

"That's no rumor. He told me himself. Seems the bos'n convinced him that you had connections in Washington and now he thinks I'm trying to get you to use those connections against him. That's why I had to take you off my watch."

He'd wondered why the new watch list put him with the chief engineer, Haggen, instead of Posey. McCain slammed his fist on the chart table. "I think maybe our captain is sick in the head. What do they call it, paranoia?"

Posey's face turned red and his mouth puckered as he said, "Chief, neither of us are doctors. That kind of talk is out of place."

"You're right," McCain admitted. "I'll watch what I say. And if the right situation comes along, I'll apologize to him. That should take the heat off." He stuffed the phone set into its metal storage box, smiled and said, "But I want you to realize that I'll be giving up the only pleasure I've found on this bucket of rust."

The muscles in Posey's neck relaxed and his eyes smiled as he said, "Thanks, Chief." He went to check the radar. McCain went below.

Back inside his room, McCain took off his shoes and stretched out on his bunk. He wondered why he felt so tired, and then he remembered he'd been up since the argument between Adams and his wife. That was about 0300. He picked up a dog-eared copy of *Reader's Digest* and tried reading the "Humor in Uniform" page. But his eyes were just too heavy.

With the magazine spread open across his chest, he closed his eyes and thought about one afternoon in Cheyenne. He, along with Tommy and Ruth, was sharing a back booth in the soda shop. He had looked at Ruth and felt a sense of pride knowing that she had chosen him over all the other boys. She didn't care that he was shortest guy in the senior class. And neither did Tommy, who was the tallest and had lettered in every varsity sport. They were the three musketeers of Cheyenne High.

McCain's thoughts raced ahead to graduation day. How happy they were for each other. The world was waiting for the three of them to share. But when Ruth and Tommy went off to college, McCain was all alone. He tired several jobs, but work didn't help the loneliness. He talked to his mother about college, but on a cleaning lady's salary she said she couldn't afford the tuition. The small town started closing in around him. So one day he took the bus into town and joined the Navy.

He'd only been in the Navy a year when his mother's heart gave out. The Red Cross tried to get him home in time, but she couldn't wait. He was on his way from the airport when she took her last breath. He didn't even notify Tommy and Ruth. Soon as the funeral was over, he gave power of attorney to a lawyer to wrap up the details and left Cheyenne for good. When four years later he received an invitation to be the best man at Tommy and Ruth's wedding, he refused and sent them a check.

Since that time, he often thought about Ruth and wondered how it would have been if she were his wife. But then he'd picture her and Tommy and how happy they were together. He doubted if he'd ever get married. That was unless something happened to Tommy and Ruth would let him take his place.

Tap. Tap. Tap. McCain opened his eyes. Someone was at the door. "Come on in," he shouted as he rose up and swung his legs over the side of his bunk.

It was Dixon. "Chief McCain, de captain wants to see you in his cabin. Says you get there on the double." He turned and left the room.

Dixon's message sent the pleasant thoughts of home back inside his memory and replaced them with the repugnant anticipation of another go-around with Captain Adams. He wasn't going to let him get the better of him this time. Posey's plea was serious and he realized he wasn't making headway by his constant battle with the old man. With a vow not to lose his temper, McCain slipped on his shoes and headed for Adams's cabin.

He found the captain waiting at his door with a message form in his hand. He handed McCain the form and said, "You know what they're talking about here?"

McCain took his time reading the message before looking up at Adams and saying, "Yes, sir. ComEasternSeaFrontier wants to know why we were so late in reporting Johnson's absence. Autopsy on Johnson's body shows he'd been dead several days before we sent out the AWOL reports."

Heavy lines appeared on Adams's brow. "I knew I shouldn't have signed those papers." He stepped back into his cabin. "Come in. You got me into this mess, now you get me out of it."

McCain followed him inside and closed the door behind him. *So he thinks I got him into this mess, what a laugh.* He would have loved to make his point, but remembered his promise to Posey. His mind raced to come up with a plan to take advantage of this new situation. In less than a minute, he said, "Captain, this could really be serious. Could really hurt your career. I've got an idea, but it has to be between you and me. No one else must know about it." The muscles in Adams's face seemed to relax. McCain was sucking him in.

"What you got in mind?" he asked.

"Do we have a deal on keeping it quiet?" McCain countered.

The frown lines reappeared. He was debating with himself. Finally he said, "Give me a hint, then I'll give you my answer."

When he didn't say no, McCain knew he had him hooked. "Hell, Captain, things get lost in the mail all the time. I'll type up a report, backdate it, and we'll send them our file copy. No way in hell they can prove you didn't send it when you was supposed to."

"How about the dates on the reports I signed in Bayonne?"

McCain gave him a reassuring grin. "Not to worry, Skipper. Those reports were desertion notices. The ones I'm going to backdate will be seventy-two-hour AWOL reports. Believe me, the Navy will buy anything as long as it's in writing."

A wry smile replaced Adams's scowl. "Great idea, Chief. Our secret, right?" Before McCain could answer, the frown reappeared and he said, "How do I know you won't tell Posey? Seems like you two are thicker than tow-wire grease."

With an even wider grin and complete confidence in his voice, McCain said, "I've heard that rumor, Captain. But it's not true. He's treated me pretty good, so I've treated him the same. But between you and me, Posey's not exactly my idea of a take-charge naval officer."

Much to McCain's surprise, Adams put his arm around his shoulder and looking genuinely pleased, said, "You've got him pegged right. I can't rely on him for anything. Glad you see it my way. Go get those papers ready. I'll sign them and we'll get this monkey off our backs."

"Aye aye, sir," McCain said as he did an about face and reached for the doorknob.

Before McCain could turn the knob, Adams said, "One more thing, Chief. Now that I think about it, I may have been too hard on you. What say we start over? This time on the right foot." He stuck out his hand.

McCain shook his clammy hand and said, "Would like nothing better. I haven't felt good about the whole thing. It probably wasn't all your fault. I deserved a lot of it. Great idea, starting over." McCain left with Adams beaming.

Now McCain felt he had more of a handle on things as he hurried back to his room. Inside he pulled out the IBM Selectric and typed out a message to Commander Eastern Sea Frontier saying the AWOL reports on Johnson must have been lost in the mail and that copies would be forwarded upon arrival in Guantanamo Bay. Then he jerked the form from the typewriter, rushed to Adams's cabin and knocked on the door. "Captain, it's McCain. I'm ready for your signature."

The door jerked open. Adams stood there looking as if McCain was his best friend. "Hi, Chief. You got those forms typed already?"

Funny how being partners in crime had improved his attitude. "Not yet," said McCain. "But I think it'd be a good idea to send this message.

You initial it, and I'll take it up to the radio shack."

"Let me look at it." He took the message, quickly read it, and said, "Great idea, Chief. This'll show those desk jockeys we're on the ball. Give me that pen."

McCain handed Adams a Bic pen, and said, "You're right, I've been around here for so long, I know exactly how they operate. When they get this dispatch they'll buy our story hook, line and sinker." McCain put a heavy emphasis on "our."

"Chief, when we get into port, I'm going to buy you a box of those cigars you smoke. Least I can do." He scribbled his signature beneath the last line of the message and handed it back.

"That won't be necessary, Captain," McCain said as he started to leave. Then realizing he was on a roll, he faced Adams again and said, "I would appreciate you taking the leash off when we hit Gitmo. Sometimes I just like to leave the ship and walk around a bit. Gives me time to think. It's a pain in the ass having to get permission all the time."

Captain Adams stepped forward and patted McCain on the back. "Hell yes, Chief. You know when your workload will let you go ashore. If I'm handy, you can mention you're leaving. If not, just tell the quarterdeck watch when you expect you'll be back aboard. From now on we're going to get along real well."

Hoping he sounded like he really meant it, McCain said, "Thank you, Skipper." He closed the door and climbed the ladder to the radio shack.

The chart house was empty. Hall must have been on the bridge. McCain went on through the chart house and into the radio shack. Rossi was sitting at the teletype reading another comic book. He looked up, saw who it was, and said, "Well, if it ain't Little Caesar. Heard someone threw a dog wrench at you. Too damn bad they missed. You want something? If not, get the fuck out and leave me alone."

McCain glared at the pimply-faced radioman and thought how he'd love to punch his foul mouth back into his head. "Better watch your lip and stay in your own pay grade, Rossi. The captain wants this message sent." McCain dropped the form on top of the open Superman comic book. "For your information, wise guy, I figured it was you that tried to coldcock me with that dog wrench. Now I know it was."

"Oh, yeah. What gives you that idea?" He smirked insolently.

Once again McCain was tempted to knock the grin off his face. But instead, said, "I never told a soul what happened that night. If you knew about it, either it was you or you know who did."

"You some kind of fucking Sherlock Holmes?" Rossi sneered.

"No. Just smarter than you are," McCain said.

Acting as if he had to have the last word, Rossi said, "If you're so fuckin' smart, what ya doing on this ship?"

It was McCain's turn to grin. "Don't you know? I'm here to make your life miserable." He pulled out a chair and sat down facing Rossi. "As long as you keep mouthing off, I'm going to bust your balls." McCain took a deep breath and wondered if it was a good time to mention the money Rossi owed Household and Beneficial Finance.

For some reason, Rossi's arrogance seemed to wane and he said, "You shouldn't have tripped me. I could've been hurt. You started it. Remember?"

Figuring Rossi was in retreat, McCain said, "Rossi, you're not fit to wear the uniform of my Navy. I knew it from the first minute I stepped on board." McCain pulled out a cigar, tore the cellophane off and lit up. "I don't like your smart-assed mouth. I've never had to put a man on report before, but you're pushing me to the point where I'm about to break my record."

Rossi's grim expression told McCain that his message was getting through. He looked down at the message and said, "I'll get this out, right away."

"That can wait a minute," McCain said as he stood up and stared down at the weakened Rossi. "You know damn well, if I write you up, Captain Adams is going to have to take my side." Even as screwed-up as Adams was, McCain was counting on there being no way he could let a third-class petty officer be insubordinate to a chief. "If you want to test the process, just say so. I'll be happy to oblige you."

Rossi looked like a whipped pup as he said, "At first I was only joking, but when you tripped me…"

"Did you throw the dog wrench? It's between you and me."

Rossi stared at the deck and said, "I was trying to get even." He reached down and pulled up the right leg of his dungarees. "See this."

There was about three inches of skin missing from Rossi's shin bone. "I did this on the hatch combing."

"When?" McCain asked.

"When you tripped me," said Rossi.

"No shit," McCain said. "Guess I'd be pissed too."

"Chief?"

"Yes."

"What really happened to Johnson?"

The question took McCain by surprise. Was Rossi trying to change the subject? Did he know something? Was he trying to let bygones be bygones? He'd play along for now. "Damned if I know. You got the message. You know as much as I do." McCain sat back down. "Hell, you probably know more than I do. You knew Johnson. I never met the man, or whatever he was."

"You sound like you know about Johnson being queer?" This time his grin was friendly.

McCain said, "Trumbull told me."

Rossi nodded. "Did he tell you about the night Johnson disappeared?"

"Said he left him in Ziggy's."

Rossi bit his lip. "Did Trumbull tell you who he was with in Ziggy's?"

"He said Captain Adams was there. Were you there too?"

"Yep." Rossi looked as if he wanted to say something else.

"Anybody else from the ship?" McCain asked.

Rossi said, "Not when Trumbull left."

"How about when you left?" McCain asked.

"I was the last to leave," said Rossi.

Maybe this was leading to something. McCain said, "Did Johnson and the captain leave together?"

Rossi nodded. "So did the XO. The three of them left together."

McCain pulled the skin on his chin and wondered how in the hell Posey got into the picture. Finally he said, "Trumbull didn't mention Posey being there."

"That's because he wasn't there when Trumbull left."

"He wasn't? Just when did he get there?"

"I'm not sure, Chief. I was in the back shooting pool."

"Who with?"

"A second-class commissaryman named Lisker. He's stationed on the base."

"When did you first notice Posey?" McCain asked.

"It must have been almost an hour after that phone call Johnson made to him."

"How do you know that?"

"I heard him," Rossi said.

"You heard Johnson call Posey?"

"Yeah."

"Tell me about it."

Rossi shrugged. "What's to tell? Lisker and I were in the back shooting pool. Johnson comes back there, picks up the phone, drops in a quarter. Next thing I hear is him asking to speak to Daniel Posey."

Getting this story was like standing a mid-watch. It seemed like it would never end. "Did you hear him talking to Posey?"

"Nope."

"You didn't hear anything?" McCain asked.

"Like I said, I was shootin' pool. What the hell did I care what they were saying?"

"You didn't think it strange that Johnson would be calling his XO at that time of night?" McCain asked unbelievingly.

"Not really. They were pretty chummy," Rossi said.

"Any idea who answered Posey's phone?"

"What do you mean?" asked Rossi.

"You said you heard him ask for Daniel Posey. Any idea who he asked?"

Rossi shrugged his shoulders. "I suppose it was the officer Mr. Posey shares an apartment with."

"You know who the officer is?"

"Nope. He's a lieutenant. Posey brought him aboard for dinner once or twice. Dixon told us he was the XO's roommate." Suddenly a quizzical cloud formed in Rossi's eyes. "Why so many questions? Johnson's dead. One less queer ain't going to break the bank."

"I take it you didn't like Johnson?" said McCain.

Rossi snarled, "I don't like no cock-suckin' queers."

"You didn't kill him did you?" McCain asked.

The question brought the old Rossi charging back. "Fuck you, Chief. I ain't answering any more questions."

"Watch you tongue," McCain said jokingly as he snuffed out his cigar. "I was only kidding. Johnson probably fell in the drink and drowned. But I am curious why the CO, Posey and Johnson were all in Ziggy's that night. It might help me get along with them a little better." McCain scratched his jaw and said, "I think you can understand that."

Rossi relaxed. "Sure I can. I ain't got a single fucking friend on this ship. I even did the CO a favor, but it didn't help."

He must be talking about the loans from the two finance companies, but he'd let it go for now. "Sounds like we're in the same boat. Tell me what the three of them were doing when you first noticed Posey."

Rossi wrinkled his brow and got up. He walked to the door, stared out into the chart house, turned, came back and sat down. Seeing no one else around, he said, "Near as I can remember, I was taking aim on the eight ball in the corner pocket. Directly in line with my cue, I saw Posey at their table."

"What were they doing?"

"I don't know. Just talking, I guess."

"Did they look like they were arguing or anything?"

"It did look as if Johnson was doing most of the talking. But arguing..."

"How long did Posey stay after you noticed him?" McCain asked.

"Not long. I made a run. Then while I was waiting for Lisker to miss, I saw the three of them get up and go out the door."

"And you never saw Johnson after that?"

"Hell, no." Distrust showed in his eyes. "Are you trying to accuse me of something?"

"Of course not. But didn't you find it strange when Johnson didn't show up the next morning?"

"Not really. Hell, when a second-class pulls a liberty with the CO and exec, I just figured they gave him a few days' leave. Stranger things have happened on the *Lakota*."

"Did the old man or the exec know you were in Ziggy's that night?" asked McCain.

Rossi shook his head and said, "Not unless Johnson told them. There was one of those partitions with diamond-shaped holes between them and me. I could see them but I doubt if they could see me."

"After Johnson failed to report for duty," asked McCain, "did you mention to the CO or Posey that you were in there?"

"No way, Chief. I don't say nothing to them people."

McCain checked his Timex. Just enough time to eat an early lunch and then relieve the watch. "Good idea to keep your mouth shut. What say we do the same thing about our talk today?"

Rossi grinned as he used his right thumb and forefinger to pretend he was zipping his mouth shut.

McCain gave him a friendly pat on the back and said, "Better get that message off." On the way out the door, he turned and said, "No more flying dog wrenches, right?"

Chapter Fourteen

Day Four—Afternoon

At 1140 McCain climbed the two flights to the pilothouse. Chief Warrant Officer Haggen, his new watchmate, was being briefed by Chief Hall. Seaman Crisano had already relieved Seaman Haley at the helm.

Boatswain's Mate Third Class Tucker stood at the chart table with the deck log open. He saw McCain, made a quick entry as having been relieved, and said, "The course and speed are in the log. No ships in the area. The tow is on six hundred feet of wire. No strain. Man, I'm starved. Crisano says we're having stuffed pork chops. How are they?"

McCain picked up the duty pencil and said, "They're great." Before he had a chance to write a word, Tucker disappeared down the ladder. McCain glanced at Crisano and said, "Seems like Tucker's worked up an appetite."

Crisano grinned. "You know them rebels when it comes to pork chops."

McCain made his log entry and joined Haggen on the port wing where he was staring at the tow. "Howdy, Chief; welcome to my watch. Posey tells me you're a good quartermaster. Says you really wanted to be a boatswain's mate."

"I can say yes to the second part. How good a quartermaster is for you to decide."

Haggen nodded and said, "I'm sure Posey wouldn't have said it if it wasn't true. As for me, I don't care much for these deck watches. Give me an engine room. That's where I feel at home."

"Not for me," said McCain. "Working in an office is bad enough, but at least it's above the water line. Can't imagine spending hour after hour in that heat and noise. And if something happens, I want to be able to jump overboard."

"To each his own." Haggen pointed his binoculars in the direction of the barge. "Ever done any towing before?"

"Never," McCain said as he watched the barge riding slightly off to port. "How come it's not directly behind us?"

Haggen lowered his binoculars and said, "Every tow acts a little different. Each one seems to have a mind of its own. Some ride to port, some to starboard, and some directly astern." He once again lifted his glasses and peered aft.

"Anything I should be doing different now that we have a tow?" McCain asked.

"Every hour we'll freshen the nip," he said, still staring aft.

"Freshen the nip?" McCain asked.

Without looking at McCain, Haggen said, "To cut down on the wear to the wire, every hour we let the tow out or take it in a few feet. On this watch we'll let it out; the next watch will bring it in."

"That'll be my job?" asked McCain.

"It'll be your job to call the towing-engine room and tell the watch what to do. You'll also enter it in the log. The tow watch will give you the strain on the wire. You'll log that too."

"Sounds to me, that other than freshening the nip, it's just like any other underway watch."

Haggen lowered the glasses, walked to the pilothouse chart table, and, in a serious voice, said, "Not quite. When towing, the length of our ship is from the bow of the tug to the stern of the tow. That makes for a very large vessel."

"What could go wrong?" asked McCain.

Haggen shrugged and said, "Lots of things. The catenary could drag bottom or hang up on a sunken ship…"

"Catenary?" McCain asked, not recognizing the word.

"The catenary is the sag or dip in the tow wire. When you're towing with six hundred feet of wire, the center of the catenary rides pretty deep." He opened the drawer of the chart table and took out a small booklet. "There's a table in here that will give you an estimate of how deep the wire is riding."

"Why don't we just use less wire?" McCain thought he was asking a logical question.

Haggen went back to scanning the horizon. "The weight of the catenary acts as a spring that makes the tow ride smoother."

McCain wasn't quite sure he understood why, but he'd ask Hall later. He changed the subject by asking, "How about he weather?"

Haggen dropped the glasses to his chest. "Towing in heavy seas is not a lot of fun. Anytime we can, we avoid running into rough water by pulling into a harbor of refuge and waiting for it to blow over. We may be late in arriving at our destination but the ship and tow will be intact."

McCain was impressed with the black-gang officer knowing so much about deck seamanship. "Who taught you the ropes?"

Haggen stared McCain in the eye and said, "Ross Adams taught me everything I know."

He couldn't picture Adams taking the time to go into such detail. In a voice that bordered on sarcasm, McCain said, "He must have been a good teacher."

Haggen's comeback was just the opposite. "Damn right he was. He was a different man in those days. As good an officer as I'd ever served with."

McCain was about to comment on how the man had changed when Haggen went inside the pilothouse and checked the radar.

When he returned, McCain asked, "Anything else I should know?"

Haggen trained the binoculars on the barge. "See that piece of plywood attached vertically to the forward hatch?"

McCain lifted his own glasses, spotted the plywood, and said, "I see it."

"If you look close you'll see, mounted on that board, a light fixture and an alarm bell. If the tow springs a leak, that light flashes and the bell rings."

"How does it work?" McCain asked.

"It's controlled by an aspirin," he said with a hint of mystery in his voice.

"Come on now, you're shitting me. An aspirin?" McCain couldn't picture any circumstance where an aspirin could play such an important role.

"You'd better believe it. You can't see it from here, but there are two wires running down from the battery to about a foot above the barge's bottom. Those two wires are joined at their tip with an alligator clip. Between the jaws of the alligator clip is a common aspirin. If the barge takes on water, the aspirin melts, the jaws close and the circuit is closed, causing the light to flash and the bell to ring.

"Well, I'll be damned," said McCain as he pulled out an Optimo. "Guess there is a lot to learn. I was hoping to qualify for OOD, but guess that's out for a while."

A grin spread across Haggen's face. "Tell you what. I'll teach you all you need to know to qualify. But you've got to give me the name and phone number of that split-tail you was with last night."

McCain turned his back, looked over his shoulder, and said, "Sorry, but I can't give you her name." He went inside the pilothouse and peered into the radar scope.

A minute or so later, Haggen passed on his way to the starboard wing. "Can I see you out here, Chief?"

By the time McCain got outside, Haggen was leaning against the bulwark. He looked McCain in the eye and said, "Let's forget what I said about the woman. Guess I was a little jealous. I spent the night baby-sitting Greene and Jackson. They both got so damn drunk, neither one of them could hit their asses with both hands."

McCain found the subject boring, but didn't want to insult Haggen. "What time did you get back aboard?"

"It was way before midnight."

"Where was Posey?" asked McCain.

"I guess he didn't leave the ship," said Haggen. "I think he spent the evening in the wardroom watching TV. He told me that Adams said he had to stay on board."

What a mess, thought McCain. He stared at Haggen and said, "A few minutes ago you said Captain Adams was a good officer. Do you still believe that?"

"The *Lakota's* a different ship now," said Haggen pensively.

"Better or worse?"

As if he was returning to the past, Haggen said, "When I first came aboard she was a great little ship. Top-notch crew and a good wardroom. The officers got along great."

McCain found that interesting. "What went wrong?" he asked.

Haggen rested his elbow on the pelorus stand. "Hard to pinpoint exactly when things started going downhill." He paused for a second or two. "Adams was already CO when I came aboard. Our bos'n was named Egbert and the exec was a jg named West. West made lieutenant and was transferred. Posey relieved him. A couple weeks later, Egbert completed his thirty years and retired. Greene took his place."

McCain remembered from Adams's service record that he'd been on board for almost two years. He tried remembering when Haggen reported on board, but couldn't. "When did you report?"

"A month or so after the skipper," he answered.

Trying to get back on track, McCain said, "Did you notice a change in the captain before or after Greene and Posey reported?"

"It wasn't the officers. If anything it was that cunt, Kitty."

"The one I saw in his stateroom?" McCain asked.

"That's her," he said in a way that seemed to leave a bad taste in his mouth.

"What'd she do to make him change so much?"

Haggen smirked. "To make a long story short, she made Adams forget he had a wife and a ship and…"

"How'd she do that?"

"Good question. Don't know how she did it, but he went crazy. She was the only thing that mattered. If she wanted something, he had to get it for her."

"Like what?"

Haggen shook his head before saying, "A fur coat, a car, new furniture, you name it."

Now they were getting someplace, McCain thought. "Where'd he get the money?"

Haggen stared at the deck and shook his head again, "When his pay ran out, he started borrowing."

"Borrowing from who?"

Haggen raised his head. McCain saw the pain in his eyes. Haggen started to say something, and then changed his mind. Finally he said, "I don't want to talk about it." He walked to the bulwark and looked down at the water for a second. He then turned and said, "Right before my eyes, I saw an officer I admired turn into a bum. Now I have no more respect for him than I do for a skid-row derelict."

"That bad?"

Once again he shook his head. "Worse. When he couldn't borrow any more from us officers, he started hitting up the crew. Then he replaced the money in the recreation fund with an IOU."

"I heard about that," said McCain. "That is pretty bad."

"It gets worse. After losing the respect of the officers and crew, he turned to Johnson. Practically let him run the ship."

Now it was McCain's turn to shake his head. "Johnson was just a second-class PO. How could he take over?"

Haggen sighed. "I'm a little ahead of myself. Six or seven months ago, we had a tow to Norfolk. While there, Adams must have got his wife pregnant. A few weeks later she wrote him a letter telling him she was expecting. And just one day after receiving his wife's letter, Kitty tells him she's also knocked up."

For a second, McCain almost felt sorry for Adams. He couldn't imagine getting hit with a double whammy like that. "How'd he take the news?"

"Hard to say. He crawled into a shell and didn't want anything to do with us officers."

"Was that when Johnson took over?"

"Yes. It seemed to me that Johnson was holding something over the old man's head."

"Any idea what it was?"

Haggen shrugged. "Could have been most anything. Johnson was no damn good. The world is better off without him. He seemed to be a good yeoman but was a real troublemaker. Look how he tried to get Posey to take over the ship."

"Wasn't you in on that?" McCain asked.

"Yes, I was, but Posey said it was the only way to wake Adams up to what he was doing. Said it was just a matter of time before headquarters got wind of why he kept volunteering for trips and how his personal life was affecting the ship and crew. Posey was sure that if that happened, Adams's career would be over."

"Can't argue with that," said McCain. "But why blame Johnson?"

Haggen gritted his teeth and said, "From what I hear, it was Johnson who planted the whole thing in Posey's head. And when it backfired, Adams was worse than ever."

"In what way?"

"He started fighting with everybody. He and Posey went round and round. Then he relieved Posey of all his duties. I don't think he trusted any of us. Only person he talked to was Johnson and sometimes Hall."

"Things don't seem much better now," said McCain.

"Not much," said Haggen. "But at least Johnson is out of the picture."

The words staggered McCain. Did Haggen realize what he'd just said? Could it have been Haggen who got Johnson out of the picture? If it wasn't him, does he know who it was? This would take some thinking about. To keep Haggen from seeing his wheels turning, McCain quickly asked, "Why do you suppose he'd only talk to Johnson?"

"We all wondered about that. Especially when Johnson talked Posey into the mutiny. I got my own ideas, but don't think I should say what they are."

Too bad, thought McCain. He decided to prod a little. "Before you discovered Johnson's part in the mutiny, what did you think of him?"

Haggen hunched his shoulders. "Like I said before, at first he seemed like a pretty good yeoman. But then word got out that he was queer."

"Did you believe it?"

"I tried not to, but then…"

When Haggen started to walk away, McCain said, "What made you change your mind?"

Through tight jaws Haggen said, "The son of a bitch tried to make a move on me."

"What did he do?" McCain asked with a shocked look on his face.

"I don't want to talk about it." Haggen retreated toward the pilothouse. Before going inside, he turned back and said, gruffly, "Call the tow watch and freshen the nip. Then go down to the chart house and get a loran fix."

"Aye aye, sir," McCain said.

Chapter Fifteen

Day Four—Evening

Relieved from watch, McCain went down to the crew's mess and filled himself a mug of coffee before going into his room and closing the door. With an hour to kill before supper, he decided to use the time to make a list of the things he wanted to go over with Tommy.

At first it looked as if the killer was either someone ashore or Captain Adams. But now the list had grown to include Lt (jg) Posey, Chief Warrant Officer Haggen, and any number of enlisted men. Obviously Johnson was not well liked. Sure he was gay, but was that enough to give him the power he seemed to have over the officers and crew? A second-class PO convincing his XO to start a mutiny was unbelievable. Damned good thing Hall kept his head or Posey would be in deep shit. But did the mutiny have anything to do with Johnson's death? If only he could lay his hands on that journal and get the dead man's side of the story. Where in the hell could Johnson have hidden it?

Starting with the scene he'd witnessed while at Joan's house, he picked up a pen and started making a list. Did Adams know Johnson had written to his wife? Was there any truth to the allegations Johnson put in his letter about making it with the old man?

And what was Adams looking for when he checked the mail? He was probably pulling out the dun letters, but maybe it was something else. Trumbull did mention that Adams thought Posey was some sort of spy.

And why had Trumbull felt it necessary to keep secret the fact that he'd left Johnson with the CO? And Rossi's story of Johnson, Adams, and Posey leaving Ziggy's together. Wonder where they went? Could it be that one of them was the murderer? McCain supposed they could have both done it, but that was really stretching. He didn't think those two could do anything together.

And where did Haggen fit into this twisted mess? No doubt he hated Johnson and, till recently, liked Adams, but was that enough of a motive to kill? Did he even have the opportunity? Maybe if McCain knew where Haggen was that night, he could put him in or out of the picture.

Just as McCain finished his officer list and started pondering the enlisted suspects, there was a knock on the door. He turned his yellow pad face down and yelled, "Come on in."

The door opened and Chief Jackson stepped in. He was wearing a dirty set of work khakis, a sweat-stained baseball cap and high-topped brown shoes. A smudge of grease adorned his right cheek. "You busy?" he asked.

"Not at all," said McCain. "What can I do for you?"

"Don't really need nothing. I just thought we might shoot the shit before chow." He pulled the side chair away from the desk and with the back of the chair facing McCain; he threw his leg across the seat and straddled the chair. He wrapped his arms around the back and rested his chin on the top edge. McCain couldn't help but think that it looked as if the chair and sprouted a head, arms and legs.

From his desk drawer, he pulled out two cigars and offered one to Jackson.

He refused the cigar, took out a can of Copenhagen, twisted off the cap, and using his thumb and forefinger, pulled out a hefty pinch of the black powder and stuffed it between his bottom gum and lip. After packing the tobacco down with his tongue, he said, "Snuff for me. I can have both hands free and I don't have my eyes full of smoke. Want to try some?" He offered McCain the container.

McCain used his palm to refuse the offer and said, "No thanks; I'll stick to my Optimos. I'd probably get sick if I tried that stuff."

"To each his own," said Jackson before leaning over McCain's polished stainless steel sink and spitting out an amber glob of tobacco juice.

McCain jumped up and immediately flushed the sink with hot water. He'd take some soap to it later. He reached into the wastebasket, took out a paper soda cup and handed it to Jackson. "Here," he said. "Use this to spit in."

Jackson set the cup next to his chair and said, "Word's out you're off the old man's shit list."

"Guess so," said McCain. "It's about time, don't you think?"

"How'd you pull it off?"

"What difference does it make? But you don't seem surprised that I did it."

Jackson shifted his gaze down to the deck and said, "Everyone thinks you must have loaned him money."

"You think that would do it?" asked McCain.

Jackson leaned back, crossed his arms across his chest, and said, "Shit. He'd do anything for money."

"You really believe that?" McCain asked sarcastically.

"Damn right I do," said Jackson.

Hoping he might get something new about Adams, McCain asked, "Can you give me an example?"

Jackson thought for a second and then with a wry grin, said, "For fifty bucks, he'd let any of us take off for a week and wouldn't let Johnson deduct it from our annual leave record."

"No shit," said McCain. "I thought only yeoman did that. Was Johnson getting a cut?"

"Damned if I know." Jackson reached down, picked up the cup, and spit. "You wait. Now that you're buddies he'll probably hook you into working with him."

McCain thought of the old saying, *A woman's ass and a whiskey glass made a horse's ass out of me.* It fit Adams to a tee. "Why does the captain need so much money?" he asked, wondering if he'd get the same story he got from Haggen.

Through a shit-eating grin, Jackson said, "Pussy, man, pussy. Cut open his brain and all you'd find is a bunch of little pussies floating around. Between his wife and that cunt, Kitty, the poor bastard's ready for the poor house."

Nothing new there, thought McCain. "What did you think of Johnson?"

Jackson rolled his jaw, spit into the cup and through gritted teeth said, "I hated the little bastard. He thought he was too good for the rest of the white hats. Only sucked up to the officers."

McCain wondered if he meant that literally. Might as well get the subject out in the open. "I've heard he was queer. Did he ever make a move on you?"

With a disgusted look in his eyes, he said, "No way, man. I'd have killed the son of a bitch."

"How about the rest of the crew; are there any rumors about them?"

"Only friend he had was Trumbull. It's like I told you, he thought he was too good for anyone else."

"Do you have any idea of what Johnson thought about Chief Hall?"

"Hell, I have no idea. Hall's a strange duck. Keeps to himself. He's a nice guy, but I don't think he's said ten words since you hijacked his room and he moved in with me."

Jackson's words didn't surprise McCain in the least. He'd try some more, "What do you know about Kitty?"

This time he seemed to be caught off guard. Heavy lines furrowed his brow. He spit into the cup again and then said, "Kitty was going with me first. I introduced her to the old man and next thing I knew, she dropped me and started going out with him."

"Did that piss you off?" asked McCain.

"Hell, no. I knew from the start that I couldn't afford her." He spat again. "At first it bothered me a little. Now I'm glad that it's him and not me paying the price."

"Do you still speak to her?"

The look in his eyes told McCain that he probably does. Why was he holding back? Finally Jackson said, "A couple days before Johnson went over the hill, she came aboard looking for the old man. When she found out he was ashore, she asked for me."

"Did you talk to her?"

"Yes."

"What did she want?" asked McCain impatiently.

"Well, the quarterdeck watch said she was waiting for me in the captain's cabin. So I went up there and soon as I got inside, she started asking me a bunch of questions about Johnson."

"Johnson?" McCain asked in a surprised voice.

"That's right, Johnson. Seems she got it in her head that Johnson and the old man had something going. I told her I didn't know anything about it."

"Did she believe you?"

Jackson shrugged. "I don't know, but she said that if she ever caught them together she was going to kill the little fag."

"Those were her exact words?" asked McCain.

"That's what she said."

"So what happened then?"

He shifted in his chair. "I told her I had to get back to the engine room. That woman is crazy; I wanted to get away from her."

Another suspect to add to his growing list, thought McCain. He wondered if Tommy was going to think he was exaggerating. Hoping Jackson had something else he could use, McCain asked, "Did she say anything else?"

Jackson shook his head. Then, using the crook of his forefinger, he reached into his mouth and pulled out the cud of snuff. He dropped it in the cup and tossed the cup into the wastebasket. "What time is it?" he asked.

McCain glanced up at the clock above the sink and said, "Seventeen hundred."

Jackson got up and said, "Let's go get some chow. Rice is serving pot roast tonight. You just wait till you taste it."

Seated at the chief's table between Jackson and Hall, McCain took from the mess cook's hands a heaping plate of thick slices of beef, potatoes, carrots, parsnips, turnips, and onions floating in thick brown gravy. Rising steam sent a heavenly aroma flowing into his nostrils. His mouth salivated in anticipation. McCain glanced at Hall and said, "This is the best feeding ship I've ever served on." He forked off a chunk of the tender beef and stuck it in his mouth. It was out of this world.

Hall used a paper napkin to wipe his mouth and said, "We are lucky in that regard."

Jackson, through a mouth full of food, said, "Chow is chow. All it has to do is make a turd." He started laughing, causing a lump of potato to fall to his lap.

Hall lowered his head in disgust. McCain wondered how the two of them survived in the same room. But that was their problem. He picked up an oversized fresh-baked roll, tore off a chunk, and sopped it in the gravy. It then dawned on him that if he wasn't careful he'd soon be growing out of his uniform.

Halfway through the meal, Jackson threw back his arms and let out a belch. Then after scratching his crotch, said, "Got to go down and check the plant. Snipes don't have time to sit around."

Jackson had almost reached the door leading into the head when Hall said in a low voice, "Why in the hell don't you stay down there." When he realized that McCain had heard him, he said, "That man is disgusting. I wonder what kind of parents produced a mutation like that."

"I think he just does it for effect. He knows it bugs us," said McCain. "Maybe we should have a talk with him."

Hall shrugged. "Let's just let it go for now. We sure don't need any more trouble."

"You're right," said McCain as he pictured Jackson spitting in his polished sink. "Jackson and I were just chewing the fat in my room. If it wasn't for his foul habits, he's not a bad guy."

Hall stared at McCain in disbelief for a second. "You'll never convince me of that." He went back to eating his meal.

Having eaten enough for two men, McCain took his plate into the galley and dropped it in the sink. Then, with a fresh mug of coffee in his hand, he headed back to his room. As he passed the chief's table, he looked at Hall and said, "See you later."

Back in his room, McCain set the mug to one side and turned over the pad he'd been writing on. His heart dropped. The page was empty. Had he forgotten that he'd torn it off? He shook his head. No, when Jackson came in, he was sure he had just turned it face down and hadn't touched it since. Someone was in his room, and that someone took the list. He scratched his head. Who in the hell could have done it? And why would anyone want to? It was only a list of names and not important to anyone unless they were able to put two and two together. He hoped that wasn't the case, but whoever took it must be wondering why he'd made the list, especially if the thief's name was on it.

Most of the enlisted men were in he crew's mess with McCain. That would make one of the officers the likely suspect. Or it could have been Dixon. Or it could have been one of the radiomen passing McCain's room on his way to or from the radio shack. He knew it wasn't Ben Wishbore because he was still eating. He wouldn't put it past Rossi, but he was on watch. Bos'n Greene, Tobey and Curtin were on watch on the bridge.

That narrowed the suspects down to Dixon, Captain Adams, Posey, or Haggen. Any one of them could have seen McCain head for the mess, waited till he was out of sight, and ducked into his room. He'd watch real close to see if one or more of them changed their attitude to him. Maybe, with a little luck, the culprit would give himself away. One thing for sure: no more lists. From now on he'd have to rely on his memory.

McCain decided that for now he'd discount Dixon. He was too busy taking food from the galley to the wardroom. It was doubtful that he'd have time to take the list. McCain's next contact with Haggen would be on the mid-watch. Those four hours of close contact might be long enough to get an inkling if it was him. What McCain needed now was some reason to meet with Adams and Posey. He'd start with the CO by using the need for signatures on the back-dated AWOL reports.

Twenty minutes later, with the papers in his left hand, McCain knocked on Adams's door with his right.

"Who is it?" came gruffly through the door.

"Chief McCain, Captain."

"Come right in, Chief." McCain could hear a smile in his voice. He opened the door and stepped inside. Adams, wearing skivvy shorts, a T-shirt, and calf-length socks, was stretched out on his bunk. A dog-eared copy of *Playboy* lay open at his side. He picked up the magazine, swung his legs over the side of his bunk, laughed and said, "I only read the interviews." He closed the *Playboy* and tossed it behind him.

The magazine reminded McCain of Jackson's description of the contents of Adams's brain. He chuckled and said, "I've said that a time or two myself." Adams seemed in an awfully good mood for someone who might have discovered that his chief yeoman was keeping written records of him and his officers.

Adams pointed to the papers in McCain's hand and said, "Need something signed." As he reached for the papers he said, "Grab a chair. I'll buzz Dixon and have him bring us some coffee." The CO got up and pressed a black button next to the sound-powered phone. He then went to his highboy and dropped the desk leaf. He was still signing the duplicates when there was a knock on the door. "Get that, will you, Chief?"

McCain opened the door to Dixon, who stood with a bored look on his face. When he saw McCain, his expression changed and a funny look appeared in his eyes. McCain yelled over his shoulder to Captain Adams, "It's Dixon. Do you want him to come in?"

"Tell him to bring a carafe of coffee and some of that cake we had for lunch."

Before McCain had a chance to repeat the order, Dixon turned and headed for the galley. McCain closed the door and said, "That guy has shifty eyes. Have you had any trouble with him having sticky fingers?"

"Naw, he's too damn lazy to steal. Biggest problem with Dixon is that he hates whites."

"I've noticed that. The day I reported aboard, Bos'n Greene told me how lazy he was. He also left no doubt that there was bad blood between the two of them."

Adams laughed. "You can say that again. A couple of times the bos'n was ready to strangle him."

"I believe it, "said McCain. "How about the rest of the officers?"

"As far as I know, nobody likes him. Officers or enlisted men, and he feels the same about them. But the guy he hated most was Johnson."

"Johnson?"

Adams laughed again. "You bet. If Johnson had been murdered, Dixon would be my number one suspect."

What brought that up, McCain wondered. Was he playing cat-and-mouse? Was it possible that he did have the list and was trying to throw McCain off course? He studied Adams's expression and asked, "What was the problem between them?"

He shrugged, "Damned if I know. But there sure was bad blood between them."

"Dixon doesn't look dangerous to me," said McCain.

Adams shook his head, "Maybe not, but I sure wouldn't trust him. Did you ever notice the hate in his eyes? If I were the bos'n, I'd be afraid to go to sleep at night. Just a matter of time before one of them blows."

"One of them?" asked McCain.

Adams nodded. "That's right. One of these days Greene is going to be just drunk enough that when Dixon spouts off to him, he's going to lose control. When that happens, I wouldn't want to be Dixon."

McCain wished he knew why Adams seemed so relaxed. Usually he was tight as a drum. Suddenly a quick tap and the door swung open. Dixon came in with the coffee and two pieces of carrot cake. Adams said, "Put it on the desk tray. I'll pour."

"Yes, sir, Captain. Anything else, Captain?"

"That will be all, Dixon."

Dixon bowed and backed out the door.

McCain said, "I've never heard him talk like that before. Is that the way he always is with you?"

"Only when there's an audience. When I'm alone, he's out-and-out surly."

"Why let him get away with it?" asked McCain.

"I'd rather take his lip than have him spit or piss in my food." Adams grinned but McCain knew he was serious.

"How do you know he isn't doing that too?"

"I don't," said Adams. "But if I worried about it, I'd starve. I doubt that he is, but when it comes to Greene…"

The thought of it made McCain almost gag. What a horrible thought. He stared into his coffee cup for a second and then pushed it aside without taking a drop.

Adams took a sip of coffee. "Don't worry," he said. "I checked the cups before I poured."

"It's the damned pot I worried about. I think I'll pass on the java." McCain picked up the AWOL forms and said, "I'd better get back to work."

As McCain was on his way out the door, Adams said, "Haggen tells me you'd like to qualify as an OOD underway."

McCain turned back and said, "I sure would. There sure can't be too many yeoman qualified. But..."

Adams grinned. "You did me a favor. I told Haggen to get you ready. By the time we leave Gitmo, you'll have your own watch."

"Thanks, Captain. I really do appreciate it." McCain left the cabin feeling quite confident that Adams didn't have the list. But McCain still thought his captain was the killer and no matter how many favors he did for him, he wasn't going to stop believing that. That is unless he found someone else to take his place. He headed for the ship's office to talk to Tobey about the feud between Dixon and Johnson.

Tobey's office was empty but not locked. McCain figured it would be a good time to take another quick look for the hiding place of Johnson's journal. He stepped inside leaving the door open. At first he scanned the bulkhead hoping he'd discover some nook or cranny he'd overlooked before. When he finished scanning, he'd found nothing new.

Disgusted, McCain plopped down in Tobey's chair and stretched out his legs. As he leaned back and gazed at the overhead, he noticed the round finned register attached to the heating duct. From that angle it looked as if it twisted on and off. Could that be? His gut churned. A perfect hiding place, why hadn't he noticed it before? When McCain stood up and tried to reach it, he discovered he was several inches too short. Damn it, he thought. Having no other choice, he slid the chair under the duct, climbed up and gave the register a twist. It moved. Another twist and it came loose in his hands leaving a twelve-inch-diameter hole.

Holding the register in his left hand, he used his right to reach into the left channel of the duct. It was empty. He turned around and stuck his arm into the right channel. It too was empty. He should have known it would've been too good to be true. He quickly replaced the vent, stepped down from the chair and noticed Tobey standing in the open door with a coffee mug in his hand. How long had he been there? How much had he seen?

"What you doing, Chief?" he asked.

McCain pulled out his handkerchief and wiped the seat of the chair. He then wiped his hands, pushed the chair back into desk opening, and said, "I was on my way to the mess deck when I noticed the vent looked like it was wobbling. I didn't want it to fall on your head, so I got up there and tightened it. It should be all right now. But I'm glad you're here, I've got something I want to talk to you about." Tobey stood there with a blank look on his face. Did he know McCain was lying?

Finally Tobey looked up at the register and said, "Good thing you saw it. Don't think a bong on the head from that thing would feel too good." He stepped inside, put his cup on his desk, and sat down. "You wanted to ask me something?"

"Just something I'm curious about." McCain lit up an Optimo and said, "The old man told me Dixon and Johnson hated each other. Do you know if that's true and if so, why?"

"I think I do, but it's just a guess."

"What's your guess?"

Tobey took a sip of coffee and said, "I think it was because of Dixon's leave record."

"I don't understand," said McCain while thinking that leave records played an awfully big role on this little ship.

"It's simple," said Tobey. "Dixon took more leave than he had on the books and he wanted Johnson to take care of it for him."

"And Johnson refused," asked McCain.

"Guess so. I heard them arguing about it."

"Do you remember who said what?"

"Not everything, but I do remember Dixon saying something about Johnson doing it for everybody else." He pursed his lips for a second. "Oh, yes. Dixon claimed that Johnson wouldn't do it for him because he was black."

Now we have race for a murder, thought McCain. This case was getting worse by the hour. He stared at Tobey and asked, "What do you think? Did Johnson hate blacks?"

"Probably," said Tobey.

McCain blew out a puff of smoke and crossed his arms. It was a good time to test what Jackson had told him. "Was Johnson tearing up leave papers and not entering them in the records?"

Tobey stared with doubt in his eyes. It was obvious he was not comfortable talking about the subject. Finally, he said, "Not mine. I made sure every hour was charged."

"I'm sure you did. But, how about the others?"

Tobey started to say something, and then stopped.

McCain didn't let him get away with it. "You were going to say?"

Tobey looked very up tight as he said, "Chief, what's done is done. Johnson's dead and I don't see any reason to talk about it."

"Do you see any reason to cover it up?" asked McCain.

"I think I've said enough." He drained his coffee mug and said, "I think I'll get a refill." He got up and hurried toward the crew's mess.

McCain followed him out, but instead of going toward the mess, he turned left and went into his room. He was pissed at himself. Because he pressed so hard on the leave issue, he didn't learn a thing about who it was that sneaked into his room and took the suspect list.

He suddenly thought of the letters from Johnson's locker. Did the thief get them? He pulled out the center drawer beneath his bunk, reached under a stack of skivvies, and breathed a sigh of relief as he pulled out the bundle of letters. From the size of the stack, it looked as if they were all there.

So far he'd gone through more than half of the letters and found nothing that helped in the murder investigation. While he had them out, he decided to take the time and go through the rest of them. That way, if they did disappear, he wouldn't be wondering what he'd missed.

McCain pulled off the rubber bands and started leafing through the stack. He'd put a check mark on the stamp of each one he'd already looked at. When the check marks ended, he was left with ten letters.

The first five were as boring as the previous ones. McCain had written and received many letters but none of them could compare to the homo bullshit these guys wrote to Johnson. Whatever these guys did to one another, Johnson must have been one of the best.

The sixth was a little better. It was from a girl, obviously not a friend, that lived in Bayonne. By reading between the lines, McCain was able to ascertain that she appeared to be the wife of one of the sailors on the base, and that she'd found Johnson's name and address in her husband's wallet. By the tone of the letter, she believed her husband and Johnson were having an affair and when she had confronted him he admitted it. She ended the letter with a warning that if Johnson didn't knock it off he'd be sorry. McCain set the letter aside. Soon as he got the chance, he'd ask Trumbull if he was aware of the relationship between Johnson and the woman's husband. He'd also pass the woman's name on to Tommy to check out on his end.

The remaining four letters contained nothing of value. He put all the letters, except the woman's, into a pile and wrapped the rubber bands around them. No use holding on to them any longer. Tonight on the mid-watch, he'd give the letters a silent burial at sea.

Chapter Sixteen

Day Five—Early Morning

They were an hour into the mid-watch when McCain turned to Haggen and said, "How about a fresh cup of coffee? It looks as if it's going to be slow for a while."

"Good idea, Chief. Take your time." He thought for a second, and said, "If you can find a piece of cake or pie or something and don't mind carrying it up the ladder, I'd appreciate you bringing me a piece."

McCain nodded. "Be glad to." He stepped inside the companionway and hurried down the two flights to the main deck where he noticed a movement of the drape covering the entrance to the wardroom. He pulled the drape aside and discovered Dixon standing there in his skivvy shorts and T-shirt. A shit-eating grin covered his face. What was he doing up at 0100 hours? Where was he coming from or going to? Obviously he'd just entered the wardroom. Could it be that he'd just paid a visit to McCain's room? McCain frowned and said, "Up kind of late aren't you?"

He showed McCain his teeth and said, "Just doing my job, Chief."

McCain, not liking the mind-your-own-business surliness in his voice said, "Job. What have you got to do at this time of the morning?"

Dixon's grin changed to a sarcastic scowl as he said, "Us slaves be on duty twenty-four hours a day. Don't ya all know dat? Man, I thought you chiefs knew everything."

"Cut the shit, Dixon. What are you doing here?"

Dixon gave McCain another dirty look and said, "Cool it, man. Can't you take a joke? I was sound asleep when all of a sudden I woke up wondering if I'd turned off the burner under the coffee pot. So, dedicated man that I is, I hit the deck and scampered up here to check." The shit-eating grin reappeared.

McCain had a hunch he was being conned, but went along with Dixon and asked, "Had you shut it off?"

"Sure did. I'm such a good nigger, should've know I didn't forget."

"Cut the act, Dixon." McCain turned to the door and said, "Come with me. I want to make sure nothing is missing from my room."

"You ain't calling me a thief, is you?"

"I'm not calling you anything, yet," McCain said.

"An' you better not. You mudderfuckin' pencil pushers are all the same. Think you're better than…"

McCain, in a raised voice, said, "That's enough, Dixon." He was sorry he'd gotten into this confrontation but wouldn't back down now. He knew Dixon had him by the balls. Without a witness, he'd never be able to charge him with insubordination, and he was smart enough to know it. Before it went too far, McCain figured it was time to put an end to the jousting and get back on watch. In a calmer voice, he looked Dixon in the eye and said, "I take it you didn't like Johnson."

"You can say that again. He was a mudderfucking, cocksuckin' honky."

McCain took that to be a yes and decided to lay it on the line. "You can bet your last dime that I'm not like Johnson. But that's not important. What I'm trying to figure out is why someone was in my room during the supper hour tonight. Did you see anyone go in or out?"

His wise-ass grin appeared as he said, "I was so busy packing grub and worrying about my leave record, I didn't have time to see much."

So he's still trying. "What's wrong with your leave record?"

Obviously not expecting the question, Dixon thought for a second and then said, "I used a couple more days than I had on the books so I asked Johnson for a favor."

"What did he say?"

"He said he would if I paid him some money."

"Did you give him any?"

"Hell, man," Dixon said. "I don't have no money to give to his cocksucking friends."

McCain shrugged his shoulders and asked, "If you had given him money, do you think he would have altered your leave record?"

"Hell, yes, man. He was doing it for everyone else."

"Are you sure they were paying him?" McCain asked.

"Some were paying him. Some were paying the captain."

"Are you sure? Those are pretty serious charges."

Dixon, through a toothy smile, said, "Am I sure? Does the KKK hate niggers?"

McCain, having got Dixon's point, hesitated for a second and asked, "If I take care of your leave record, do you think you can remember seeing anyone going into or coming out of my room?"

"I might be able to." He gave McCain another grin. "I sure don't want my pay docked."

Tiring of this game of mental checkers, McCain said, "Damn it, Dixon. I told you I'd wipe that excess leave off your record. Now tell me what you saw."

Dixon held up one hand and said, "Man, you sure got a short fuse. The only one I saw in your room was Mr. Posey."

"The exec was in my room."

In his usual sarcastic way, Dixon said, "You got a hearing problem? I saw Mr. Posey come out of your room. Wasn't any business of mine what he was doing in there. Did he steal one of your stinking cigars?"

"Who said anything was missing?"

"Well, you're making such a big deal out of it. Hell, don't make no sense if nothing's missing?"

He was right, thought McCain. "There were some papers missing."

Dixon rubbed his bony chin. "You thinks me or Mr. Posey took them?"

"I'm not accusing anyone," said McCain.

Dixon's grin was back in full force. "Maybe you threw them away by mistake. My ole mammy was always doing that and then blaming my old man."

McCain couldn't take any more of Dixon's wisecracks. He pulled the drape aside and started out the door. "Maybe you're right; I'll go through my wastebasket."

Dixon's hand shot out and grabbed McCain's arm. "You going to take care of my leave?"

McCain pulled loose from his grasp and said, "I told you I would. Now go hit the sack. I've been away from the bridge too long already."

After watching Dixon go down the ladder to the crew's compartment, McCain went into his room, reached into the drawer under his bunk and took out the stack of letters. As he was tearing them into shreds, he noticed the yellow sheet of paper in the bottom of the wastebasket. He pulled it out and discovered the missing list. Did Dixon know it was there? McCain was sure he'd checked the basket earlier and it was empty. Besides, when he went to go eat, the page was still attached to the pad. He didn't know who tore it off the pad and dropped it in the basket, but he was sure it wasn't him. But was it Dixon or was it Posey? Whichever one it was must have thought it would be a good idea to return it. One thing for sure, this little fucked-up ship had more mysteries than a book store.

When McCain finished shredding the letters and the yellow sheet of paper, he took the wastebasket to the fantail and dumped its contents into the ship's wake. The wind caught some of the pieces and sent them fluttering into the air. He watched till he was sure none of the pieces landed back on the ship. Convinced they were gone forever; McCain went into the galley and cut two huge squares of yellow sheet cake. Then with the cake and two mugs of coffee resting on a tray, he carefully eased his way up the ladder to the bridge.

At the top of the first flight, he discovered Rossi standing in the doorway of the chart house. If Dixon didn't put the list back, could it have been Rossi? Being on watch in the radio shack would give him the opportunity to run down to McCain's room, throw the list in the waste basket and be back on watch without missing a message. "Slow watch, Rossi?" McCain asked.

Now that they'd patched things up, Rossi was downright civilized. "Slow is not the word," he said. "I haven't copied a word in the last hour. Sure makes time drag."

McCain nodded and said, "Know what you mean. I'd like to stay and keep you company but Haggen's waiting for his cake." McCain left Rossi standing there as he resumed his climb to the bridge.

Haggen was waiting at the chart table. "Thought you fell overboard. Was about ready to sound the alarm." He picked up a chunk of cake and took a huge bite. Soon as he swallowed he said, "Rice can sure bake some good victuals."

McCain offered a piece of cake to the helmsman. When Crisano refused, he ate it himself.

The next two and a half hours were filled with the routine duties of getting Loran fixes, calling the towing engine watch to freshen the nip, checking the radar screen and keeping his log up to date. As he went about his duties, McCain wondered how he was going to narrow the number of suspects who might have killed Johnson. It seemed that every few hours a new person joined the list. He checked his left hip pocket for the letter from the jealous wife. It was still there. Could she be the killer? He'd have Tommy check her out.

"What's on your mind, Chief?" asked Haggen as he joined McCain on the starboard wing. "You still thinking about that little gal in Norfolk?"

"Not really. I was just wondering if I'll be able to go to sleep when we get off watch." He hoped Haggen believed that was all McCain had on his mind.

Haggen raised his binoculars, peered out over the bow and said, "I'll give you something to think about."

"What's that?"

Without lowering the glasses, Haggen said, "It'll take us another four days to get to Gitmo. That's at least three watches a day. I think that after ten more quartermaster watches, you'll be ready to qualify as OOD. I'll talk to the captain and see if he'll let you stand the last two watches on your own. I'll just observe."

McCain smiled and said, "Wow—I didn't expect to qualify so fast. But I know I can do it." He was surprised how important this had become to him. But he knew he had to be extra careful not to let his desire to qualify interfere with the investigation. He'd decide later if he was going to tell Tommy when he called him from Gitmo.

Chapter Seventeen

Day Eight—Morning

Four uneventful days settled life aboard the *Lakota* into the normal routine of a ship at sea. To McCain it felt as though he was always on watch, or always getting ready for watch, or always just coming off watch.

As Haggen promised, he had convinced the captain that McCain was ready to be certified. Yesterday, Adams called McCain into his cabin, asked him a few pertinent questions and declared him ready to take the con.

McCain would be the first to admit that during his first stint as OOD, he was a bit nervous, but by the time the four-hour watch ended, he felt like a pro. He was about to finish his second tour under the watchful eye of Chief Warrant Officer Haggen when Haggen, wearing a beaming smile, shook McCain's hand and told him he was ready to solo. But it would have to wait till they left Gitmo.

Before dawn they had spotted lights on the island. Now McCain and Haggen stood on the starboard wing looking at the tip of Cuba. They were in the Windward Passage and would be entering Guantanamo Bay shortly after the noon meal.

"Ever been to Gitmo?" Haggen asked.

"Hasn't everybody?" said McCain. He then realized he'd answered a question with a question; one of those things that really pissed him off when it was done to him. Trying to undo his mistake, McCain said, "I've been there twice; both on shakedown cruises. Once on the *McCaffrey* and the other on the *Boston*."

"I served on a cruiser myself once," said Haggen. "Best duty there is."

McCain nodded and said, "I think so too. But why do you like them so much?"

Haggen thought for a second. "Well for one thing, I didn't have to stand deck watches, but most of all I think it's because the crew is better trained and better disciplined. Besides, the warrant officers have their own quarters and mess. Even better than the chiefs have it."

McCain grinned. "I've never been able to figure out why everybody thinks the chiefs have it made. They earn every special privilege they get. It's left up to the chiefs to make sure the white hats are trained. Of course, there's a method to their madness; the better the petty officers know their jobs the less headaches for the chiefs. But why am I telling you this? You were a chief."

Haggen looked at McCain kind of funny and said, "I'm surprised you didn't go through my record. I was never a chief, just one of those lucky guys that were picked to go straight from first class to warrant. But it was probably because my chief took the time to make sure I knew my job, almost as good as he did."

McCain heard someone coming up and ladder and turned to see Bos'n Greene stepping into the pilothouse. "Ready to be relieved, Chief?" he asked.

McCain checked his watch: 0730. He then looked at the two chief warrant officers and wondered if he'd be better off trying for warrant rather than a full commission. Probably not, years of too many watches, hard liberties, and time away from their homes and families made both men appear older than they really were. When he realized Greene was waiting for an answer, he said, "I'm ready." He glanced at Haggen and said, "Time sure flies when you're having fun."

When Haggen asked Greene what was for breakfast, Greene said, "Foreskins on toast. And nobody makes them better than Rice."

McCain pictured chunks of pink thinly sliced dried chipped beef floating in a sea of white gravy over thick slices of toast. "One of my favorite breakfasts," he said. "Too bad the civilians don't know what they're missing."

"I see Rice has cast his spell on you like the rest of us," Greene said.

McCain nodded and rubbed his hands together. "That he has, and since me and the old man got our problems squared away, I'm kind of getting used to this little tub. Ain't nearly as bad as I first thought." He didn't mention that he still believed there was a killer on board and that most of the crew would never make muster on a real ship of the line.

He gave Greene the rundown on the course, speed and traffic in the area, and then, followed by Haggen, went below. When they reached the main deck, McCain went to his room to wash up. Haggen stepped into the wardroom.

It was close to an hour later when McCain downed the last of his second helping of chipped beef. He stood up, rubbed his belly, and drew a fresh mug of coffee that he carried out into the fresh air. Though the day had just started, the sun was already beating down on the metal deck. He looked up at a cloudless sky and knew that life aboard the *Lakota* would soon be too hot for comfort.

Trying to keep the steel decks from turning into hot plates, the deck crew was rigging awnings above the fo'c'sle, both wings of the bridge, and a huge section of the fantail. It would probably help some, but trying to sleep in his little cabin, with only a fan to circulate air, was not something he was looking forward too.

Deciding it was already too hot for coffee; McCain tossed the dregs of his mug over the side and returned it to the galley. He was heading aft when he spotted Posey standing alone staring at the tow. He moved alongside the young officer and said, "Haven't had much of a chance to talk to you since I switched watches. How is the old man treating you?"

Without turning his head, Posey said, "Not good. Seems to me that since he hasn't got you to pick on, he's even worse."

"No shit. I thought you said he'd ease up if I patched things up with him."

Posey shifted his gaze to McCain, who saw confusion and pain in his young eyes. "I sure was wrong," he said. "The captain even said that you felt I wasn't doing my job. I don't know why on earth you'd say that. I thought we were hitting it off pretty good."

McCain felt as if he'd been kicked in the balls. He remembered telling Adams that but never dreamed he'd repeat it. He thought for a minute, and then said, "Damn it, Mr. Posey, I only told him that to try to get on his good side. I actually thought I was doing you a favor."

As Posey stood there with a blank expression on his face, McCain wondered if he should tell Posey why he was on board. Maybe it would make him feel a little better. Before he had a chance to make up his mind, he heard, "Chief McCain, de cap'n wants to see you in his cabin." He spun around to find Dixon grinning like the ivory keys on an ebony baby grand.

"Any idea what he wants?" asked McCain.

Dixon, with a twinkle in his eye and a wry grin, said, "All he had on was his shorts. You is a yeoman, ain't you?"

McCain knew all too well what he meant; pencil pushers throughout the Navy were the brunt of many homosexual accusations. Johnson hadn't helped matters any. But it was time to put an end to this bullshit. McCain squinted, gritted his teeth and in a low firm voice said, "Dixon, one of these days I'm going to forget I'm a chief, and when I do…"

Posey stepped between the two men, and said, "Dixon, that was uncalled for. Get back to your duties now." With a sneer, Dixon turned and shuffled forward.

McCain looked at Posey and said, "I can see why the bos'n hates that black bastard."

Posey shrugged. "He's just another product of Captain Adams's failure to enforce discipline. A good CO would have squared him away in a minute."

"You can say that again," said McCain. "But now I'd better go see what he wants." As he started to leave, he turned to Posey and said, "Don't worry, I'll make sure I don't get you in any more hot water." Posey's expression failed to show even a hint of relief. What a damned shame that a good officer like the XO was being ruined by a vindictive psycho.

McCain tapped twice on the captain's door. The familiar voice of Adams called out, "Come on in. It's not locked."

When he went in, McCain discovered that Dixon was right. Adams, clad only in white skivvy shorts decorated with red hearts, was sprawled on his bunk with identical gray fans on each end blasting hot air down on his near-naked body.

Adams put his hand on his thigh and pinched a bit of cloth between his thumb and forefinger. "What do you think of my fancy shorts? Kitty bought them for me. She says they make me look sexy."

As much as McCain wanted to tell him that they looked disgusting, he held back and said, "To each his own." But that didn't satisfy him, so he followed up with, "Why don't you take a stroll through the mess deck. We'll take a vote of the crew."

Adams laughed and then said, "That should really give them a different impression of their captain."

McCain, already growing weary of being in the same room with Adams, said, "Did you call me just to show me your valentine drawers?" What a disgrace for a naval officer, he thought.

"Of course not. I wanted you to know that Haggen, Greene and I are going to play some golf this afternoon. I thought you might want to be the fourth."

Not expecting the offer, McCain wondered how he was going to get out of this one without pissing him off again. He put on a sorrowful expression and said, "Damn, Captain; under normal circumstances I'd like that, but when you're as short as I am, you just can't find the right-sized clubs to rent in the pro shop. I probably should have brought mine." He paused for a second. "Besides I hear Gitmo has a strange course."

"Strange?" he asked.

McCain shrugged. "That's my word. Seems that I read somewhere that since Castro cut off the water supply they can't grow grass on anything but the putting greens. So when playing the rest of the course, you carry an Astroturf door mat with you and each time you hit the ball you have to put down the mat, spot your ball, and go through with your swing. My game is bad enough without going through all that."

"Well, if that's the way you feel. I just thought I'd ask." McCain didn't know if the look in Adams's eyes was one of insult or disappointment.

Hoping he sounded believable, McCain said, "I really do appreciate the offer, Skipper." Actually he found that trying to be nice to his commanding officer was more difficult than locating Johnson's journal. The thought gave him an idea. What if Adams had the journal? Maybe, while he and the others were out chasing their balls, McCain would be able to find a way to get into the CO's cabin and have a look-see. "Want me to check if Chief Hall or Jackson wants to play?"

With no enthusiasm at all, Adams said, "Try Hall. Unless I miss my guess, Jackson will make a beeline for the Chief's Club. I've already warned Greene that he'd have to hold off his drinking till we hit the nineteenth hole."

Thinking he was trying to be funny, McCain said, "That must have broken the bos'n's heart."

"I don't think he liked it too much," said Adams in a more serious tone than McCain expected. "He'll still have plenty of time to make up for it."

"Speaking of time," asked McCain. "How long are we staying in Gitmo?"

"We're leaving in the morning. We'll be taking some Jamaican workers with us so they'll have a chance to see their families," Adams said.

This was a surprise; McCain never dreamed that they'd be having passengers. "How many?" he asked.

"Oh, ten or fifteen. That's about all we have room for. We're also taking an engineer to test the quality of the sand."

McCain shrugged and said, "I thought sand was sand."

"Me too," said Adams. "But they tell me only certain types are used for concrete."

McCain reached for the doorknob and said, "I'd better get to Hall before he makes other plans."

He was halfway out the door when he heard, "Chief."

Over his shoulder, he said, "Yes, Captain?"

"You can go ashore anytime you want. Let that asshole Posey stay on board." There was a hint of satisfaction in his voice.

"Thanks," McCain said. What he really wanted to say was, *If only you were half the officer Mr. Posey is, you'd have a much better ship.*

Soon as he closed the door, he hurried up to the chart house and gave the message to Hall. Then before Hall could object, McCain retreated back down the ladder.

Now if he could only get Posey off the ship for a while, he'd have clear sailing in his search for the journal. Chances are that none of the enlisted crew would give him a problem. Their quarters were already so hot that any of them not already ashore drinking beer would be stretched out under the awnings.

Chapter Eighteen

Day Eight—Early Afternoon

Soon after the entrance to Guantanamo Bay appeared over the bow, Captain Adams set the special sea detail. McCain had just finished strapping on his sound-powered phones when the CO said, "Chief, tell the towing engine room to reel in the tow."

"Aye aye, sir," said McCain before repeating the order into his mouthpiece.

Adams then gave the order to reduce the number of turns to where they were barely maintaining headway. The reduced speed cut the resistance on the tow wire and allowed the distance between the *Lakota* and the barge to quickly shorten. When the distance was down to a few feet, Adams ordered, "All stop."

Soon as the barge bumped the fenders protecting the *Lakota*'s stern, Boatswain's Mate Third Class Billy Joe Tucker, with the end of a hawser in hand, jumped aboard.

Adams called out, "Ahead slow. Pay out twenty feet of tow wire." McCain repeated the orders into his mouthpiece.

While McCain was repeating the orders, he watched Tucker take his end of the heavy rope aft on the barge. Seaman Curtin pulled the other end forward and took a turn around the *Lakota's* capstan. When Tucker signaled that his end was made fast, Bos'n Greene pushed forward on the handle that engaged the gears. As the capstan turned, the barge started making a 180-degree turn. It was only a few minutes till the barge, stern to, was made fast to the starboard side of the tug. McCain couldn't help thinking that they must look like Hemingway's *Old Man and the Sea*.

A short while later they were passing between the modern-day Pillars of Hercules guarding the entrance to Guantanamo Bay: Carter Field to port and McCalla Field to starboard.

An hour later they moored port side to Pier One. As before, Adams's ship handling had been flawless. Soon as the special sea detail was secured, McCain rushed down to the main deck, crossed the gangway and headed for the post office to pick up the ship's mail.

By the time he got back to the ship, the foursome had already left for the golf course. McCain hurried into his room, opened the mail pouch and dumped the contents on his bunk. First he separated the official mail and took the personal mail into the crew's mess and distributed the letters. Among the letters, he noticed several from Household and Beneficial Finance. He felt good that it was about time the men knew about the scam being inflicted on them.

In seconds, McCain heard, "What the fuck is this?" It was Rossi yelling as he waved an open letter. Almost immediately thereafter similar outbursts came from Quartermaster Third Class Smith, Shipfitter Second Class O'Neil, Radioman First Class Wishbore and Boatswain's Mate Third Class Tucker. Commissaryman First Class Rice stood silently staring at the two letters in his hand and then shifted his gaze to McCain. His bulging white eyeballs surrounded by his ebony face had the pleading look of a whipped dog.

McCain eased next to Rice, leaned close and whispered, "Don't worry about the letters. I told you I'd take care of them." Rice seemed to relax a bit and he tried to smile but it was obvious he was still very uncomfortable.

When Wishbore saw McCain talking to Rice he must have put two and two together and said, "Do you know anything about these letters, Chief?"

McCain stretched out his hand and said, "Let me take a look at them?"

Wishbore handed McCain the letters he'd received. Already knowing what they contained, McCain pretended to read them, then handed them back and in a voice loud enough for the others to hear, said, "It's pretty simple. These companies claim that you borrowed money from them and you haven't been making your payments. Pay your bills and they won't send you any more letters."

McCain's words were no sooner out of his mouth than he was surrounded by Tucker, Smith, O'Neil, and Rossi, all trying to talk at once. "Hold it down," he said. When he was sure he had the floor, he said, "It looks to me like you guys have got a problem. Are these the first letters you've received?"

As usual, Rossi was the first to answer, "It's the first ones I've received," his Brooklyn accent more pronounced than ever.

In a quieter, but equally concerned voice, Wishbore said, "I don't owe one cent to anybody."

"Me either," O'Neil blurted out.

The others stood, as if in shock, nodding in agreement.

McCain pushed through the men, grabbed a mug and filled it with coffee. "I've been around a long time and I've never heard of either one of these companies trying to gyp anyone out of money they didn't owe. At one time or another, all of you must have signed some kind of papers." He knew they had, but he wanted to see the expressions on their faces.

Tucker looked around at the others, and said, "I did. I signed some papers for Captain Adams but he said he was going to make the payments."

Through a nodding of heads, a round of "me too" spewed forth from the others.

McCain shook his head and took a sip of coffee. "I hate to tell you guys this, but since you signed the papers, you've got to make the payments."

"No fucking way," yelled Rossi as if they were all hard of hearing. "I'm going to see the old man."

After the men left no doubt they agreed with Rossi, McCain stepped in front of the door leading to officer's country and said, "Take it easy. The captain is ashore, you'll have to wait till he gets back." He was hoping that they'd really be stirred up by that time and ready for bear.

It should be quite a show, but now, if he was going to carry out his plan, he'd have to get Posey off the ship.

He went to Posey's cabin and knocked on the door. When it opened, he said, "I'm going to be working on the mail; no use for both of us staying aboard. If you want to go ashore, I'll cover for you."

Posey gave McCain a grateful grin and said, "Tell you the truth, I do have a friend stationed here and would like to give him a buzz. Maybe we can get together."

Without seeming too pleased, McCain said, "You can go ashore any time you want, and don't worry about the captain. He said they were going to have a few drinks when they finished their round. That means he'll probably be in a good mood. I'll just tell him your friend came aboard and I volunteered to stand by for you."

"Thanks, Chief. I should be ready in about ten minutes. I'll let you know before I leave the ship."

It was about fifteen minutes later when McCain walked out on deck with Posey. As he crossed the gangway, Posey turned and said, "Are you sure you don't mind standing by for me?"

"I'm sure. Have a good time with your friend. Maybe it'll take your mind off Adams and the ship."

"Thanks again, Chief. I owe you one."

McCain felt like saying *Damn it, just go so I can get to work,* but instead, he nonchalantly waved his right hand and watched Posey move up the pier and take a seat at the bus stop. Soon as Posey was seated, McCain spun around and headed for the captain's cabin.

One night, while on watch, McCain had discovered in the chart table drawer a master key that fit all the stateroom locks. Assuming that it would also fit Adams's cabin, he removed it from the drawer and had been carrying it around with him, just waiting for a chance to use it. Now, from inside his room, he watched till the passageway was clear and, with key in hand, hurried to Adams's cabin. He stuck in the key, twisted to the right and the door opened. He stepped inside and locked the door behind him.

McCain went directly to Adams's desk and switched on the lamp. Unlike the *Lakota*, the desk was shipshape as it could be. McCain was amazed how a man whose personal life was so much in disarray could be so meticulous about his personal papers and his ship handling. The only item on top of his desk was a letter from his wife held down by a bronze chipping hammer. He picked up the heavy hammer and saw that it was a going-away present from the members of the deck force on his last ship.

He pulled out the top right-hand drawer and discovered several large manila clasp envelopes. Each one was labeled in Adams's handwriting.

He unlatched the prongs on the envelope marked "HFC & BFC letters." Inside were dozens of unopened letters addressed to the six debtor crew members. Several others, all opened, were addressing to the Commanding Officer, USS *Lakota*. He opened one of the letters and found it was a plea for the CO to help get the members of his crew to honor their debts. What a waste of time. He shoved the letters back into the manila envelope and closed the clasp.

The next manila envelope was marked, "Personal Letters." A quick check confirmed McCain's hunch that they were from Adams's wife and girlfriend. He didn't feel right about delving into his CO's personal life, so he set the envelope aside and opened one marked "Fitness Reports."

McCain removed the long yellow forms and started reading. The reports on Haggen and Greene were quite complimentary. In Adams's opinion, both were outstanding officers. McCain pictured the day he found Greene stretched out on the wardroom couch and shook his head.

He then checked Posey's report. His stomach knotted and he felt blood rushing to his face. He couldn't believe it. Adams had rated the young, obviously talented officer as totally unsatisfactory. McCain knew that in his hands he held the end of Posey's career. When the promotion board reads this report, Posey was sure to be passed over. How much hate could Adams have for the young officer? McCain checked the date it was written and discovered that it was before the mutiny attempt. That meant the bad report wasn't a result of the mutiny, but what else on earth could Posey have done to rate this drastic evaluation?

From force of habit, McCain pulled out an Optimo and started to light it, but then remembered where he was and that someone might smell the smoke. He closed the Zippo's lid and put the cigar back in its sleeve. He looked at the envelope again. It was empty. Why hadn't Posey attached a rebuttal? It was certainly his right to do so. In fact, as far as McCain was concerned, it was Posey's obligation to object to these obviously unjust prejudicial remarks about his performance as a naval officer. He checked the form again. Posey hadn't signed it. That meant one of two things, Posey either refused to sign or Adams had never showed it to him.

He quickly checked the remainder of the envelopes and found nothing of interest. He then went through the rest of the drawers, underneath the mattress, and the clothes closet. Johnson's journal was nowhere to be found.

McCain opened the door a crack, saw that the coast was clear, stepped into the passageway and locked the door behind him. As long as he had the key, he decided to check Posey's room. Not that he had a reason to, but it was one of those things you do when you have the opportunity. He sure didn't expect to find anything; Posey seemed too much of a gentleman to have anything to do with Johnson's death. Hell, he didn't stand up for his own rights with the old man; surely he couldn't be involved in anything close to murder. But there was the mutiny attempt that wouldn't fit his profile either. So many questions and no answers.

It was almost two hours later when McCain spotted the golfers coming down the pier. Even in the distance he could tell that Adams and Greene were feeling no pain. Haggen didn't look too bad and Hall looked cold sober.

"The captain's coming back," someone called out from the boat deck.

McCain looked up and saw Rossi sliding down the vertical ladder. He'd no sooner hit the deck when the other five debtors poured out of the crew's mess. Wishbore was in the lead. He turned to the others and said, "Let me do the talking. We don't want to make this worse than it already is." A few dissenting groans came from the others but no one voiced an objection.

Hall was the first to come aboard. He saluted the quarterdeck and colors and went straight to his room. Haggen and Greene came next. Greene stopped and said something to Wishbore. When Wishbore ignored him, he staggered up the deck.

Soon as Captain Adams stepped off the gangway, he was met by a wedge of white hats. Wishbore saluted and said, "Captain, me and these men here would like to talk to you."

Adams scowled and tried pushing Wishbore aside. "Not now. I'm not in the mood. That fucking Hall and Haggen snookered us."

Wishbore braced himself and stood fast. The others closed in and Adams stared at them through blurry eyes. "What's going on here? Get out of my way or you'll all be on report." He stepped around Wishbore, pushed his way through the others, and hurried toward his cabin. The six men were at his heels.

McCain stayed in the background and watched them go up the passageway to Adams's cabin. Before unlocking the door, Adams, with a fleck of foam hanging from the corner of his mouth, turned and faced the men. He wiped his mouth with the sleeve of his shirt and said, "I warned you bastards. You're all on report. I'll hold Captain's Mast as soon as we get out to sea. Now get out of here."

Wishbore held out the two letters he'd received. The others waved theirs in the air. Wishbore said, "Captain, we're not going anywhere till you explain why we got these letters. You know that when you asked us to take out these loans, you said you'd pay them off and assured us that we wouldn't have a thing to worry about."

The captain looked as if he'd been kicked in the groin. He grabbed the letters from Wishbore's hand and in a slurred voice said, "How'd you get these letters?"

The men all started talking at once. Wishbore turned to them and said, "Hold it, men. Getting all excited won't get us anywhere." He turned back to Adams. "Captain, we'd like to step inside and talk about this."

Suddenly all the fight went out of Adams. He looked like a whipped dog with his tail between his legs. "All right," he said. "Come on in."

Soon as they were all inside, McCain hurried to see if he could hear what was going on. It was no use. Much to his surprise, the meeting was a lot quieter than he expected. Feeling that sooner or later he'd be dragged into the confrontation, McCain retreated to the mess deck and poured himself a glass of iced tea.

He'd drained one glass and started on another when the drape opened and Wishbore, followed by the others, entered the crew's mess. Rush motioned to McCain and said, "The captain wants to see you."

"How'd the meeting go?" McCain asked.

"Not good," he said. "But at least everything is out on the table."

"Any idea why he wants to see me?" asked McCain.

"Nope." Then as if he didn't want to tell him, Wishbore said, "But, by the way he said it, I don't think I'd want to be in your shoes."

McCain shrugged. "So what else is new?" He downed the rest of his iced tea, dropped the glass in the sink, and reluctantly went to see the captain.

As he approached the cabin, Adams was waiting at the door with daggers shooting from his eyes. "You've done it again, McCain." He said as he stepped back into his cabin. "Get in here."

McCain just managed to get through the door when Adams slammed it shut and growled, "What gives you the right to disobey my orders?"

"I didn't know I did. Tell me what you're talking about."

Adams threw up his arms. "You know damn well I gave an order that all mail was to be brought to me before it was distributed."

"No, sir. I did not know that," He lied.

"What!" obviously catching him by surprise.

Putting on his most convincing voice, McCain said, "You never gave me that order."

With doubt now reflecting in his voice, he said, "You mean to tell me that Tobey never told you?"

Now was the time to play it smart. What could he say that wouldn't get Tobey in trouble? Taking a chance, McCain said, "Now that you mention it, he did say something, but I thought he meant official mail."

"I meant all mail," he said through clinched teeth. "And you've disobeyed my orders."

Using every bit of composure he could muster, McCain said, "Gosh, Captain, I didn't know I was doing anything wrong. I only handed out United States mail addressed to the crew members. It wouldn't be legal not to give it to them."

Adams's face was now the color of a bullfighter's cape. "I'm the captain of this ship. I'll decide what's legal or not."

McCain looked Adams straight in the eye and in a calm reassuring voice, said, "Captain, instead of screaming at me, why don't you tell me what you're trying to do? Maybe I can help you, like I did with the AWOL reports."

The offer seemed to take the fight out of him. With shaking hands, he lit a cigarette and started pacing the length of his cabin. After a few seconds, he stopped long enough to say, "I don't think anyone can help me now." Adams looked and sounded like a beaten man.

McCain dropped his hat on Adams's bunk, sat down next to it and folded his right leg over his left. "Captain, why don't you relax and tell me what the trouble is? I'm pretty good at solving problems."

It took the better part of fifteen minutes before Adams finished confessing how he'd asked the six crew members to borrow the money and how he'd promised to take care of the payments. McCain almost felt sorry for him when Adams said, "I really did intend to pay off the loans, but then everything seemed to go haywire."

"What happened?"

Seeming almost happy to get it off his chest, Adams said, "Kitty told me she was pregnant and that she needed money for an abortion. Then she changed her mind and said she needed money for doctor bills."

McCain took out a cigar and said, "I'm confused. What did you do with the money they borrowed for you?"

He shook his head and said sheepishly, "I gave it to Kitty. First we needed an apartment. Then we needed furniture. Then she wanted a car."

McCain spun the wheel, sent his Zippo flaming into life and held it to the tip of his cigar. When it had formed a glowing ash, he said, "With all those expenses, I can see how your lieutenant's pay wouldn't make it. But please go on."

"Most of my pay went to my wife. She's pregnant too, but the Navy takes care of her medical bills."

Shaking his head in disbelief, McCain said, "Your wife and girlfriend are both pregnant?" He already knew the answer but there was no use letting Adams know he did.

"That's not all. My wife's been shacking up with a second class boatswain's mate and I've got a strong hunch that her kid belongs to him. I'd like to divorce her, but that takes money."

"Does she know about Kitty?" asked McCain.

He sighed and said, "I didn't think she did, but after what happened in Norfolk, she seems to know all kinds of things."

McCain brushed that aside by saying, "I'd like to hear what went on in Norfolk, but let's stick to the money for now."

"I'd just as soon forget about it," said Adams looking as if he'd lost all hope.

Now McCain knew he had Adams where he wanted him. "Captain, these things happen. I'm single and have quite a bit of money in the Navy Credit Union. Let's make a list of what you owe and I'll see if I can help you out."

"No thanks," he said.

McCain was astounded. "You don't want me to help you out?" To give him time to think, McCain took a long drag, blew out the smoke and then repeated the process. "Mind if I ask you why?"

Adams hung his head and stared at the deck. After a minute or so, he looked at McCain and said, "I don't know if I can trust you. Johnson told me he was going to help me out. Said all he needed was some money to prime the pump."

"You gave Johnson money? Where'd you get it?"

He hesitated for a few seconds and then said, "It was Johnson's idea. We took it out of the recreation fund. I put in an IOU that I intended to tear up when Johnson brought me the money he said he was going to get from a friend who owned a club."

Things were finally coming together. "Did Johnson get the money?" asked McCain.

"No, he didn't." Adams appeared more dejected than ever. "He went to see the guy, but when he came back he said that he wanted more money from me." Then as if it was an afterthought, he said, "Before I could scrape up some more, Johnson went over the hill."

A couple more pieces seemed to have fallen in place. Evidently Johnson was conning Adams out of money for his bouncer friend. It must have been in Ziggy's that Johnson broke the news that he needed more. But why did Johnson make the phone call to Posey? He'd bet anything that it too was for money.

McCain uncrossed his legs and stood up. "What's past is past. Right now you're in a bind and it looks to me as if I'm the only one who can help you out. You've got to get those finance companies off the backs of your crew. And you've got to put that money back into the recreation fund."

Adams, looking like he was about to cry, said, "I know, but I don't know how to do it."

It was McCain's time to take the offense. "Damn it, Captain, I'm trying to tell you how you can do it. There's a branch office of the credit union on the base. I can go there this afternoon and have cashier checks made out to each of the men involved. I'll bring back cash for the rec fund." He paused for a second. "Are there any other debts you owe? Now's your chance to get back on your feet."

Adams leaned forward and buried his face in his hands. McCain waited for several seconds and then said impatiently, "Well, what do you say, Captain?"

The captain looked up through hopeless eyes and said, "I'll do what you say, Chief. And I swear I'll pay back every penny."

There was no way McCain believed him, but he didn't feel he was taking that much of a risk because he was sure Tommy would find a way to cover the funds he'd be laying out. He gave Adams a friendly smile and said, "I know you will. And to make it easier for you, I'll work out a payment schedule. You can give me so much every payday." McCain put on his hat and said, "Now give me those finance company letters; I'll get the IOU out of the rec fund box."

Adams went to his desk, took out the envelope containing the letters and handed it to McCain. He took the envelope and said, "I'll get to the credit union before it closes. We'll have this taken care of this afternoon."

The look of disbelief on Adams's face made McCain know that from that moment on, Adams was in his pocket.

Chapter Nineteen

Day Eight—Late Afternoon

"Chief McCain, your call to New York is ready in booth number seven."

McCain raised his hand to let the short-haired redhead manning the telephone center desk know that he'd heard her message. She had a tiny turned-up nose and big brown eyes. He considered making a play for her, but then realized that she was probably married to one of the sailors stationed on the base and decided it was a bad idea. He stepped into the booth, closed the door and said, "Tommy—you bastard. Do you know what you're putting me through?"

"One moment, Chief McCain, I'll put Commander Thomas on." The New York accent again. If she was a boy she'd have been perfect for a part in the Dead End Kids. He realized what he had just said, thinking it was Tommy, and felt his face turning red. *Why can't big shots answer their own damn phones?* he wondered.

Tommy came on the line and said, "Jack, how's the weather down there? Are you calling from pool side at the club?" His voice sounded like it was filled with pent-up laughter.

"Hell no, I'm not. Do you think this is a vacation? Well..." McCain was wasting his time, Tommy was now laughing so hard, and McCain didn't think he heard a single word he had said.

Suddenly Tommy stopped laughing and said, "Can't you take a joke anymore. Maybe you need your ashes hauled."

McCain smiled at the words they used to use for getting laid in high school. Then he said, "All I need is to solve this damned case and to get off this bucket of rust."

Now in a serious voice Tommy said, "Speaking of the case, how are you doing?"

"To tell you the truth, day by day I get more confused on who could have killed Johnson. But I do have the debt letters squared away. That is if the Navy is willing to spend some taxpayer's money."

"What are you talking about? Those debts are personal. Why should they cost the Navy anything? How much money are you talking about?"

McCain took a deep breath and said, "One thousand eight hundred and thirty-three bucks."

"Are you crazy?"

McCain had to get back on offense. "No, I'm not crazy. And don't tell me a big shot like you can't get the Navy to spring for a couple grand?" He felt a knot form in his gut as he pictured the falling balance in his credit union account.

"Jack, you know the hurdles we have to jump to get cash from the navy accounts. It can be done, but it's not easy and I don't like to go after anything where I'm pretty sure I'll be turned down."

"Look, Tommy. I've already laid out the loot. I made a decision based on the fact that I thought it was the proper thing to do. Now I'm not going to beg, but I think the least you can do is help me get my money back."

"I suppose the least I can do is listen. Tell me how you got into this predicament."

After McCain gave Tommy a complete account of how Adams conned the six sailors into taking out the finance company loans and then the IOU to the recreation fund, Tommy said, "It sounds to me like it's Adams, not the Navy, who owes you money."

"Of course you're right. But there's a lot riding on this and it's not the time to get into a pissing match with Lieutenant Adams. I've just come from the credit union and I still have the checks, so if you're not going to bail me out of this, I'll put them back into my account. And when I do, it's going to make me look like a damned welsher and I doubt if I'll ever get cooperation from Adams or the crew again."

"Come on, Jack," said Tommy. "Put yourself in my shoes. How would you feel about going to the admiral and trying to convince him the Navy should bail Adams out?"

From the sound of Tommy's voice, McCain knew he was fighting a losing battle, but in a last-ditch effort, he said, "I thought you had a pair of balls."

"You know I do, but I also have a brain."

McCain, now getting desperate, said, "If this was a goddamned drug case you'd come up with the money to buy drugs wouldn't you?"

Tommy was silence for several seconds before he said, "I probably would, but this is not a drug case."

Thinking he heard of bit of wavering in Tommy's voice, McCain held his breath and said, "I know that, but the money will be spent in the same way by giving me greater access to Adams's thinking. And since it looks more and more like he's the killer, the Navy will get its money's worth."

"Sorry, Jack. I know what you're trying to do, but you'll have to find another way. I'm not asking for the money."

"You don't sound to me like you're sorry," said McCain. "Way I see it, you're telling me I should take these checks back and have them cancelled. Are you sure you want this case solved?"

"You do what you have to do, Jack. Maybe if I was convinced Adams killed Johnson, I'd think about it some more. But the case so far is not too compelling. Listen to what I've found out and you'll agree with me."

McCain felt his gut churn as he asked, "What's that?"

It seemed like an hour before Tommy said, "Remember the woman you said had written Johnson about his relationship with her husband?"

"Sure I do."

McCain pictured the serious expression on Tommy's face as he said, "I had her checked out and discovered that she's the daughter of your bos'n."

"Greene?" McCain asked.

"Greene," said Tommy.

Having a hard time believing what he was hearing, McCain asked, "Are you telling me that Bos'n Greene had a hard-on for Johnson?"

"Sounds like it, and, to give it more credibility, as soon as she found out about Johnson and her husband, she told her father about it."

"Damn it, Tommy, just when I'm sure I've got it narrowed down to Adams you drop another line in the water."

"There's more."

McCain sighed and said, "Now what?"

"Not only did she write that letter to Johnson, she wrote one to Captain Adams."

"That's not so surprising."

"I agree. Writing the letter to Adams is not surprising, but what happened next sure is."

The conversation was getting on McCain's nerves. "Damn it, Tommy, will you stop dribbling out information and give me the whole story?"

"Okay. It seems when Adams received her letter, he went to see her at her apartment and, believe it or not, while he was there he put the make on her."

"You're shittin' me!" said McCain. "You know something, Tommy; I'm really not a bit surprised. How did he go about it?"

"According to her, he tried to convince her that she should get even with her husband and he was willing to help her."

McCain wondered if Adams really thought she'd fall for that. "You see, Tommy. I've told you all along that Adams is no damn good. Did she go along with it?"

"No. She said she kicked him out and warned him that if he didn't put a stop to Johnson trying to break up her marriage she'd tell her father about the whole thing."

"So are you telling me that Bos'n Greene knew about Adams's visit?"

"He didn't at first."

"What does that mean?" McCain asked. In his gut he already knew he had the answer.

"Like I said. She didn't tell her father at first, but on the day the *Lakota* pulled out for Gitmo, she wrote him a letter."

McCain wracked his brain for a second. If that's the case, he didn't receive it till this afternoon. Seems like he did remember Greene having a letter in the batch of officer's mail he left on the wardroom table. Finally he shook his head and said, "Tommy, of all the investigators you could have put on this case, why in the hell did you pick me?"

"Simple. You're the best man for the job. There's a lot riding on this case. The Navy's had a lot of bad publicity lately and the CNO is up in arms. According to the admiral, the CNO is chomping at the bit to make an example out of one of the big brass and the boss doesn't want it to be him."

"And for that, you pick me?"

"Jack, you're the best friend I've ever had and I know you won't let me down."

"We are friends, but you're still a bastard and still know how to find my weak spot. So you go home to Ruth and the kids and I'll get back to saving your ass. I'll give you another call when we get back from Kingston."

By the time McCain returned to the credit union, cancelled the checks, and put the money back into his account, he felt a compelling need for a cool drink, a smooth cigar, and a quiet place to think. And the best place to do all three was the Chief's Club.

The ride to the top of the bluff, where the club was located, had been exceedingly slow and because the hot Cuban sun beat down on the roof of the old gray navy bus, McCain felt as if he was sitting in a gas-fired broiler. But now, inside the large red-tile-roofed building, the air was cool. He waited just inside the door till his eyes adjusted to the dark interior before going into the main lounge where a dozen or so chiefs were bellied up to the long mahogany bar. Much to McCain's annoyance, Pete Jackson was perched on the last stool on the far right end of the bar.

Doing his best not to call attention to himself, McCain tried to keep his back toward Jackson as he ordered a beer. He picked up his glass and bottle in one hand and was heading toward an out-of-the-way table when Jackson spotted him. "McCain," he shouted from across the room. "I was wondering when you or Hall would show up. Try one of these Bacardi and lime water. Makes a great drink." In his haste to drain his glass he sent a flow of greenish liquid down both sides of his mouth. Soon as the glass was empty, he used his shirt sleeve to wipe his chin.

Against McCain's better judgment, he said, "I'll have one with you, but then I have to get back to the ship. I've got a lot of work to do."

Jackson grabbed McCain's arm and with slurred words said, "Fuck the ship. You'll have plenty of time at sea to do your work. Now's the time to get drunk," He waved to the Cuban bartender and said, "Smokey. Couple more drinks over here."

McCain pulled his arm away, trying not to show how unhappy he was with the way this was working out. He wanted a quiet place to think. Should he go back and tell Adams and the men that he didn't have the money? Or should he let them believe that everything has been taken care of? Suddenly he became aware that Smokey was waiting for his order. "I'll have the same as Jackson," he said.

When Smokey brought the drinks, McCain lifted his glass and took a sip. One thing for sure, Jackson knew his booze. Trying his best not to give away his true feelings, McCain smiled and said, "You're right, Pete. This is good."

Jackson drew back his head and through a blank stare, asked, "What'd you say?"

"I said the drink is good." Jackson still seemed to be straining to make out McCain's words. It was something McCain had noticed in that talk they had in his room. He looked Jackson in the eye and asked in a louder voice, "Have you got a hearing problem?"

Jackson drained his glass again and said, "Little bit. Too many years in the engine room. But most of the time I hear what's worth hearing." He put down his glass. "That ain't much."

"You should have it checked out," McCain said.

Jackson shrugged and said, "I did."

"And what did the doctor say?"

Jackson smiled through nicotine-stained teeth. "The sawbones said I couldn't stay drunk seven days a week." He motioned to Smokey for another round. "So I asked him if three or four days a week was okay."

Wondering if Jackson was serious, McCain asked, "What did the doctor say to that?"

Without a hint of a smile, he said, "The dumb bastard said I shouldn't drink at all."

"So why are you drinking?"

"Shit. That pecker checker don't know nothing. What could drinking have to do with my hearing?"

McCain gave up; it wasn't worth discussing any longer. "Let me buy you a drink, and then I have to go."

Through a broad smile, Jackson said, "About time. I thought you'd never get around to it." Once again he motioned to Smokey and yelled, "Bring me another one before McCain changes his mind."

Smokey nodded and grabbed a new goblet.

McCain studied Jackson's condition for a few minutes, decided he was just drunk enough to loosen his tongue and asked, "Do you know much about Bos'n Greene?"

"Sure do. He's the only man I ever saw who can drink more than me." He lifted his glass in a mock salute, and then said, "But I can get just as drunk." He started pounding the table and yelling, "Smokey, where's my drink?"

McCain ignored Jackson's outburst and then asked, "Did you know the bos'n had a daughter?"

Jackson leaned back in his chair, shook his head, and said, "Daughter? Greene has a daughter?" He let out a belly laugh. "Far as I know the only thing Greene ever made love to was a bottle of booze."

He was still laughing when Smokey said, "Here ya go, Chief," and set Jackson's refill in front of him.

McCain handed Smokey three bucks and said, "Keep the change." He then picked up his hat, looked at Jackson, and said, "I've got to go. But you'd better ease up a little or you'll be drunk before sundown."

On the way to the door, McCain decided that he might as well go back to the ship and face the music. As long as Jackson was still upright there'd be no peace and quiet in the club.

When he walked into the crew's mess and saw the six men waiting for him, McCain didn't have the heart to tell them the truth. He took a deep breath, looked at them and said, "Why don't you guys go ashore?

Try to forget about the letters. Everything will be fine." He felt guilty as hell when he saw smiles spread across their faces.

And when Rice grabbed his hand and said, "Thanks, Chief," McCain felt even worse. Although Tommy was doing what he felt he had to do, McCain still couldn't see why he couldn't bend the rules a little. Oh well, he thought, now it was time to face Captain Adams.

He found Adams on the bridge relaxing in his bridge chair with his feet resting on the bulwark. A smoldering cigarette hung from the left corner of his mouth. Obviously he was in another world and didn't hear McCain step into the pilot house. He moved behind him and said, "Captain Adams."

Adams jumped as if he'd heard a rifle shot. But when he saw it was McCain, the fright left his eyes and he said, "Chief, you scared the hell out of me. I guess I was drifting off." He snuffed out his cigarette in the cylinder ash tray attached to the arm of his chair. "How'd you make out?"

McCain, feeling no real obligation to soften the blow, said, "Not so good."

The expression of belligerence McCain remembered so well reappeared as he said, "I'm disappointed in you, Chief. You promised you'd help me out, but I can see by your face that you're about to give me some lame-brained excuse."

After just shafting Rice and the others, McCain was not about to take a chewing-out by Adams. He stepped back, gave Adams a glaring stare, and said, "Now wait a minute, Captain. I didn't get you into this mess. You've got no right to get pissed because I won't use my own money to bail you out." He did an about face and headed for the companionway leading below.

He'd only taken two steps when Adams yelled, "Get your ass back here, McCain. Don't you ever believe you can talk to me like that and get away with it. You may think you're some kind of big-shot chief yeoman, but I'm captain of this ship and you'll treat me with all the respect I'm due."

Now McCain was really pissed. He spun around and with a razor-edged voice said, "Captain, I'll not apologize for what I said. And now

I'm glad I didn't get the money. You made your bed, now you've got to sleep in it. It's the crew I feel sorry for, not you."

With daggers shooting from both eyes, Adams snarled, "Fuck the crew. They'll get over it. I told them I'd pay off the finance companies and I will."

"Sure you will," said McCain. "That'll be the day."

Adams was livid. "I warn you, McCain. I'm captain of the *Lakota* and as far as you're concerned, I'm God. And don't you forget it."

Then, using the most sarcastic tone he could muster, McCain said, "Oh—I won't—Your Holiness. Would you like your feet kissed?"

Obviously seeing that being tough was not making it with McCain, Adams changed his tone and said, "It's just that I was counting on you, that's all. You were so sure of yourself. Tell me what happened."

The tone of despair in Adams's voice eased McCain's anger. The captain was in over his head and because of it, a lot of good people were being hurt, and in one case, it looked as though a not-so-good person had been killed. McCain hated thinking about it, but even without Tommy's backing, he knew he was the only one who could bring some sanity to this little ship. Deciding to buy some time till he figured out a better solution, McCain said, "Their computer was down. If you'd have given me a chance, I'd of told you." It was funny how bullshitting Adams made McCain feel so good.

"So when will the computer be fixed?"

McCain gave him a shrug. "Don't know. But I'm sure it'll be back in operation by the time we get back from Kingston."

"Then you'll get the money?" He looked like a kid believing in Santa Claus.

McCain couldn't let him off this easy. "I'll think about it. I'm not too happy with your attitude."

Adams slid down off his chair, put his arm around McCain's shoulders, and said, "You're right, Chief, I was out of line. Let's forget about it for now. I need you. Everyone else is against me and I've got to have someone to talk to."

The poor bastard looked as if he was going to cry. "Okay, but I need a promise."

"Sure thing; you can have anything you want. Want me to take you off the watch list?"

McCain scoffed and said, "No, I don't want off the watch list."

"What is it then?"

McCain twisted to remove Adams's arm, and said, "It's about the six men who borrowed the money for you."

"What about them?"

McCain pointed his finger at his commanding officer and said, "They think I took care of everything and I don't want them to know differently."

"Sounds good to me. You can be sure I won't say a word."

"Good. Now I'm going below and try to get some work done."

Adams grabbed McCain's arm. "One more thing, Chief."

McCain pulled away and said, "What's that?"

Then with a like-nothing-ever-happened smile, he said, "I was wondering if you've got a loose twenty you can spare. I'd like to take in the 'O' club tonight."

My God, thought McCain, this man has got bigger balls than a bowling alley. He pondered for a second, took out his wallet and handed Adams two tens. "I expect them back on payday," he said.

"You can count on it, Chief. I really do appreciate the loan." The man acted as if he didn't have another debt in the world.

Suddenly McCain thought of a way to capitalize on Adams's temporary weakness. Acting like they were old friends again, he said, "By the way, Captain, what did you think of Bos'n Greene's daughter?"

The words hit Adams like a kick in the nuts. Fidgeting as he struggled for something to say, he looked as if he was standing on hot coals. "How…." He reached for a cigarette. "What are you driving at, McCain?"

Loving every minute of it, McCain said, "Driving at? I'm not driving at anything. I just asked you a simple question."

His hand shook as he lit his cigarette. After taking a puff and with smoke flowing from his mouth, he said, "How'd you find out Greene had a daughter? I thought he didn't want anyone to know."

"Why wouldn't he want anyone to know?"

"He just don't like to talk about it. That's all I know."

Man, thought McCain, how great it was when you had someone trapped in a lie and they didn't know it. Not having enough of a good thing, McCain asked, "Have you ever met her?"

True to his character, Adams, with all the confidence in the world, said, "I wouldn't know her if I tripped over her. Are you trying to tell me something?"

Feeling as if he had his CO in a hammer lock, McCain said, "Not at all. I was just wondering if she was married and where she lived."

Through a forced smile, Adams said, "I don't know anything about her. I figure if the bos'n wants to clam up, it's none of my business. And I might add, it's none of yours either."

McCain gave him one of his favorite what's-the-big-deal shrugs and said, "Loosen up, Captain. I was just asking a question." He would have given a box of Optimos to have been able to read Adams's mind.

Adams glared as he said, "Sometimes you ask too many questions."

"Sorry you feel that way, if you think the bos'n's daughter is top secret then I have no trouble with that." As McCain started down the ladder, he looked back at Adams and said, "Have a good time ashore. See you in the morning." Actually he couldn't wait for the day he could hang Adams out to dry.

Chapter Twenty

Day Nine

At exactly 1147 hours, the *Lakota*, towing the empty barge, left Guantanamo Bay. Lieutenant junior grade Rick Slang of the Civil Engineering Corps, Second Class Engineering Aid Lemay Roth, and eighteen Jamaicans were on board as passengers. The two engineers' job was to ensure that the sand they picked up in Kingston was suitable for high-quality concrete. The Jamaicans, employees of the Navy, were going home to visit their families.

It had been a busy morning. After breakfast, McCain typed out the sailing diary and passenger list. When it was finished he put out the word that he was going to the post office and would take any last-minute letters anyone wanted mailed. Rice had a letter to his wife and Adams had one for Kitty. McCain wondered if Rice had broken the news of his problem to his wife. He didn't care what Adams had to say to Kitty.

While on the base, hoping that overnight he'd had a change of heart, he gave Tommy another call. It was just wishful thinking. Tommy was still playing hardball and McCain knew he really didn't have a choice. But, if the positions were reversed and Tommy needed help, he was pretty sure he'd at least make a stab at backing him up. If only his old friend could take a look into the eyes of those six men who were counting on McCain, he would certainly be more receptive. He really didn't give a damn about Adams but the crew was a different matter. Some of them had their faults but they were minor compared to a couple of the wardroom occupants.

By the time McCain returned to the ship and handed out the mail, it was time for special sea detail. Because everything went as sooth as Rice's gravy, it had taken only a few minutes to cast off, string the barge, and set the course for Kingston.

McCain checked the new watch list and discovered that he would be taking over Posey's watch. That was good because it meant Posey had taken himself off the watch list; maybe it showed he was finally getting a backbone. Besides it was about time the XO started pulling some rank. McCain still couldn't understand how Adams had the nerve to write that unsatisfactory fitness report on a fine young officer like Posey.

It was one thing not to like someone, but to ruin his career was something else. It was a damned shame, that's what it was. He had sent Tommy a full report on the matter, which should be enough to get the chief of naval personnel to review the circumstances into why Adams wrote it. Feeling he already had enough egg on his face because of the loans, McCain wouldn't mention the matter to Posey.

His first watch wasn't till 1800 hours so McCain took a chair out of his room, carried it back to the fantail and settled down to read a few pages of Louie L'Amour's *Law of the Desert Born*.

He was still on the first page, when he felt a tap on his shoulder. He looked up into the bulging troubled eyes of George Rice.

"Chief, wonder if I could talk to you about this?" He shoved a handwritten letter in McCain's direction.

When McCain discovered that the letter was from Rice's wife, he stood up and said, "Damn it, Stew, are you sure you want me to read your wife's letter?"

Rice nodded. "It's real bad news. I don't think I can talk about it."

Red vein lines crossed Rice's ivory-colored eyeballs. The big smile that usually decorated his round ebony face was absent. McCain looked around and saw several Jamaicans staring at them. "Let's go to my stateroom. Maybe it's not as bad as you think."

The words had no effect on his expression. Shaking his head from side to side, Rice said, "Oh no. It's bad, real bad."

McCain could see that it was not the time or place to console him. He handed back the letter, picked up his chair and started forward. He'd gone about fifteen feet when he looked back and saw Rice still standing there shaking his head, staring at the letter. McCain stopped and said, "Come on, Stew. Let's go talk about what's bothering you."

Rice slowly lifted his head, carefully folded the letter and put it in his pocket. Then he moved slowly toward McCain saying, "I'm sorry to bother you, Chief. But I don't know what to do." Obvious pain highlighted his every word and movement.

McCain put down the chair and took Rice's arm. Trying to cheer him up, McCain said, "Try to pull yourself together so I can look forward to another batch of cornbread and some more of that Dakota honey."

After a brief and obviously forced smile, he said, "You help me out of this mess and I'll make you anything you want."

McCain patted Rice gently on the back. "Well then, let's get a move on." Once more he picked up his chair and hurried toward his room. This time, Rice followed close behind.

He'd no sooner closed the door to his room when he looked at Rice and saw that his black friend had broken down. Tears flowed from his large reddened eyes. But then, all of a sudden, he stopped crying. Anger replaced the hurt in his smoldering eyes. His thick lips grew tight, and in a tone, using words McCain would never have expected from this kind, gentle man, said, "I'm going to kill that motherfucker."

McCain took one of Rice's shoulders in each of his hands and gently shook him as he said, "Come on, Stew. Get hold of yourself and tell me what this is all about."

Rice handed McCain the letter again. "It's all in here."

After taking a deep breath and letting it out slowly McCain wondered what on earth his wife could have said to get him so upset. He gently started taking the pages from the envelope when Rice grimaced and said, "Our mortgage application was turned down."

McCain had already guessed the reason when he asked, "Did she say why?"

With his thick lips barely moving Rice said, "Because of those loans I took out for Captain Adams."

"Damn it, Stew. I told you I'd take care of that matter for you. When we get back to Gitmo, we'll give her a call and tell her to reapply."

With a look of disbelief, he said, "You didn't take care of anything." Surprisingly, there was sadness but no anger in his voice.

"What makes you think I didn't?"

"Dixon," he said as he looked down at the sink. "Could I have a drink of water?"

McCain quickly took a clean glass out of his medicine cabinet and filled it with water. As he handed it to Rice, he asked, "What's Dixon got to do with this?"

He took a sip, swallowed and said, "Dixon heard you tell Captain Adams that you didn't get the money."

"He what?"

"Dixon was taking a cup of coffee to Captain Adams on the bridge when he heard you tell him about not getting the money."

Another reason to hate Dixon, thought McCain. There was no longer any purpose on carrying on this façade with Rice, so McCain said, "You're right, Stew. I didn't get the money yet." Then for some unknown reason he said, "But I will, just as soon as we get back to Gitmo."

Staring down at the deck, he said, "Won't make any difference anyhow." He took another sip of water.

"Sure it will. Give me a little more time and I'll get you the money to pay off those loans. I'll even help you get that mortgage you want."

He expected Rice to show some sign of relief, but instead, he sat down on the edge of McCain's bunk and started crying like a baby again. McCain had never seen a grown man cry so hard. Tears the size of raindrops dripped from his oversized cheeks. Feeling as helpless as a trapped beaver, McCain sat down next to him and put his arm around his shoulder. "Come on, Stew, everything is going to be all right, you'll see."

Sobbing so hard he could hardly speak, he said, "It's too late to do anything, except get even."

Was Rice overreacting or was there something else in that letter? "Have you told me everything?"

He shook his head. "She wants a divorce because she thinks I borrowed that money to spend on another woman."

"Damn, Stew, that's a real bummer."

He looked at McCain through red, flooded eyes and said, "I've just got to kill the motherfucker. He's got to pay. He don't deserve to live."

The calm deliberate way he spoke convinced McCain he intended to carry out his plan. Not knowing what else to do, McCain jumped up, put his hand under Rice's chin and raised his face to where they were looking into each other's eyes. "You're talking foolishness," said McCain. "Killing Captain Adams won't help you or your family. You'll be in the brig just when your wife's going to need you most. Remember you've got a baby coming."

"No more, I don't," he said.

McCain felt sick to his stomach. "Don't tell me your wife had a miscarriage?"

Rice shook his head. "No. But she did get an abortion. She said she didn't want my baby in her belly. It's no use, Chief, that motherfucker has got to die."

Lowering himself down to the edge of his bunk, McCain put his head between his hands. He'd liked Rice from the minute he met him. Now look at the poor bastard; all because of a good-for-nothing CO who thought of nothing but himself. He raised his head, turned to the angry black man and said, "I know nothing I say can bring your baby back, but when we get to Gitmo I'll find some way to convince your wife that none of this was your fault."

Rice, showing no emotion to the words, looked as if he was in another world. "Did you hear what I said, Stew?" McCain got up and gave the cook's shoulders as shake.

Finally he showed some response. Distress had replaced the anger in his eyes as he said, "What did you say?"

When McCain repeated his offer of help, Rice said, "Don't bother, Chief. I just don't care no more. What happens to me ain't important."

McCain felt a dire need for a stiff drink and a cigar. But decided to hold off till he'd convinced Rice he was on the wrong track. Once more he took Rice by the shoulders and said, "The hell your life isn't important. You're the best damned cook in the Navy and there's no doubt in my mind that you're a good husband. And someday you're going to make some kids a great father."

The words had no obvious effect. He calmly looked at McCain and said, "I know, for a white man, you mean well, Chief, but this nigger has been kicked around long enough. It's time I stand up for myself."

McCain gave him a good shake. "That's enough of that race crap. You're my friend and I'm not going to let you destroy yourself. Just promise me you won't do anything foolish till we've had a chance to talk to Mrs. Rice."

For the first time, it appeared that he was getting through to Rice. He was no longer crying and said with a new degree of sanity, "I'll think about it. But no promises, and one thing for sure, it's best if you keep Captain Adams out of my galley."

McCain took a washcloth, soaked it with cold water and handed it to Rice. "Wipe your face, Stew. And I'd appreciate it if you don't mention anything to the rest of the crew."

After giving his eyes a quick swipe with the cloth, Rice got up and went out the door.

McCain took a deep breath and eased himself down on the edge of his bunk. He then opened a fresh box and removed an Optimo. As he was lighting up, he wondered when all this bullshit was going to end. It seemed the decent folks like Posey, Hall and Rice were getting hit harder than the others. Yet it was Adams who was trying to get people to feel sorry for him.

Was Bos'n Greene still on Adams's side? McCain hadn't had a chance to see him since he'd received the letter from his daughter. He would find out soon enough; he'd be relieving Greene at 1745 hours and again at 0345 the next morning.

He tried taking a drag on his cigar only to discover he hadn't lit it. He pondered for a second and decided he'd put it off for now. He put the cigar in the ashtray and lay back on his bunk. He couldn't get his mind off Rice. If someone had told him that the chubby, easygoing cook could get as emotional as he had a few minutes ago, he'd have never believed it.

One thing for certain, he didn't care if he ever got his money back or not, he was going to get Rice out of this mess with his wife. He couldn't bring the baby back, but he had to stop the bust-up of their marriage. In time they could have another baby. He checked his watch; an hour before chow. Enough time to rest his eyes for a few minutes.

Chapter Twenty-one

Day Ten—Morning

At first light McCain stood on the starboard wing of the bridge watching the island of Jamaica grow larger. If all went as planned they'd be having lunch in Kingston. He glanced at his Timex: ninety minutes left on his second tour as an unchaperoned officer of the deck. His first, the 1800 to 2000 on the night before, went off without a hitch, and so far the 0400 to 0800 was going just as smooth. Probably a good thing too. He had so many things running around in his head that it's a wonder he was able to take a fix or understand what he saw on the radar screen.

His latest problems started at supper. Rice had made fried chicken and it was terrible. The coating tasted like sawdust and close to the bone the chicken was still raw. Because McCain was sure the unanticipated bad meal could only be attributed to the distressing news from Rice's wife, he was more than ready to dismiss it. But inasmuch as none of the others knew about the letter, they were bitching up a storm. How soon they forgot the usual fastidious care the ship's cook put into his craft.

It was probably because the crew was so spoiled that this one bad meal was on the verge of turning into a real fiasco. When Dixon, with his right eye bruised and almost swollen shut, stormed into the galley and told Rice that the captain wanted to see him, Rice tore off his apron, threw it on the deck, and started for the wardroom. McCain jumped up, grabbed his arm, and pulled him back into the galley. When McCain first told him he'd go talk to Adams, Rice wouldn't hear of it. But with a little more convincing he calmed down to the point where McCain felt it was safe to leave the furious cook alone while he went to talk to their skipper.

When he told Adams about the letter, the CO's eyes took on a blank stare and his mouth dropped. After two or three seconds, he called Dixon in and told him to bring the officers some Spam as a substitute for the undercooked chicken. McCain went to Rice and told him to do the same for the crew. While every man on board except Jackson was eating canned pork, Jackson, who saw nothing wrong with the chicken, ate five pieces.

After things settled down a bit, McCain asked Wishbore if he knew what had happened to Dixon's eye. Surprisingly, he said that Rossi had slugged him with a solid right and then went on to say that McCain was the cause of the fight.

Never expecting a reply like that, McCain asked how that could be. Wishbore nodded and said that the way he understood it was that Dixon tried to convince Rossi that McCain was lying when he said he'd taken care of the loans. McCain was surprisingly impressed that Rossi had taken his word over Dixon's. It was a real turn of events but too bad Dixon was right. He wondered what Rossi's reaction would be when he learned the truth. Once more McCain could kick himself for making a promise he couldn't keep.

Then to make matters worse, Posey told him that Bos'n Greene refused to eat in the wardroom with the rest of the officers, and ever since they returned from playing golf, he remained holed up in his room. That explained why last night and again this morning when McCain relieved Greene, the bos'n acted more like a zombie than the tough salty character he usually portrayed.

McCain had tried to draw him out of his shell but it was no use. He just scowled, reported the course, speed, the night orders and any ships in the area. Then, without even waiting to see if McCain had any questions, the old warrant officer turned and hurried from the bridge. No doubt about it, things on board the *Lakota* were quickly slipping from bad to worse.

"How would you like an early breakfast, Jack?" Hall's words, as he stepped into the pilothouse, pulled McCain out of his deep thoughts.

"Are we having Spam?" asked McCain.

"Worse," said Hall. "Beans, cornbread and hard-boiled eggs." He bent over the radar and stuck his head into the rubber face shied. A couple seconds later he lifted his head, turned to McCain and said with a curious look in his eyes, "You got any idea what's going on here?"

"What do you mean?" McCain asked as if surprised by the question.

Hall's expression couldn't be more serious as he said, "I mean this ship is going to the bottom in a hurry. It was always bad, but now…"

McCain continued to act ignorant by saying, "What makes you think I would know anything? I've only been on board for a few days."

"I know," said Hall with a hint of aggravation in his voice, "and it's in those few days that things have gotten worse."

The accusatory tone brought McCain up short. He was about to let Hall have it when he realized that the chief was really worried and confused. To give himself time to cool off, McCain strolled through the pilothouse and onto the port wing. He was staring at the island when Hall came alongside. McCain looked him in the eye and said, "Are you trying to blame me for Rice's rubber chicken?"

"It's not that." He shook his head. "It's the bos'n who has me worried, he's ready to crack."

"You think that's my fault?"

When Hall didn't answer, McCain said, "Tom, I'm as concerned as you are, but to blame me is ridiculous. You know damned well that this ship had more than its share of problems before I ever crossed the gangplank. My guess is that Johnson's death started bringing all those problems to the surface. And now the boil has come to a head and is about to burst."

Hall stared at the deck and nodded. "Maybe you're right."

Deciding it was time to change the subject, McCain said, "Beans and cornbread. If they're cooked right make a pretty good breakfast. How were they?"

"I don't know. When I saw what Rice was making, I settled for a slice of toast and coffee. Now if you're ready, I'll relieve you and you can go find out for yourself." He stepped over to the chart table, studied the chart for a minute, and then said, "Looks as if we'll be pulling in right on schedule."

"Yep, and for lunch we can go ashore and have barbecued goat."

For the first time since coming on the bridge, Hall smiled, and said, "Not for me. I'd rather have rubber chicken."

McCain lifted the binoculars from around his neck and handed them to Hall. "Are you trying to tell me that you're not going ashore or just not going to sample the food?"

"Both," he said. "You guys can go ashore. I'll take the duty."

"Sounds good to me. That civil engineer we brought with us told me of a good place to pick up some local action. And, according to him, it's not one of the regular dives. This place has class."

"Oh yeah, what's the name of the joint?"

"Cloud Nine."

Hall grinned as he said, "Sounds like an opium joint."

Realizing he was right, McCain broke into a laugh and then said, "Come to think of it, it does doesn't it. But I'm sure it isn't." He took out his handkerchief and blew his nose. "Now if you'll take the con, I'll go down and give Rice's beans a try."

"I've got it," said Hall.

Either Rice had calmed down to the point were he regained his culinary skills or he'd made cornbread so many times he could do it in his sleep. It was delicious, and so were the Campbell's pork and beans. Of course it would be pretty hard to screw them up. He didn't sample the hard-boiled eggs.

McCain was on his second helping of cornbread when Rossi sat down beside him and said, "Can I talk to you for a minute, Chief?"

"Sure, Rossi." McCain took a sip of coffee, laughed, and said, "You're not going to dog wrench me are you?"

A grin spread across the lanky radioman's pimply face. "Hell no, I'm here to speak on behalf of the guys you helped out. We want to invite you to go ashore with us so we can buy you a beer or whatever it is you drink."

Feeling like a complete fraud, McCain said, "Damn it, Rossi, there's no need for that."

"Shit, Chief, we all know that, but we feel we owe you that much." There was actual respect in his voice.

What a bummer, McCain thought. They all think he's a hero and he didn't do a thing for them. He was about to confess when he decided to wait till they got back to Gitmo and he could try again to put a lot more pressure on Tommy. "Where you going to take me?" he asked.

"The Red Rooster, the most famous dive in Kingston. You'll love it," he said proudly.

The name didn't sound as appealing as the Cloud Nine, but he couldn't pass up the chance to pull a liberty with some of the men. It might even improve morale a bit. "Okay, I'll have a beer or two with you bunch of bums. But I'm paying my share. Mrs. McCain didn't raise no freeloader."

Rossi's shit-eating grin reappeared. "What say you meet us at the gangway at 1300?"

"Sounds good to me," McCain said as he rose from the table. "Now I think I'll go out on deck and see how close we are." He downed the last of his coffee, carried his plate into the galley and dropped it in the sink. When he stepped out on deck, he saw Rice standing with his head bowed and foot resting on the lower lifeline.

He moved next to him and said, "Good breakfast, Stew. I still say you make the best cornbread I've ever tasted."

When Rice turned his face, McCain gasped. He looked terrible. Huge bags hung below his bloodshot eyes. The bags, resting on top of his overly puffed cheeks, made it look as though overnight his face had turned into two black, red-headed Pillsbury Dough Boys. Obviously he had not slept the night before. McCain put his hand on Rice's shoulder and said, "Stew, it's important that you pull out of this. You've got to believe me when I tell you I'm going to do all I can to get your wife back and your mortgage approved. But I have to wait till we get back to Gitmo."

In a voice totally lacking any sound of hope, he said, "Don't know if I'll be making it back to Gitmo. I've been looking at the water and thinking that on the way back, I'll just take me a swim."

His words struck McCain like a sledgehammer. He grabbed Rice's arm and said, "Damn it, Stew, don't talk like that."

Then as calmly as if he was talking about the weather, Rice said, "It's either that or kill the captain. He killed my baby and don't deserve to live. As long as he's walking this earth, I'll never get another night's sleep."

McCain felt as helpless as a newborn baby. "Stew, you've got to promise me that you won't do anything till we've had a chance to square things away. When I'm done, Captain Adams won't bother you, or any of the rest of the crew, again.

Still staring intently at the water rushing by, he shook his head and said, "I really wants to believe you, but you couldn't take care of the loans."

"Stew, I swear on my mother's grave that this time I won't let you down. But till we get back to Gitmo, please don't say anything to the other men. No use getting them upset too."

He gave McCain a quick glance and said, "Ain't goin' to tell them nothing." His gaze returned to the passing clear green water.

McCain knew he had been excused and further talk would be useless. He climbed the starboard stairway to the fo'c'sle deck and followed the lifeline to the extreme forward point of the bow. He placed his foot on the bull nose and stared at the approaching island.

"Won't be long now, McCain," Haggen said as he joined the ship's yeoman. "Ever been to Kingston before?"

"Can't say that I have." He then pointed to a white cliff and asked, "What's going on up there on the mountain? Looks like a bunch of earth movers."

Haggen nodded. "You hit it right on the button. They're mining bauxite."

"Learn something new every day," said McCain.

Haggen pointed to some building on the other side of a low finger of land. "Know what that town is?"

"Probably Kingston."

"Nope," said Haggen. "That's Port Royal, the old pirate town. Kingston is the larger city at the far end of the harbor."

Suddenly, they heard over the loudspeaker: "Chief McCain, come up to the bridge; time to set special sea detail."

Both men looked up at the bridge and saw Adams staring down. McCain gave Adams a nod and a wave. He then turned to Haggen and said, "Guess I'd better get up there."

As he was walking away, Haggen said, "I'll be in the engine room."

Chapter Twenty-two

Day Ten—Afternoon

It was a few minutes before noon when the *Lakota* boarded a pilot and turned control of the barge over to a harbor tug that moored it to the port side of a rickety-looking pier in Kingston Harbor. Under direction of the pilot, Captain Adams moored the *Lakota* across the pier from the barge.

Soon thereafter, lunch was served and once again it was not the usual bill of fare that McCain had learned to expect from Rice. Nevertheless, he figured it was better to eat canned chicken-noodle soup and cold-cut sandwiches than take a chance on eating ashore.

Besides McCain had no right to complain about the menu since it was his idea in the first place. He was coming out of his room to grab a cup of coffee when he overheard the mess-cook trying to wake up Rice. When it was obvious Rice was not responding, McCain rushed down the ladder to the crew's compartment to make sure nothing had happened to his distraught shipmate. When he saw how soundly the ship's cook was sleeping, McCain told the mess-cook to heat up the canned soup and slice some cold cuts. The unusual bill of fare reminded him of what Jackson had said a couple days earlier: "What the hell, it makes a turd don't it?" McCain shrugged his shoulders. It hadn't been funny then and it still wasn't.

As McCain was eating his bologna and cheese sandwich, Rossi came over to him and said, "Don't forget, you promised to go ashore with us."

McCain nodded. "What time?"

"How about 1300?"

McCain checked his Timex: 1215. Plenty of time to get cleaned up. "Thirteen hundred it is. I'll meet you on the quarterdeck."

When he stepped onto the quarterdeck, all the loan company victims, except Rice, were waiting. Surprisingly, every one of them, even Rossi, wore dress whites and looked more like regulation navy men than McCain ever believed they could. Smiling, he said, "With a bunch of squared-away swabbies like you guys, I won't stand a chance with the women."

Tucker answered up. "Long as you got the green, the girls will love you."

"And we all know you got the green," Rossi chimed in with a friendly grin on his long narrow face.

McCain looked up at the sky; not a cloud in sight. The sun beat down on them like the fires of hell. "I've got enough to buy the girls a couple drinks, but I'll have to wait and see if I want to dip my wick into one of them." He pointed to the pier. "We'd better get going before we have sunstroke."

Shipfitter O'Neil said, "Shit, Chief, any port in a storm is the way I look at it. Ain't no such thing as bad pussy. Only some is better than others." The chorus of yeah's left no doubt O'Neil was not alone in his beliefs.

Wishbore stepped toward the gangplank. "Let's not stand around talking about pussy. Let's go get some."

McCain said, "Lead the way, Sparks."

They crossed the gangplank and headed up the pier toward two tall red-brick buildings. One had a large Tia Maria coffee liqueur sign painted on the side facing the pier. The other was decorated with an equally large Red Stripe beer sign.

At the head of the pier they were met by several Jamaicans, all yelling the names of the gin mill that had hired them to try to entice the thirsty, sex-starved sailors to their individual places of business. In the front row was a charcoal-colored teenager yelling the virtues of the Red Rooster. Wishbore pointed at the near-naked youth and beckoned him forward.

With his wooly-braided dreadlocks bouncing against the sides of his head, the barefoot boy ran across the stone-strewn street to Wishbore and said, "Hey, mon. Red Rooster best beer and girls in Kingston. Me take you. Uncle's the boss. Give you a good time, cheap."

Wishbore nodded and spun his finger in a circle. "We'll all go."

Obviously figuring his commission, the kid's face broke into a smile that would light a room. He threw back his shoulders, gave the other hawkers a look of superiority and took off toward town. The white-garbed sailors, grouped around a khaki-clad chief, followed a few steps behind.

By the time they worked their way up the main drag and into the alley that would take them to the Red Rooster, McCain had gotten used to the heavy smell of horse manure and gasoline exhaust that permeated the humid air. From the dozens of goats, chickens, and hogs running wild in the streets he almost felt as though he was back on a farm in Wyoming.

Sweat was pouring down every part of his body when they finally arrived at a red two-story house built into the side of a hill. The young guide stopped and said, "Okay, mon, we here. In Red Rooster you get much fucky-sucky. Not much money." He opened a wooden screen door and invited them in.

McCain followed his shipmates into a large dark room that felt surprisingly cool. One windowless wall was consumed by a rough wooden bar. The rest of the space was used for about twenty uncovered beat-up wooden tables with four equally beat-up chairs each. A close inspection of the carvings on the tables would probably tell you every ship that had visited Kingston in the last twenty years. The floor was covered with faded linoleum that had foot paths worn into the surface between and around the tables.

They were greeted by a giant black woman who said, "You chil'n come in here. Mama and her girls will take care of you." She turned toward the stairs leading to the second floor and yelled, "You ladies get your black asses down here. We got visitors."

Suddenly the air filled with screams and the building shook as ten or twelve women of various ages, shapes and heights, all wearing bright-colored sack dresses, came bounding down the rickety stairs. McCain was tempted to turn and get the hell out of there, but he'd promised the men he'd have a drink with them.

Like iron filings drawn to a magnet, two girls attached themselves to each of the men. McCain wound up with a little almond-skinned teenager and a jet-black middle-aged woman with a solid gold front tooth. The teenager introduced herself as Virgie. The older woman said her name was Goldie.

Wishbore, taking charge, pushed some tables together, then with a girl on each side, took a seat. Mama came and stood at the head of the table. "What you chil'n goin' drink?"

Tucker said, "What you got, Mama?"

"We got rum. We got rum and Coke. We got rum and water. We got rum and ginger. An' we got Red Stripe beer." She reached down and scratched her groin. "You ladies get up and take care of your men." She turned, waddled across the room and squeezed behind the bar.

McCain, now even more regretting that he'd agreed to this, ordered a Red Stripe. Goldie went to the bar and came back with two half-pint bottles of white rum, two bottles of Coca Cola, a brown bottle of Red Stripe and three glasses. When he saw the dingy-looking glasses, he decided to drink from the bottle.

Glancing around the table he noticed that Wishbore, Tucker, and O'Neil also had the tall brown beer bottles before them. Rossi, Smith and all the women were drinking rum. All except Rossi had mixed their rum with Coke. Rossi took his straight with a squeeze of lime. Evidently the five men had pooled their drinking money before coming ashore and made Wishbore the treasurer. He paid for the first round and then another.

In between sips of beer, McCain learned that Goldie was married and had five children. Virgie, who said she got her name because she was a virgin, offered him the opportunity to relieve her of that burden. "For twenty dolla' I let you get my cherry," she said.

Not wanting to be the person who would make it necessary for her to change her name, McCain declined. Then he ordered and paid for another round of drinks.

By the time they were ready for the next, Rossi and his two women were staggering toward the stairs. A few minutes later, Wishbore handed the remainder of the pooled drink money to Tucker and along with the younger of his two women followed in the footsteps of Rossi. That was the start of the flow.

When only Tucker and a handful of women remained, Tucker stood up and said, "I hate to leave you alone Chief, but Susie here…" He put his arm around the light-skinned woman and squeezed her closer to him, "has me horny as hell. If I don't do something about it, my buttons are going to start flying off my pants."

McCain pictured the old Captain Jack comics as he grinned and said, "Go on up and get your ashes hauled. I've got to be going anyway." He pulled out his wallet and removed another twenty and two fives. He handed the twenty to Tucker and said, "Add this to your drink pool and tell the guys that I enjoyed the drinks and I'll see them back aboard."

Then he gave Virgie and Goldie five each and said, "It was nice meeting you, but I have to leave."

Virgie grabbed the money and stuffed it between her breasts, "Why won't you let Virgie show you a good…"

Goldie latched on to his arm and pulled him toward the stairs. "You not going till Goldie gets to play with that peter of white gold. You not be sorry. Come…"

McCain pulled away, grabbed his hat and headed for the door. On his way out he heard Goldie call out, "What'sa matter, you don't like girls?"

He grinned. If Goldie only knew that if he didn't get out of there fast, he'd soon be upstairs with Virgie. He knew damn well she wasn't a virgin, but she had a pair of tits that he was finding harder and harder to resist examining closer. Besides, he'd already stayed longer than he'd planned.

Outside, he followed the alley till he came out on the main drag. A minute or so later he found a vacant taxi, crawled in, and told the driver to take him to the Cloud Nine.

Chapter Twenty-three

Day Ten—Evening

The Cloud Nine turned out to be located on the second floor of a commercial building in Kingston's legitimate business district. McCain climbed the stairs, opened a stained-glass door and found himself in a room with plush white carpeting, red-leather chairs and couches. Flowing through the air was the aroma of jasmine and the sound of soft music. This place was so different than the Red Rooster that it verified the opinions that Kingston was populated by only two classes of people: the rich and the impoverished. McCain had yet to see any sign of a middle class.

Seated at marble-topped tables scattered around the room were several men and women dressed in business or evening attire. McCain's gaze swept the room looking for the bar. Failing to spot one, he moved further into the room and was met by a young Oriental woman dressed in fishnet stockings, a short starched black-crinoline skirt and a white short-sleeved blouse. "Chief McCain?" she asked.

"You've got me, sweetheart," he answered wondering how she knew his name. Undressing her in his mind, he created a picture that made him yearn for a chance to confirm his mental images. "What can I do for you?" he asked in his time-tested pickup tone.

With a smile that sent his already overheated blood gushing toward his crotch, she said, "Your friends asked me to show you to their table." She turned, looked over her shoulder and said, "Please follow me."

How McCain loved walking behind women. Especially women built like this one. By the time they were halfway across the room, he spotted a table occupied by the civil engineer, Rick Slang; Dan Posey; Jim Haggen; and a civilian he didn't recognize.

Soon as McCain reached their table, Posey rose to his feet, looked at the unknown civilian and said, "Ron, this is our yeoman, Chief McCain."

Ron, a middle-aged, dark-complexioned man, got up and stuck out his hand. "Glad to meet you, Chief. I'm Ron Thompson." Ron looked at the waitress and said, "Penny, bring the chief whatever he wants."

Posey said, "Ron is the contractor supplying the sand we're hauling to Gitmo."

McCain didn't let on that he'd already recognized the name from the paperwork they received before they left Cuba. He gave Penny another I-would-love-to-have-you smile and said, "I'll have a planter's punch. If you stick your finger in it, I just know it'll be delicious."

Showing no signs of receiving his non-verbal communication, Penny jotted something on her pad and headed for a pair of swinging doors in the back wall, leaving him staring at her cute little wiggle till the doors swallowed her sexy frame. He pulled out a chair next to Posey, sat down, looked around the table and said, "Mind if I smoke?" Without waiting for an answer, he reached inside his uniform jacket and brought out an Optimo.

Soon as his cigar appeared, Thompson reached into his shirt pocket and took out a long black cigar. He tossed it across the table and said, "Try that baby, Chief. I guarantee it's the best Cuban leaf."

McCain picked up the cigar, admired the way it was rolled; not too loose and not too tight. Then after affectionately caressing its smooth outer wrapper, he inserted it between his teeth. Out of nowhere appeared a white-gloved hand holding a flaming match. Attached to the gloved hand was a tall Jamaican waiter wearing a black tux.

McCain accepted the light and as smoke rose up to the ceiling, Haggen laughed and said, "I swear, Chief, that stogie is almost as big as you are."

"You think so?" said McCain. "Just remember that it takes a damn good man to handle one of these stogies. I don't think you'd better try one."

Haggen's laugh disappeared and Posey said, "That's what we need; dueling cigars."

"No thanks," Haggen growled. "I don't need a turd-shaped roll of tobacco to make me a man."

"Come on, you guys," said Posey. "Let's leave the fighting on board ship. Now is the time to relax for a change and maybe get to know one another a little better."

"You're right," Thompson said. He motioned to the tall waiter. "Have Penny bring us another round. And make sure she puts all the drinks on my tab."

"Yes, sir, Mr. Thompson." The waiter gave a slow deep nod, turned and silently glided through the swinging doors.

Lieutenant Slang looked at McCain and asked, "Have you been taking in the city, Chief?"

McCain gently put down his cigar, and said, "Some. I just came from a joint that if I hadn't seen it for myself would never believe it existed. It was as bad as or worse than the joints in the back alleys of Tijuana."

"What's the name of the place?" asked Thompson.

"The Red Rooster."

Thompson grinned. "You met Mama?"

McCain nodded and said, "She's one of the biggest women I've ever seen. If P.T. Barnum had found her, I'm sure he would've had her in his circus."

"That's true," Thompson said. "But she's good people, with a heart as big as her belly. Her place may not be fancy, but you get your money's worth: good booze and clean girls."

McCain was glad to hear that. At least the guys might not come down with the clap. He picked up his cigar, gestured around the room and said, "If it's all right with you, I'll take this place any day."

With the waiter back in his stealth position, Penny delivered the round of drinks just as Slag turned to Posey and said, "I've got to hand it to you Dan. I don't think I could stand a tour of duty on the *Lakota*, especially with a CO like Adams. You know he had the balls to put the finger on Thompson for a kickback?"

Slang's words didn't surprise McCain a bit. But Posey frowned, shook his head and said, "I never thought he'd go that far."

McCain turned to Thomson, "Just how did he put the proposition to you?"

Thompson shrugged. "He sure didn't beat around the bush. He came right out and accused civilian contractors of always ripping off the Navy, and it was about time to get even. He even warned me that if I didn't give him five hundred bucks he'd see to it that Slang didn't certify my sand."

The words sent Haggen into a tizzy. He slapped the table, and said, "I don't believe it. Captain Adams may have some problems but he wouldn't do anything like that. And I'm not drinking with anyone who says he would."

As Haggen stood and started to leave, McCain took hold of his arm. "Let's hear the rest of the story."

Haggen jerked his arm out of McCain's grasp, glared down at him and said, "I told you before that Adams treated me okay. I'm not going to stick around." He turned his glare to Posey and said, "And you, Mr. Posey, would be better off if you got out of here too." Then without waiting for Posey's response, Haggen spun around and trotted toward the door.

Soon as Haggen was out of hearing distance, McCain asked Thompson, "How'd you wind up your encounter with Captain Adams?"

Once again Thompson shrugged. "I just told him to go to hell." He paused for a second, and then said, "Soon as I left Adams, I went to Rick Slang and told him the whole story."

Thompson and Slang started laughing like a couple of schoolboys, then when they realized that the rest of them had no idea what was so funny, they stopped laughing and Thompson said, "Poor damn bastard Adams didn't have a clue that Rick and I went to school together. In fact, I wouldn't be down here in this business if Rick hadn't written me a letter saying the Navy would be buying a lot of sand."

McCain wondered if it was kosher for Slang to have tipped him off like that. He also wondered if Rick Slang was sharing in the profits. But that was not his job to figure out. He just said, "It's a small world."

Thompson downed the last of his drink, stood up and checked his watch. "I think I'd better run down to the pier and see how the loading is going." He motioned to the waiter. "Reggie, you make sure the drinks keep coming and don't let these boys spend a dime. You got that?"

Reggie gave Thompson a deep bow. When he straightened up, he said, "Yes, sir, Mr. Thompson. They won't want for anything. You know you can count on Reggie."

Thompson reached in his pocket and pulled out a roll of bills large enough to stuff up a toilet. He pulled off two fifties and handed them to the tall black waiter. "You take one and give the other to Penny."

For the first time Reggie's somber face broke into a smile. "Thank you, Mr. Thompson. I sure will, Mr. Thompson. And Penny thanks you too, Mr. Thompson. You make sure you hurry back, Mr. Thompson." The man's tightly thatched head bobbed up and down like the float on a catfish line.

McCain thought of Virgie and wondered if she'd ever been tipped fifty bucks. As he was remembering the enticing bulge of her tits, Slang stood up and said, "Think I'll go with you, Ron. If Adams does try to make trouble, I want to be able to testify that I kept a close eye on the sand's quality while it was being loaded."

"Good idea." Thompson looked down at Posey and McCain. "You guys stay as long as you want. And if by chance you should get some company they'll be my guests too."

When they'd gone, Posey turned to McCain and said, "Well, Chief, it looks as if we're all alone."

McCain lifted his planter's punch and emptied it down his gullet. He held up the glass and said, "Yep, and we might as well take advantage of Thompson's hospitality." In seconds Penny placed a fresh drink before him. "Thank you, babe." He said as he looked her up and down while quickly forgetting about Virgie.

Posey handed Penny his empty daiquiri glass then reached out and pulled its replacement close to him. "I suppose you're right. But it makes me feel like a freeloader."

"Don't let it bother you," said McCain. "Just think how pissed off our captain would be if he knew we were being wined and dined by Thompson." He laughed and gave his knee a quick slap. "If that wouldn't send him into orbit, nothing would; especially when he hasn't got enough loot to hit the beach for a lousy beer." McCain took a healthy sip of his drink. "And there's not a soul on board who'll loan him a dime."

"You're right about that, Chief."

McCain looked at the squared-away young officer and asked, "Mr. Posey, what ever made you decide to go into the Navy?"

A light seemed to go on in his eyes as he said, "I've no problem answering that, but, while we're ashore, why don't you call me Dan?"

McCain almost felt like he was talking to Tommy. But he still wanted an answer to his question. "Okay, Dan, but why did you join the Navy?"

Posey grinned. "This may surprise you, but both my father and grandfather were chief boatswain's mates. Both career navy." Pride was written all over his face. "From the time I was old enough to walk, they planned a navy career for me. And for me to be anything less than a commissioned officer would not have fulfilled their expectations."

"Good for them," said McCain. "If I had a son, I'd want him to be an officer."

Posey nodded and said, "They worked hard on it. God only knows how many letters they wrote before they got me an appointment to the Naval Academy." You could see his eyes cloud over when he said, "You should have seen the two of them when I graduated. It was almost as if it was the two of them that were being commissioned. They were so proud of me."

McCain pictured the three men. "Do they still feel the same way?" The words were no sooner out of his mouth than he realized how dumb the question was.

A sign of grief showed in Posey's eyes. "Dad does, but Grandpa died two days after I graduated. It was like he was just waiting for that day before he passed on."

"That's a damned shame. Are you going to stay in?"

The young officer took a deep breath, let it out slowly and said, "I have to. Just before he died, Grandpa made me promise that I would." Somehow there seemed to be a hint of doubt in his words.

"That's not a good enough reason," said McCain. "An officer has to love the Navy or he's just an imposter." He then stuck a fresh cigar in his mouth and once again Reggie's gloved hand was ready with a light. He puffed till the tip formed an ash. "Thank you, Reggie."

McCain took a couple for puffs. "You take Adams now. He may be a no-good son of a bitch, but he does love the Navy. And if he hadn't let pussy take control of his brain he'd be a damn good officer. I've never seen a better ship handler."

Posey seemed to roll the words around in his head for a minute before saying, "You're right about that. But I too love the Navy, only I'll never be able to treat people the way he does. Maybe I am in the wrong game."

"I don't know much about being an officer," said McCain. "But I do know that when you take command, you stop being an ordinary member of the wardroom. From that point on, you can't afford to be buddies with the other officers." He took a deep puff and sent a smoke ring fleeing toward the ceiling. "I had an admiral tell me once that being CO of a ship was the loneliest job in the world."

Posey stared for a second and then said in a pleading voice, "It can't be any worse than an XO who's on the old man's shit list."

Serious as his expression and words were, McCain couldn't help thinking how funny they sounded. He let out a short guffaw, and then remembering where he was, looked around to see if others were watching. He sighed and said, "I guess you've got me there. So you still think you're going to make a career out of the Navy?"

"I'm sure going to give it a try."

"Because you promised your granddad?"

Posey nodded and said, "And my dad."

"And they were both chiefs?"

"Boatswain's mates," he said proudly.

Realizing that this liberty was quickly turning into a wake, McCain grinned and said, "Well, I won't hold that against them."

Posey responded with a blank stare.

Suddenly McCain thought of that day he went through Adams's desk. "Has Captain Adams made out a fitness report on you?"

He shrugged and said, "Not that I know of. I wondered about it, but things being the way they were I didn't want to push the issue."

"I don't blame you." McCain took another sip of his drink, took two puffs on his cigar, thought for a second and said, "Maybe I shouldn't tell you this, but while we were in Gitmo, I was going through some papers in the CO's cabin…"

Posey's mouth dropped open and it looked as if he was waiting with bated breath for McCain's next words. After a couple seconds, he asked, "What kind of papers?"

"Some of them were fitness reports."

"Did you read them?"

"Yes," McCain said. Then trying to sound as kind as he could, he said, "I'm sorry to say that yours was so bad that it's a cinch you'll be passed over for lieutenant. And you know what happens then."

"I know," he said. "After that, it's just a matter of time before I'm a civilian."

Posey looked so sad, McCain was sorry he'd said anything. Then looking for a way to lighten the load, McCain said, "Look, Dan, it doesn't have to be that way; you can fight an unsatisfactory report. I've seen it done and you can count on me to help you do it."

"I'd appreciate that, Chief, but how can you help?"

McCain chomped down on his cigar and said through clinched teeth, "I've got good friends in high places and I can write."

"Are you sure that will help?"

"It's sure worth a try." He ruthlessly snuffed the life out of his cigar in the ashtray, leaned toward Posey and said, "Now listen up. When he shows you the report and asks you to sign it, you tell him you want to attach a rebuttal. Tell him you'll sign it but under protest."

"Won't that just send him further into orbit?"

"So what, you've been putting up with his temper for almost a year. I'm sure you can do it for a while longer."

Posey bowed his head and said, "I guess I can."

McCain reached across the table and patted Posey's arm. "Now as soon as he shows you your report, you do as I told you and then let me know. Tomorrow morning I'm going to start drafting your rebuttal. We'll have it ready when we need it."

"I sure hope it works. My dad's not well and if I get kicked out it will kill him." He pondered for a second. Then with a cruel glow in his eyes he gritted his teeth and said, "And if anything happens to Dad, I'll get even."

"I wouldn't blame you, but let's hope it don't come to that." McCain checked his Timex: 1900. "Dan, I hate to leave you alone, but I think I'll go back to the Red Rooster and check on the crew." The fact was that he was thinking more about Virgie's tits than the five sailors.

Posey looked relieved. "Thanks for the advice, Jack. I think I'm going to stick around here for a while. Rick and Ron should be back soon."

As he was going down the stairs, McCain met Slang and Thompson on their way up. He thanked Thompson for the drinks and told them were he was going. After a quick handshake he hurried down the stairs and out the stained-glass doors.

Chapter Twenty-four

Day Eleven

It was early afternoon before Thompson's trucks finished filling the barge's seemingly insatiable belly with river-bottom sand.

Shortly after the last truck pulled away, the harbor tug pulled the loaded vessel away from the pier to where the *Lakota*, having already shed her moorings, stood waiting with her stern facing the oncoming barge like a bitch dog waiting to be mounted.

Soon as the tow was in place, the crew attached the heavy towing bridle and secured it to the tow wire. When they were safely out into the channel, Adams gave the order, "Ahead slow," sending a shudder through the ship as she eased forward to tighten the strain on the wire.

When sufficient slack was out, Adams said, "Ahead one-third." Posey shifted the handles on the engine-order telegraph to the corresponding position. Adams then gave the helmsman his course and they were on their way back to Guantanamo.

At breakfast that morning, McCain's drinking buddies were walking around like zombies. Even Posey had an "I wish I could have a couple more hours' sleep" look in his eyes. McCain hadn't seen Haggen yet, and, according to Posey, the bos'n was still cooped up in his cabin.

Rice's deep sleep seemed to be beneficial. Although his eyes were still puffed and the pissed-off look on his face was still visible, his chipped-beef breakfast was back to what it used to be.

The most notable change was in Captain Adams. At 0630 hours, McCain had stepped out of his room and ran face to face with his CO, who was coming out of the wardroom. He was wearing freshly pressed khakis, his eyes were clear and he was clean shaven. His lips broke into a smile. "Good morning, Chief, I feel great this morning. I've got a hunch that things are really turning around."

When McCain didn't answer, Adams said, "I was looking for you yesterday, but you'd already gone ashore. I thought maybe we could've had a couple beers together." He flexed his muscles again and said, "Now, I'm glad I missed you. No hangover. No deeper in debt and I'm feeling like a new man." He reached out and gave McCain a gentle punch on the shoulder. "See you later, Chief. I'm going out and get some of this fresh morning air. It's bound to get hot later."

All McCain could do was stare and nod. He couldn't stand anyone that chipper so early in the morning. Especially when the other guy was cold sober and he was fighting off the effects of too much rum and Red Stripe.

When he pulled out his handkerchief to wipe his nose, he was immediately hit with the lingering aroma of Virgie's sweet musky body. He smiled as he thought about the way she had grabbed the handkerchief out of his pocket and wiped the sweat from between her tits. "Tomorrow you smell handkerchief and remember how we make love," she had said. He took another sniff; she sure was right.

He stepped out on deck and looked out over the water. They'd soon be outside Kingston Harbor. He felt a little let down, their next stop would be Gitmo and he didn't have much of anything new to report to Tommy.

At 1500, Adams secured the special sea detail and McCain took over as OOD to finish the remainder of the 12 to 1600 watch. After supper, he stretched out on his bunk and started reading his book. He'd only read two or three pages when his eyes grew heavy and he drifted off to sleep.

Chapter Twenty-five

Day Twelve

McCain was sound asleep when a half-hour before midnight Tobey knocked on his door and told him it was time to relieve the watch. He got up, slipped into a fresh suit of khakis, washed the sleep out of his eyes, stepped into the passageway and started up the ladder. He'd only taken two steps when he changed his mind, turned back, and went into the crew's mess, where he drew a mug of coffee to take with him.

At the top of the ladder he met Posey coming out of the pilothouse. "Have they settled down yet?" Posey asked.

Not having the slightest idea of what he was talking about, McCain said, "I don't know. I didn't hear anything out of the ordinary." Then it dawned on him that he was supposed to be relieving Greene. "What are you doing here? I'm supposed to be relieving the bos'n."

"You were, but it seems our friend Jackson went ashore and brought back three quarts of 151-proof rum that he shared with Greene. Needless to say, the bos'n was too drunk to stand his watch."

"No shit. I never would have thought that Greene would neglect his duties."

"It's worse than that," said Posey.

"How could that be? What do you mean?"

Posey stared at McCain for a second, and then said, "I can't believe you didn't hear anything."

McCain took a deep breath and said, "Damn it, Dan, tell me what in the hell you're talking about."

Posey's eyes took on a harried look as he said, "Not only is Greene stoned out of his skull, he now says he's going to kill Captain Adams."

"I don't believe it," said McCain. It has to be his daughter's letter, he thought.

"You can believe it all right. I wasn't there but, according to Haggen, at about 1900 he and Adams was in the wardroom watching a movie when the bos'n barged in, called Adams a no-good son of a bitch, and said he'd never get the chance to hit on his daughter again."

Slowly shaking his head, McCain pictured the scene in his mind. "What happened next?"

Posey wet his lips. "Haggen sent Dixon to find me. It took several minutes for me and Haggen to calm the bos'n down enough to get him out of there."

"What was the captain doing?"

"He was like a mouse till he saw we had Greene under control, then he called him a drunken bum and a stupid old man with a pickled brain." Posey wet his lips again. "Drunk as he was, Greene understood Adams perfectly and tried to break free. I'll tell you this, for a man his age, the bos'n is strong. It took both of us to drag him out of the wardroom and into his own room. All the time we were struggling with Greene, Adams kept spouting off."

"What was he saying?"

"I was pretty busy, but it was about Greene's daughter being as bad as he was. That was when the bos'n swore that Adams wouldn't make it through the night."

Damn, thought McCain, and to think I slept through the whole thing. "How'd you wind up?"

"When we finally got the bos'n back into his room, Haggen poured a water glass of rum and Greene downed it in one gulp. Couple minutes later, he was out like a light."

"Has anybody looked in on him?" McCain asked.

"No need to. Haggen ordered Chief Jackson to stay in the room with him and told him to call us if he started to wake up."

McCain shrugged, "Everything must be all right now. Far as I could see, there's nothing moving down there. There wasn't even anybody in the crew's mess. I thought it was a bit strange, but I just figured everyone was making up for the sleep they lost in Kingston."

Posey yawned and stretched his arms. "They probably are and I don't blame them. I can't wait to crawl into the sack."

McCain went to the chart table, turned back to Posey and said, "Give me a rundown on what's going on and I'll relieve you."

Three hours into the watch everything was looking as smooth as Virgie's light-brown skin. The tow was running slightly off to port. The pull on the wire was a little heavy but if the weather held it wouldn't be a problem. Tomorrow he'd call Tommy and fill him in on Adams's attempt to bribe Thompson and on the fight between Adams and Greene. He'd also put Tommy to work straightening out Rice's problems. And this time he wouldn't take no for an answer.

McCain had just looked into the radar screen when he heard someone running full speed up the ladder. He glanced up just as Rossi came dashing into the pilothouse. "Chief, I think the bos'n has killed the captain." Like a kid having to go to the head, Rossi shifted his weight from one foot to the other while at the same time waving the message form he held in his hand.

For a second, McCain didn't want to believe what he was hearing. Probably because he was afraid something like this was going to happen and didn't do enough to stop it. "Settle down, Rossi. Tell me what you saw."

Stuttering, Rossi said, "I copied this message!" With a shaking hand he handed McCain the form. "It was for immediate action, so I took it to the captain like I'm supposed to." His eyes were almost as big as baseballs and his body trembled as if he was standing on a vibrator. "I knocked on the captain's door and there was no answer so I turned the knob…"

McCain looked around and saw that Smith, his quartermaster, was standing behind him and listening to every word. The helmsman, Seaman Steed, with one hand on the wheel, was turned and staring in their direction. When McCain shouted, "Mind your helm, Steed!" he went back to watching the compass. McCain ignored Smith and told Rossi to go on.

Rossi took a deep breath that didn't help his stuttering and said, "I tried the door. It was unlocked. I just figured the captain was sleeping because his reading light was on and so was his desk light. I walked in and..." Rossi's voice faltered and he looked as if he was going to pass out.

McCain glanced over his shoulder at Smith. "Go down and get the XO. Don't say a word to him; just tell him I need him on the bridge immediately." In less than a second, he heard Smith running down the ladder. McCain then took Rossi's arm and guided him to the captain's bridge chair. Soon as he was seated, McCain asked, "Tell me what you saw in there."

From the fright in Rossi's eyes, McCain knew the young radioman was reliving the experience. "First I saw the bos'n. He was sitting on the deck; his head was down and he had something in his hand. Then I saw Captain Adams."

"Where was the captain?"

Looking as if he was about to gag, Rossi said, "He was folded up on his side next to the bos'n. Blood was coming from his head."

"Is he still there?"

"Yes."

The sound of footsteps running up the ladder interrupted their conversation. Posey burst into the pilothouse. "What's the problem, Chief?"

McCain looked at Smith and said, "Don't leave the pilothouse and make sure Steed keeps us on course." He took Posey's arm and said, "Let's go out on the wing. Rossi, you stay where you are for a minute."

McCain leaned close and whispered to Posey, "Rossi thinks Greene has killed the captain." He searched Posey's eyes for a response. There was nothing to speak of. "Now listen up," said McCain. "What I'm about to tell you is for your ears only. I'm an NIS investigator and you've got to take charge of the ship so I can look into whatever it is that has Rossi so upset. While I go below, I'll have Rossi come out here and tell you what he saw." McCain was amazed that the tragedy still hadn't registered in Posey's eyes.

Inside the cabin, McCain found Adams lying face down on the deck with a wicked hole the size of a silver dollar in the left rear quarter of his skull. Greene, grasping the blood-covered brass chipping hammer in his left hand, was also on the deck but leaning against the desk.

McCain bent down and pressed his fingers against Adams's neck. He felt no pulse; the body felt cool; his face was purplish and his skin had a waxy translucent look. The smell said that he'd emptied his bowels and bladder. The bos'n had the slow even breathing of a passed-out drunk. The obvious conclusion was that Greene killed the old man and then went to sleep. There would probably never be an easier murder to solve.

As McCain was leaving the scene, he met Smith coming down from the bridge. "Mr. Posey wants Mr. Haggen to report to the bridge so he can come down here to see what's going on."

They were the last words McCain wanted to hear. He nodded to Smith. "After you finish telling Mr. Haggen, go down to crew's quarters and wake up Wishbore. I'm going to wake up Chief Hall."

"You got it, Chief. Anything else?"

"Yes. Don't tell Wishbore why I want him. The word will get out soon enough. What's important now is to keep things under control."

With a worried expression on his face, Smith asked, "Why do you think Bos'n Greene did it?"

McCain knew Smith deserved an answer, but one question would only lead to another. "That's not for you to worry about. Just do what you've been told and at the proper time I'll see that you're one of the first to know the whole story."

"Thanks, Chief." Smith moved on to Haggen's door and started knocking.

McCain went past Smith, gave a quick knock on Hall's door, turned the knob and went in. When he turned on the light, Hall jumped up and took a stance as if to defend himself. "Take it easy, Tom. We've got a problem and I need your help."

Hall quickly put on his glasses. "What's going on?"

McCain gave him a general outline of the situation and then said, "I want you to stand guard outside the CO's cabin. Don't let anyone in there, and that means everyone."

Hall nodded. "I'll be right there." He was still pulling on his trousers as McCain went out the door.

Wishbore came running up the ladder from the crew's quarters. "You need me, Chief?"

"Yeah, Sparks. I want you to go up on the bridge and get Rossi. Then both of you go to the radio shack and wait for me. While you're waiting, see if you can raise Gitmo. Have someone get a hold of the base intelligence officer and tell him that Special Agent Jack McCain must talk to him as soon as possible."

Wishbore's mouth dropped open. "You're a special agent?"

"I am," said McCain. "You'll learn more later. Rossi can tell you everything that's happened so far, but keep him calm and away from the rest of the crew."

Wishbore's expression said he wanted to ask more, but after staring for a second, he said, "I'm on my way."

In the bos'n's room, McCain found Jackson sprawled out on the top bunk. Could he be dead too? But then he took a breath and McCain moved closer. He was still alive all right but the stench of stale rum on his breath almost knocked McCain over. Even knowing he was performing an important duty, Jackson couldn't pass up the 151-proof rum. And it was obvious he couldn't hold it either.

It wasn't hard to figure out what had happened. Greene must have woken up and saw Jackson passed out so he went to Adams's cabin to finish his argument. A lot of this was Haggen's fault—he should have had more sense than to rely on Jackson. It was like hiring Jessie James as a bank guard.

McCain left the bos'n's room and saw Hall coming toward him. Over his shoulder he spotted Posey opening the door to the crime scene. "Mr. Posey! Please don't go in there."

"I told him he should wait for you," said Hall.

Posey stopped, turned to McCain and said, "Chief McCain, you may be some sort of spy for the Navy, but now I'm commanding officer of this ship and I'll give the orders." He stamped his left foot and said, "You understand?"

McCain pushed him aside and said, "Cut the dramatics. I know you're the CO but this is a murder investigation and you're not going in till I take some photos. And then we have to get Greene out of there and locked up someplace. Now we can work as a team or I'll do it on my own and you can report me to whom the hell ever you want to."

Posey drew back as if slapped across the face. "Okay for now, but…"

McCain looked at Hall, pointed to Greene's room, and said, "Tom, go in there and get Jackson out. Then go through the place and make sure there's no more booze or anything Greene might use as a weapon." He waited till Hall was out of sight before saying to Posey, "But, my ass. You stand guard here while I get my camera."

Posey's arrogance mysteriously disappeared as he said, "You talk worse than Adams did. Get rid of one bully and up pops another."

McCain had had enough. He backed Posey against the closed door and said, "Look, Posey. We don't have time for this bullshit." Then he rushed to his room and came out carrying his Polaroid camera and a box of film.

He hurried to where Posey was standing stiff as a marlin spike, gave him a quick look, and said, "Captain, if you'd step aside and let me pass, I'd appreciate it."

The word captain brought the hint of a smile to Posey's face and gave him the confidence to say, "I want Bos'n Greene out of there, right now."

"Not till I take some pictures," said McCain. He pushed past Posey, went in and locked the door behind him. He checked his Timex: 0317. Seventeen minutes since Rossi came bounding up the ladder. The room was just as he had left it. Greene, with strings of white spittle dripping from the corners of his mouth, was still out cold with the chipping hammer in his hand. McCain hoped the clotted blood on the sharp peen of the head showed up in the photo.

He quickly snapped ten more shots. After each shot he laid the exposed negative on Adams's bunk for the images to fully develop. Then without knowing why, he opened the drawer where he'd seen the fitness reports. The envelope was still there. He thought about removing it, but decided he'd have time for that later.

When satisfied that the photos were of sufficient quality to show the scene as he'd first found it, McCain took a pair of scissors off the desk and used them like a pair of tongs to grab the heavy chipping hammer. He then slid the hammer into a large clasp envelope, gathered up the photos and left the room.

Out in the passageway, Hall was waiting with their new captain. McCain pulled Hall aside and said, "Get two men to haul Greene out of there. Make sure they don't touch Adams's body." He then turned to Posey and said, "It would be a good idea if you made sure nobody else goes in there."

Suddenly from the top of the stairs, he heard, "Chief McCain, Captain Rollins from Gitmo is holding for you."

Rossi's words caused Posey to say, "I'll take that call."

McCain gave him a "get lost" look and said, "Rollins is the base intelligence officer. I put in the call to him and he'll want to talk to me. Just be patient and I'll fill you in later."

As McCain started up the ladder, he heard Posey say, "From now on you clear everything with me."

"Yes, sir," McCain yelled over his shoulder. Talk about power going to somebody's head, he thought.

After reporting the murder and passing on his opinion as to what happened, Captain Rollins agreed to helicopter a forensic team out to the ship to gather evidence and take the body back with them.

Before the helicopter arrived, McCain checked Adams's room one more time. Posey wanted to go in with him, but when he put his foot down, Posey backed down. The dumb bastard didn't realize that it was for his sake that McCain wanted to take another look.

Inside the room, he went straight to the desk and took out the fitness report envelope. There was no use muddying the water with an unsatisfactory report on the ship's executive officer. The fact that Posey hadn't signed it made it unofficial and he had no qualms about removing it from the envelope and giving it to Posey.

McCain flipped through the papers and then went through them again. Posey's report was missing. Maybe, while they were in Kingston, Adams had forged Posey's signature and mailed it to BuPers. Maybe he found himself a way to get even for not being able to go ashore. No wonder he looked so happy yesterday.

Three hours later, the forensic team had finished their investigation. With the chipping hammer and photos in their possession, they zipped Adams's corpse into a body bag and flew away. The team leader, a marine captain named Steve Kane, had brought new orders for the *Lakota*.

When they finally arrived in Gitmo and moored the barge, marine guards from the brig came aboard and took Greene into custody. While the *Lakota's* fuel and fresh water tanks were being topped off, McCain called Tommy.

A little over an hour after he'd hung up, the *Lakota* was underway for Bayonne.

Chapter Twenty-six

Day Seventeen—Morning

Five days after Bos'n Greene was taken off the ship in handcuffs McCain kept recalling the events that made that day the most unforgettable in his memory. It was a day that started with Adams's murder and ended with the temporary CO, Dan Posey, acting like a little Hitler. Not only toward McCain but toward the crew in general.

The only bright spot was that Rice seemed to be doing a little better. McCain had talked to him several times and assured him that everything was being put back in order. In fact he had devoted a good portion of his telephone conversation with Tommy on Rice's problems and was quite optimistic that his old friend would be able to convince the bank and Mrs. Rice to change their minds.

The hardest part of the trip back to Bayonne was the lack of watch standers. Now that Captain Posey was too much of a big shot to put himself in the rotation, it left only Hall, Haggen and McCain on the watch list; four hours on, eight hours off. Standing OOD watches had ceased to be fun.

McCain raised his binoculars and scanned the horizon; nothing in sight. He stepped inside the pilothouse and checked the clock: 1000 hours. Two hours before he'd finish his watch. About six hours later they should be entering New York Harbor. Tommy's latest message said that he, along with some FBI agents and New York City police officials, would be waiting for them at the pier.

McCain pictured the disappointed look on Tommy's face when he learned that his trusted investigator didn't have the answers they needed to put the case to bed. For quite some time, McCain believed it was Adams who had killed Johnson. But when they found the CO with his head bashed in, he woke up to the fact that either there were two killers or Adams didn't have anything to do with Johnson's murder. If only he could lay his hands on that damn journal.

Another problem was that he was beginning to have second thoughts about the bos'n being Adams's killer. He wasn't sure why he felt that way or who else it could be, but the sinking feeling in his gut suggested that Greene might have just happened to be in the wrong place at the wrong time. He'd spent much of the last five days trying to convince himself that they had the right man in custody.

"Chief, I just checked the radar." Toby looked worried. "We're heading into a storm and it looks like a big one."

McCain rushed inside the pilothouse and sank the upper half of his face into the soft rubber light shield. The top third of the screen was one solid blip of weather. He turned to Tobey and said, "Go tell Captain Posey about the storm and that I recommend we change course."

"You got it, Chief. Want me to bring you a fresh cup of coffee while I'm at it?"

"No thanks, I've already had three cups and I've still got almost a full cup on the chart table. But it might be a good idea to warn Rice about the storm. I think by lunchtime we'll be bouncing like Dolly Parton's tits in a foot race." As he stuck his head back into the face shield he heard Tobey laughing till he was halfway down the ladder.

Within minutes Captain Posey was on the bridge. Without saying a word he motioned McCain aside so he could check the radar screen himself. When he straightened up he looked at the helmsman and said, "Maintain your present course. We're going through it. I'll show you people what real ship handling is all about. I'll make Adams look like an amateur." Then with a weird glint in his eye, he disappeared back down the ladder.

Curtin, the helmsman, shook his head. "What happened to Mr. Posey, Chief? He used to be an all-right guy. Now he's as bad as Captain Adams ever was. I've never seen anybody change like that."

McCain felt like telling Curtin that he agreed with him, but with things like they were, he couldn't side with the white hats. "Mind your helm. You know you shouldn't be talking."

Curtin looked like a whipped child. "Sorry, Chief," he said in a barely audible voice.

The change in Posey was the talk of the ship. Even Chief Hall got his ass chewed for a slight tear in one of the charts. It had been erased and corrected so many times that the paper was worn through. No way was the tear Hall's fault, but Posey jumped on him like seagulls on a garbage barge.

As bad as the morale was when McCain came on board, it was a luxury liner compared to now. Maybe that was to be expected; thirty men cooped up on a small ship can be a pain in the ass, but when one of the thirty might be a murderer, friends tend to be few and far between.

Just as the radar had promised, less than an hour later the *Lakota* was pitching and rolling. In one way they'd been lucky. This was the first really rough weather they'd encountered since leaving Bayonne. But for several hours now the barometer had kept falling steadily. Now green water washed over the bow, covering the pilothouse windows with a salty spray. McCain switched on the wipers and wondered why Posey wasn't up there with him.

Without thinking, he took a swig of cold coffee and almost gagged. Either the coffee or rolling ship caused his stomach to feel queasy. His head ached; cold sweat broke out on his brow. Then it dawned on him that he was seasick, and he knew if he took another drop of the coffee he'd probably throw up. The long tour of shore duty and so far good weather were taking their toll.

With a cold sweat on his brow and a rolling sensation in his gut, McCain walked out on the wing of the bridge and tossed the contents of his mug over the side. Soon as drops of liquid started splattering against his face, he realized he was standing on the windward wing. Thank God it was only coffee and that he'd been successful in fighting back the urge to vomit.

As he wiped his face with his handkerchief, he heard, "Who's the idiot that threw that coffee over the side?"

He quickly glanced down and saw Posey, looking as wet as a bird caught in a down spout, staring up from the open boat deck. Soon as Posey saw McCain's face he shook his fist and headed for the bridge.

McCain, knowing he was about to catch hell, ducked into the pilothouse, looked around, put down his mug and met Posey at the top of the ladder. "Sorry, Captain," he said. "I should've known better but the coffee was cold and didn't taste right." Funny, but he didn't feel as sick as he did before.

Posey brushed past McCain and went to the center of the pilothouse. Then, with his feet spread for balance, he said through gritted teeth, "Chief, I think you're a Jonah! I'm relieving you of your watch before we all get killed. Go below, I'll talk to you later."

Just as he started toward the ladder, the ship took a twenty-degree roll to port. In an attempt to stay upright, McCain grabbed the door frame as Tobey held fast to the chart table. At the same time, in spite of his wide stance, Posey lost his balance, slid across the slippery deck, wrapped his arms around the bridge chair, and yelled, "Enter that in the log."

Toby tossed McCain a quick wink, turned to Posey, and asked, "You want me to put in the log that you slid across the deck?"

"No, you stupid idiot. I want the log to show that I relieved the watch."

Soon as the ship steadied itself, McCain smiled at Posey and said, "Thank you, sir. I'll be in my office." Under the circumstances, he thought "office" sounded better than "cabin."

Three times, on the way down from the bridge, McCain was forced to stop and hold fast to the stair rail. The wet steel, slippery as a Wyoming brook trout, made the journey even tougher. When he finally reached bottom, he rushed to his office, threw open the door, and let out a groan. Instead of finding his normal place of refuge, he found his room in shambles.

Soon as he saw the broken metal bracket, he realized what had happened. It must have been the same roll that sent Posey scooting across the pilothouse. Evidently the file cabinet broke loose and tipped over. It now rested on its side with all its drawers open and files scattered everywhere.

The sight made him feel as low as whale shit. By the time he got this mess cleaned up they'd be back in port with Johnson's murder still unsolved. And to make matters worse, that urge to vomit had returned. He gulped a couple times and held his breath till the nausea passed; then he went to work.

First thing he had to do was get the file cabinet back in place. With all five drawers already out, it shouldn't be too heavy. He took two thick manuals, laid them on the deck and rolled the cabinet face down with the upper edge of the top drawer opening resting on the books. When he stuck his hands between the two manuals and started to lift, he felt the tips of his fingers hitting something strange. His heart skipped a beat, it felt like duct tape. Could it be the journal? The mere thought sent his heart beating like a woodpecker's head on a bug-infested tree. He quickly rolled the cabinet on its back and stuck his hand inside. A composition notebook was taped to the top end of the cabinet.

He ripped off the tape and started reading. "Holy shit," he exclaimed. "It's the journal." He turned to the last few pages and said to the empty room, "I'll be damned." Then as if once wasn't enough, he said it again and again.

Then to make sure no one could see what he was doing, he stuffed the journal under his pillow and continued his struggle to get the file cabinet back in place. After successfully getting it upright, he kept one eye on the unsecured file cabinet while he went to the door and called for someone to give him a hand. The drape to the crew's mess moved to one side and Rice stuck his head through.

"Do me a favor, Stew. Get me piece of line so I can tie this damned cabinet down."

When Rice returned with the line, McCain was still struggling against the ship's pitching and rolling trying to hold the wayward cabinet in place. "Hurry up and tie one end of the line to that bracket holding the desk. Then wrap it around the cabinet and secure the other end to the bunk stanchion.

Soon as the heavy-set cook started tying the last knot, McCain realized what had been bothering him about Adams's killer. Rice was left-handed. The bos'n was right-handed and the blow that killed Adams landed on the back left quarter of his skull. That meant the killer was either ambidextrous or left-handed.

There was no mistake about it. He thought back to the day he first reported aboard and went to see Greene in the wardroom. Clear as day he remembered the bos'n using his right hand to drink coffee, shake hands and even to scratch his balls. Besides, from the very minute he entered the crime scene, he had a hard time believing that, drunk as he was, Greene could have swung that hammer with enough force to crush Adams's skull. Was it possible that Rice went through with his threat and killed the old man? The ship took another heavy roll, sending the unsecured drawers sliding across the room pushing loose papers and folders in their path. Murderer or not, he said, "Give me a hand cleaning up, will you, Stew?"

"Be glad to, Chief," he said in the friendly tone that McCain had grown to expect. "I've got plenty of time. The sea's too rough to cook; we're having sandwiches for lunch."

"That's good," said McCain. "If you can just help me get these drawers back in the cabinet and gather up these papers. It doesn't matter which ones go in which drawer till we stop this damned bouncing. I'm beginning to feel like I'm stuck inside one of those front-loading washing machines." No change of expression on Rice's jet-black face meant that either the simile went over his head or he didn't find it amusing.

Soon as all the folders and loose papers were stuffed into the drawers, McCain said, "Before you go back to the galley, I've got to ask you a question." He wondered if he should first warn Rice of his rights but then decided he'd just as soon not make his friend's first answer official. For sure Rice wasn't going anywhere and McCain knew that, should it become necessary, he'd get another opportunity to interrogate him.

"What you want to ask me?"

McCain took a deep breath and let it out slowly. Then he stared Rice straight in the eye and asked, "Did you kill Captain Adams?"

His eyes opened so wide they looked like black olives stuck into ping-pong balls. Then he relaxed a bit and said, "That's not funny, Chief. I know what I said to you, but no way did I kill the captain. Do you really think I did?" His tone was pure sincerity.

Shaking his head, McCain said, "Not really, but I just noticed that you're left-handed and I'm pretty sure that whoever killed Captain Adams was also left-handed."

"Well, it sure wasn't me," Rice said as he shifted from one foot to the other.

McCain waited for a second before asking, "Have you got something else to tell me?"

Rice stared down at the deck and in a low voice, said, "I don't know if I should."

McCain put his arm around the cook's shoulders and said, "Stew, you can tell me whatever you want. It's just between you and me."

After a full ten seconds, Rice said, "Only one other man on the *Lakota* is left-handed."

The words started McCain's belly churning. If it wasn't Rice it had to be the other man. "Who are you talking about?"

He hesitated again, and then said, "Mr. Posey."

Suddenly a picture of Posey signing the deck log flashed across his brain. Rice was right. Posey was using his left hand. He was still reliving the scene, when the ship's bow dipped into a deep trough and took a heavy roll to port. A shudder surged through the hull as the *Lakota's* screw lifted out of the water. Then, after what seemed an eternity, she righted herself and the screw once again churned the angry water. He took a deep breath and wondered what he was going to do next. One thing was for sure; he was going to need help.

He let go of the bunk stanchion, turned to Rice, who was holding tight to the sink, and said, "Stew, I need one more favor. Would you go ask Mr. Haggen and Chief Hall to come to my room? And please don't say anything to anyone."

Soon as Haggen and Hall joined McCain in his room, he reached under his pillow and took out Johnson's journal. "We've got real problems," he said as he waved the journal at them. "This is Johnson's journal. I first learned of it from Trumbull and I've been searching for it ever since."

Haggen shrugged. "So Johnson kept a journal. What's the big deal?"

"I'll tell you what the big deal is. According to this entry," McCain put his index finger on the open page, "that was written the day before Johnson disappeared, he was going to convince the Navy and Mrs. Adams that her husband and Posey were both homosexuals."

"Bullshit," said Haggen. "How was he going to do that?"

"I've known all along that Johnson had written a letter to Commander Eastern Sea Frontier and asked for a meeting. Now I think we know why."

In his usual calm voice, Hall asked, "Did Johnson say what he wrote in the letter? Why did Posey get so mad that he'd kill Adams? And I haven't heard anything that tells me who killed Johnson. Don't you think you might be barking up the wrong tree?"

"Well, there's always that chance, but every crime needs three essential elements: motive, method and opportunity. I'm sure all three are present in the case against Posey in the murder of Adams. As to Johnson's murder, things are a little murkier, I'm hoping Posey will open up and fill in the missing pieces."

Hall looked confused. "So, you still haven't said why Posey hated Captain Adams."

"Trust me. We'll have all the answers soon. But we can't stand around here talking." McCain looked at Hall and asked, "How much longer before we hit New York Harbor?"

"I can just guess, but it seems the storm is letting up, so I'd say seven or eight hours at most."

"Okay," said McCain. "The first thing we have to do is take command away from Posey." He stared at Haggen for a second before saying, "Jim, you're now acting CO. How about you and Hall coming up to the bridge with me?" Suddenly their conversation was cut off by another heavy roll to starboard. McCain waited for the ship to right itself before saying, "Tom, you chart us a course that'll get us into port without tearing the ship apart. I'm going to place Posey under arrest and bring him down here. I want to try to get a statement from him."

With their assignments firmly in place, the three of them made their way up the slippery ladders to the bridge. Soon as they stepped into the pilothouse, the ship rolled to port, sending them scampering across the deck. Posey, holding tight to the radar stand, said, "What are you people doing on my bridge? All of you get below, immediately."

While Haggen and Hall held fast to the chart table, McCain moved next to Posey and put his hand on his shoulder. Then in a low steady voice, he said, "Mr. Posey, I want you to turn the con over to Mr. Haggen so you and I can go below. I'm pretty sure you know why."

Like magic, the arrogance drained away from Posey's expression; his face paled and his eyes assumed the forlorn look of a beaten man. He hung his head in shame and said, "I'm glad you know. I've been thinking about jumping overboard, but I couldn't do it." Then in a complete turnaround, he stiffened his back, looked McCain in the eye, and said, "Would you make sure my dad knows I had my own command; even if only for a few days?"

In spite of what he had done, McCain couldn't help feeling sorry for the complicated young naval officer as Posey lifted the binocular strap from around his neck and handed the glasses to Haggen. He then saluted and asked, "Am I relieved, sir?"

Haggen took the binoculars, returned the salute and said, "You are relieved, Mr. Posey."

Posey's beaten-dog expression returned as he hung his head and walked slowly, with McCain holding his arm, toward the companionway. McCain stopped just long enough to say, "Tom, you take the log and make sure everything that I've told you and everything that you have witnessed here is written down. All three of us will sign it later." He then followed Posey down the ladder.

At the foot of the ladder, Posey looked at McCain and asked, "In my room?"

McCain nodded, "I think that would be best."

Once inside, McCain warned Posey of his rights and asked him if he wanted to make a statement. When Posey said he would, McCain picked up a lined pad from Posey's desk, clicked down the point of his pen and said, "Okay, I want you to start the night Johnson called and asked you to meet them at Ziggy's bar."

Posey's eyes went wide. "How'd you know about that?" he asked.

"Mr. Posey, let's get started on the right foot. From this point on, I'm the one asking the questions. After I'm through, if you want to know something I'll consider whether or not I can tell you."

Posey looked at McCain, took a deep breath, sighed, and said, "Okay. On the night Johnson called, I was home with my roommate. He sounded strange on the phone and said that Captain Adams wanted me to meet him at Ziggy's bar. And he said that if I didn't bring some money I'd be sorry. When I got there I discovered that Adams and Johnson were both shaking me down. Johnson said he needed it for some guy he was having an affair with. Adams didn't say why he needed his share, but I already knew that ever since he'd hooked up with Kitty he owed everybody in town."

"Did you give them money?"

"Yes. After Ziggy cashed a hundred-dollar check for me, I gave Johnson twenty-five and the rest to Adams." A strange looked came over Posey's face, like he was trying to remember or maybe forget what happened next.

After a few seconds, he said, "When Johnson got up and went to the head, Captain Adams leaned close to me and told me that Johnson was dangerous and it was in both of our best interests to find a way to get him out of the picture. His words scared me, but I had a feeling he was right."

"What happened next?"

With a zombie-like expression, Posey said, "When Johnson came back from the head; Captain Adams asked me and Johnson to go with him to another bar. I didn't really want to go, but I didn't know how to get out of it, so we went out to my car and I drove us into town where we went to the Blue Moon. After one drink, Captain Adams changed his mind and wanted to go back to the ship."

"Is that what you did?"

Posey nodded. "When we got back on the base, Captain Adams said he had to take a leak. So I found a dark spot behind a railroad car next to the edge of the pier and we all got out. Then all of a sudden Captain Adams wrapped his arms around Johnson, threw him to the ground, and yelled for me to get a rock or something."

McCain recalled the medical examiner's report on Johnson's body as he said, "So you did as you were told?"

"Yes, I just couldn't think right. I picked up a heavy chunk of concrete, and while the Captain held him down, I slammed it against Johnson's head." He looked as if he was about to be sick. "I'll never forget that sound. It was like dropping a cantaloupe. I don't think Johnson had any idea of what hit him."

Well, that explains the bits of cement in the wound, thought McCain before asking, "Did the blow kill him?"

"It had to. You should have heard the sound. No way anyone could live after being hit like that."

"Did you check his pulse, or try to see if he was still breathing?"

"No, there was no need to."

"What happened next?"

Posey closed his eyes and said, "Captain Adams made me take Johnson's arms while he took his feet and we tossed him into the water."

"So now, you and Adams were co-murderers?"

"I guess so," said Posey as he sighed hopelessly. "But it didn't help matters between me and the captain. It seemed to give him more power over me and he kept making me give him money."

"Now tell me how you killed Captain Adams."

Through a wry smile, Posey said, "I don't feel bad about that. After you relieved me on watch, I came down from the bridge and heard the bos'n yelling in the captain's cabin so I listened at the door."

"Could you hear what was being said?"

"I heard Captain Adams say, 'Take that, you drunken bastard.' Then there was dead silence. I opened the door and saw the captain bending over the bos'n. At first I was sure he'd killed him, but then I saw he was still breathing."

"So what did you do?"

"I grabbed that silly paperweight Captain Adams was so proud of and hit him as hard as I could. I then wiped my prints off the hammer, stuck it in the bos'n's hand and wrapped his fingers around the handle."

"That was what did you in," said McCain.

Posey's eyes widened, "How?"

"You put it in the wrong hand." McCain closed the pad he had been writing on and said, "Now I'm going to ask you something off the record. Did you take that fitness report out of the envelope?"

"Yes," he said. "I tore it up and threw it over the side."

McCain nodded slowly and said, "I'm glad you did. Even though you've killed two people, your dad won't have to know what Adams said about your seamanship. And I don't think it's my duty to tell him. It's the least I can do for a fellow chief."

Chapter Twenty-seven

Day Seventeen—Late Afternoon

At 1600 hours, the *Lakota* eased her way into Pier One at the Naval Supply Depot, Bayonne, New Jersey. Because Chief Hall had more ship handling experience, Haggen gave Hall the job of bringing the ship alongside the pier. Hall made it look easy; not a flake of paint scratched off the hull.

Soon as the moorings were secured, Tommy, followed by three men in civilian clothes, jumped from the pier onto the deck. After Tommy and McCain exchanged regulation salutes, McCain said, "Follow me, gentlemen." He then led the way down to the wardroom.

As McCain had instructed, Dixon was standing by with a fresh pot of coffee. While Dixon poured, Tommy introduced two of the men as FBI Agents Pickert and Mifflin. The third man was a lieutenant of the NYPD. Soon as they settled in their seats, McCain gave his finding of how and why Posey killed Petty Officer Johnson and Lieutenant Adams.

When finished, he turned over Johnson's journal and Posey's signed confession to Tommy. He studied them for a minute and then handed them to Senior FBI Agent Pickert.

Pickert turned to the police lieutenant and said, "Since both murders took place on federal property, we probably won't need your services for now. But you're free to stick around."

The officer stood up. "I've better things to do. Have one of your agents come down to headquarters and we'll turn over anything we've got to him." They shook hands and McCain told Dixon to show the officer out.

"Where's the accused?" asked Pickert.

McCain rose from his chair, and said, "I'll bring him in."

In less than two minutes, McCain pulled the drape aside and nudged Posey into the wardroom.

As Posey stood with downcast eyes, Pickert asked, "Are you Lieutenant Junior Grade Daniel Posey?"

In a meek voice, Posey said, "Yes, sir."

Pickert reached into his back pocket and brought out a pair of handcuffs. "Mr. Posey, I'm placing you under arrest for the murders of Petty Officer Johnson and Lieutenant Adams." He handed the cuffs to Mifflin, who moved behind Posey and snapped them on.

Tommy said, "You guys go ahead. I've got a few other non-related details to take up with Chief McCain. I'll call your office in the morning."

McCain watched, without a shred of satisfaction, as the two FBI agents led Posey out of the wardroom, up to the forecastle deck to the gangway and onto the pier. He glanced at his old friend, Tommy, and said, "If he wasn't so easily led astray, Posey could've been a damned good career naval officer." He shook his head, "You know, Tommy, if we had a way to settle this homosexual problem in the Navy there might not have been a reason for these two murders."

Tommy stared for a second, and then said, "I suppose you're right. And we'd still have that good naval officer with a long career ahead of him."

And we'd have a retired chief boatswain's mate who could still look at his son with pride, thought McCain. To change the subject, he asked, "What were you able to do for Rice?"

Tommy beamed as he said, "Good news there. Let's go into town, grab a bite to eat and I'll tell you all about it.

McCain looked across the table at Tommy and said in amazement, "You mean she didn't have the abortion?"

"Nope. She thought about it but couldn't bring herself to have it done. She's some lady. I can see why Rice was so upset about losing her. But everything is going to be all right now." Tommy checked his watch.

"In fact, right about now she should be arriving at the airport, where we've got a car waiting for her. The Rices are going to have a second honeymoon paid entirely by some bigwig civilian friends of the admiral."

"That's great," said McCain. "Now for the other guys…"

Tommy's raised palm stopped him in mid-sentence. "Don't say it," he said. "The finance companies have all been paid in full."

McCain was pleased but, at the same time, a bit pissed. "I thought you said you couldn't do that?"

He smiled, "I know, but I got to thinking and convinced the admiral that we'd have enough publicity with the murders without having those loan companies airing their gripes in the press."

McCain nodded. "But you should have done that in the first place. This has been the worst seventeen days of my life. Having to lie to those guys didn't help matters any. I'm even thinking about putting in for a transfer out of NIS and going back to pushing pencils on a cruiser or some other ship with a nice plush chief's quarters."

"You can't," said Tommy.

"Why can't I?"

"Because I'll turn down your request." He grinned. "By the way, tomorrow you're being replaced on the *Lakota* by a second-class yeoman."

"Good. Now I can go back to DC."

"Afraid not," Tommy said impishly.

"What in the hell are you planning now?" asked McCain.

"I don't know if you're going to like it, but we're going to be working together again."

"You mean I'm being assigned to the Eastern Sea Frontier?"

"Nope, we're going aboard a destroyer tender in Newport. There are accusations that some male officers are hitting on enlisted women. We're going to check it out and if true, put a stop to it."

The End

Printed in the United States
46689LVS00003B/55-102